WITH THIS RING

GEORGIA LE CARRE

With This Ring

Copyright © 2020 by Georgia Le Carre

ISBN: 978-1-910575-97-0

Many, many thanks to:
Caryl Milton
Elizabeth Burns
Nichola Rhead
Kirstine Moran
Brittany Urbaniak
Tracy Gray

AUTHOR'S NOTE

To all my awesome, beautiful readers,

Thank you for the support you have shown in 2019 and here's to you having a wonderful year full of happiness, love, laughter, and stories galore.

Love,

Georgia

Chapter One

FREYA

https://www.youtube.com/watch?v=9TQKyDD9Yig

"**F**reya!"

I looked up from the dirty vodka martini I was mixing.

"Monsieur Garlic-Cock wants you, darling," George said in his totally inimitable way, as he paused by the service station, a tray of ten cocktail glasses expertly balanced on the palm of his hand.

I could have asked him how he knew Monsieur Bisset's cock smelled of garlic, but I just laughed at his sass, and said, "Tell him he knows where to find me."

"There goes my tip," George said sourly and sashayed away, a gorgeous smile on his lips.

I looked in the direction of the middle-aged French businessman. He raised his glass and nodded at me. Monsieur Bisset flew into town once a month and he usually ended up in our bar to celebrate his victories in the boardroom. His goal seemed to be female attention, usually mine, but he was not too fussy. After a certain point in the night an orifice to wet his cock was more than enough. Of course, being filthy rich he couldn't understand why I kept rejecting his advances. I told him I didn't need money once, and he took that to mean I was holding out for more. In his eyes, I was a lowly waitress who should be grateful that such a fine gentleman as him had looked my way.

I pushed the dirty martini over to Dan, the curly-haired American guy, sitting at the bar. He was a regular, a funny guy. He gave me a wink which I returned before I moved on to mixing the next drink on my order list.

"I see I'm not the only one after you," he commented.

"Would I be as desirable if you were?" I quipped.

"Fair enough," he agreed, taking a long sip of his drink. He put his glass on the bar and grinned at me. "Fuck, this tastes as good as I can only imagine you will."

I took the flirt in good stride. It was part of the job. You want to be a barmaid in an underground cocktail bar in Lower Manhattan, then you can't be a paid-up member of the #metoo movement as well.

"Come on. Give me a chance, babe," he cajoled. "It's been months."

I reached up to the top shelves for a new bottle of rum. I needed it to make a Long Island Iced Tea. As I unscrewed the top I responded to Dan's unwise remark. "If I ever do Dan, beware. It might end with me sucking you dry—"

He tapped the counter excitedly. "But that is exactly what I want!"

"With a sexual harassment lawsuit," I dead-panned.

"I'll take that too," he said, after a brief contemplation.

My laughter rang across the bar.

"Just make it worth it," he joked.

I blew him a kiss, then delivered the Long Island to the amused, bearded man sitting next to him. He tipped his fedora to me, and I flashed him what I'd been told was my most electrifying smile. Julia came by then with a tray in hand, and passed on another message from Bisset. "He says there's a five-hundred-dollar tip waiting for you if you bring the drink to him yourself." She looked a bit jealous as she said it.

I shook my head to cover my irritation. "Tell him thanks, but my place is behind the bar."

The message was relayed and a few minutes later Monsieur Antoine Bisset himself, made his way over. "You have me wrapped around your little finger, haven't you," he said, his accent thick with French charm and alcohol.

"No one has you wrapped around their little finger, Monsieur," I say firmly. And that was no lie. I imagined him to be a man neither easily fooled nor manipulated.

He took his seat and watched me while I worked, until his ogling started to irritate me.

"What else will you have today, Monsieur?" I asked, with a big plastic smile.

He sucked in his breath. "You are a wild child, Freya."

I waited patiently while he ran his gaze from the top of my fiery red hair, down to my chest, lingering there deliberately, then coming back up to my eyes.

"The usual," he said finally, his eyes glittering.

I nodded and went to the locked cabinet to retrieve the $4,700 bottle of Louis XIII cognac that was kept specially for him.

I picked up one of the large glass goblets I'd been keeping warm on top of the coffee machine and poured a healthy amount of the ridiculously expensive drink into it. I swirled it to further warm the drink then, with the proper reverence for the price of the drink, placed the goblet on a coaster in front of him. "Should I send the bottle over to your table?"

"God no! It'd be wasted on those fools. Not one of them would know the difference between cooking brandy and one of the finest cognacs in the world," he said. "I might take it with me on my way out. Perhaps it'll be enough reason for you to stop by my hotel room and share a glass with me." Without breaking eye contact, he slipped his usual hundred towards me.

I took the cash, folded it, and tucked it into my back jeans pocket. "There will never be a reason in the world big enough, Monsieur." I smiled to take the sting away.

He took an elaborate sniff of the potent fumes, then a sip of the sinfully smooth luxury of his drink. "Ahhh ..." he moaned at the pleasure. "You know, that pussy of yours is not going to lick itself. Someday you're going to come to your senses and come with me, Princess."

Dan roared triumphantly. "Join the line Mon-fucking-sieur."

Nothing personal, all just part of the job, I told myself as I turned away to take care of the other patrons waiting to be served. That's when my eyes suddenly met *his*.

I froze.

Right there in the midst of the crowd ... he was watching me. His gaze was icy blue ... and cold, and unmistakable and just as always, my stomach flipped.

I blinked, and briefly lowered my head in disbelief.

He was here?

Why?

When I had myself under control I lifted my stony gaze to him, but he was gone.

A frown furrowed into my forehead as my eyes roved across the bar. Every sound and sight beyond that of his haunting gaze faded into the background as I searched around the dimly lit space for him, but he had disappeared like a puff of smoke. After a few seconds I started to wonder if I'd just imagined him.

But why the hell would I?

I hate him. He was an arrogant, insufferable, rude, sancti-monious, annoying, ignorant, uncivilized, brutal thug. Immediately, I abandoned the search for such a low-life, and turned around to settle my breathing. It was uneven, and it aggravated me to no end that even imagining seeing him never failed to stir the most unpleasant storms inside me.

"Bastard," I swore under my breath as I turned to a customer waiting to get my attention. But it was now a feat to focus on his order. He had to repeat it twice. I nodded and set to work, but my mood had turned sour. The rest of the night became an ordeal. I kept expecting him to turn up even though I had told myself a thousand times that he was just a figment of my imagination.

I usually headed out of the bar with a little skip in my step at the end of my shift at 3am, but thanks to the memory of that devil, I felt taut and irritable.

I'd just turned the block when I found Bisset waiting on the deserted side street, his foot against the wall. I wasn't surprised, but I was disappointed. Despite his clumsy advances and smutty jokes, I'd considered Garlic Cock fairly decent and able to respect set boundaries. Meeting outside the bar meant there was no going back.

Chapter Two

FREYA

"You're waiting to harass me, Monsieur?" I asked coldly.

He smiled charmingly. "Never, *mon chéri*. I thought, maybe, the bar is too crowded for you to … express your interest. Perhaps, you are shy in front of your employers and colleagues. I thought maybe—"

I cut him off. "You figured wrong. I'm not interested in you."

"That's unfair, baby girl. Just look at you … I'm about to lose my mind just staring at you."

I sighed. "Look, don't make this ugly. Maybe you have drunk too much, but if you stop now we can laugh about this the next time you come to the bar."

"I'm not drunk."

"Well, I'm going home. Alone."

He stepped in my path, his hands spread out and I could smell the alcohol I had fed him, pungent and overindulgent.

"My car and driver are right around the corner," he slurred. "It's running, waiting for you. Let's go for a drive. I'll show you some very beautiful places. Secret places. Where rich people go to feed their needs. You'll never get the chance to see them on your own."

My stomach turned at the thought of the ugly things he had in mind. "I've lived in this city for five years. I've seen all that I need or want to see of it."

"No, you don't understand," he rasped urgently, his eyes shining. "This city has an underbelly. An exciting place that only those in the know can hope to experience. I promise you will love it."

"Thanks, but no thanks." I attempted to walk past him again.

Suddenly his face changed. The affable Frenchman was gone. Here was the real thing. The thing I would have seen if I had said yes at any time. "What will it take?" he asked, "because I'm not going home without you tonight."

I lost my patience. "Out of my way," I said and tried to push him aside, but he grabbed my hand and turned me violently around. It twisted my wrist and the pain made me wince.

He drew me to him and brought his nose close to my neck. Sniffing me he pressed his unimpressive cock against me.

"Do you feel what you do to me? Just give me one night," he pleaded. "I'll fuck you so good you'll never forget me."

I was as still as a tree. "Let me go."

Of course, he didn't listen.

I gave him one more chance. "Monsieur, let me go."

Instead the fool pressed his lips to my skin for a kiss.

I pushed myself back and smacked a blow so hard across his face I knew he saw stars.

Shocked, he staggered away from me and hit the wall. His mouth was agape with disbelief. "You fucking bitch," he said in wonder as he pulled away the hand he had held to his bruised face. "You hit me!"

I shrugged. "I did warn you."

He came for me then.

I wanted to roll my eyes into my skull.

He grabbed my shirt and pulled me up to his face. "How dare you? You fucking cheap whore!"

I struck his wrist hard with the edge of my hand, and he howled in pain. You can't blame a man for making that racket when his limb has shifted out of joint. To his credit, he lunged again for me, but his legs crumbled under him from sheer pain. It sent him crashing to the cold ground. Some people standing outside the kebab shop in the distance turned at the sight of his drunken howl.

It was not the end of the matter though. That ridiculous cognac had put fire into his veins.

"I'm going to kill you," he screamed and once again came for me. I waited and at the right moment swung my frame around just in time to land a swift kick across the unprotected side of his face.

He flew backwards, and collapsed on the ground, a battered, pathetic mess. I glanced at the square heel of my boots and wondered just how much damage it had done to him. I felt a bit guilty: I did take all the hundreds of dollars he pushed across the bar to me. The money would go towards the orders for fashion samples that Britney and I would need in the next few days. Anyway, someone had to teach him some manners. He would think twice about using this technique to approach another woman.

"Sorry Monsieur," I said.

I was just about to walk away when I felt a commanding presence behind me. All the hairs on my body instantly stood and I swiveled around in response to the danger I could sense. There was indeed danger. A man detached himself from the shadows. It was the last man I wanted to see. The owner of the pair of icy blue eyes that had disrupted me in the bar and put me in my bitter mood.

Maxim Ivankov.

So he really had been present at the bar. I couldn't wait to find out why. He walked up to me and stood with the street-light directly overhead. It made him appear even more forbidding and brutal. I could feel my heart start to thump.

"Why the fuck are you on my tail?" I snarled.

He smiled darkly, and it startled me, just like it always had.

"It's nice to see you too," he drawled. His voice was like waves crashing upon rocks. It could take centuries but in the end it would pulverize the rocks into sand. "What's it been, seven years?"

"Well, thanks for helping."

He gazed down at Antoine, and shook his head. "You didn't need the help. The idiot didn't know what he had coming."

"Neither do you apparently," I said and instantly felt a frisson of fear strike me at the threat I had just issued to the one man I knew could hurt me with just his gaze.

"What did you say?" he asked, his voice sending chills down my body and I knew I had overstepped my boundaries. We were mortal enemies and the less involvement I had with him the better for me.

"Fuck off," I muttered under my breath, and began to walk away.

At first there was nothing but the sound of my footsteps. I prayed he wouldn't come after me. He didn't.

"Call your father," his voice rang after me.

My heart slammed into my chest. For a second I couldn't move. What did that imply? Was my dad alright?

His father and mine had been bloody rivals for as long as anyone could remember. Between them, death was usually almost always on the table.

I whirled around to confront him, but he was gone, as silently as he had arrived.

Chapter Three

FREYA

I didn't slow down until I arrived at my apartment and my heart was racing in my chest as I locked the door behind me.

"Freya!" Britney called as she headed from the kitchen towards me, a teddy bear head band holding back her messy hair, and a pot of noodles in her hand. She appeared at the doorway as I was locking the door behind me. I turned around to face her.

"Hiya."

"You're finally back. I was waiting for you. We have to finalize the sample details before tomorrow so we can send it off."

"Yeah, okay. Just give me a couple of minutes." I tried not to sound panicked.

She gave me a funny look. "You okay?"

I forced a smile. "Of course. I just need to make a phone call first."

"Sure, no problem. Your Chinese is in the microwave btw."

Then she turned around and went back into the living room. I watched her plop down on the couch and immediately get lost in a reality show on VH1.

I pulled out my phone, my hands trembling slightly. I unlocked it as I hurried to my room. Maxim's appearance meant that a big shift in my life was about to happen and it would be one I would most probably hate. He would otherwise have never made such a pointless visit. He had no ties with me, and neither I presumed, would he have the spare, unassigned, minutes to squander.

I shut my bedroom door behind me and dialed my father's number, but he didn't pick up on the first ring like he normally did when I called, and for a moment I wondered where he was... Perhaps he wasn't in Moscow. Budapest then? Or Paris?

I began to scroll through my contacts hastily to look for his other numbers until I realized I was not calling his personal one, the one he kept between us. I dialed again and when it was answered, I collapsed to my bed.

"Dad?" I called out anxiously.

"*Moya Printsessa*," he said.

The endearment made me clench my jaw. When my father called me My Princess I always knew it was time to beware. Something horrible was coming my way. "Where are you?"

"New York," he answered in his thick accent. "I landed two hours ago."

I was confused. "You're here? Why didn't you tell me you were coming?"

"I wanted to surprise you." His laughter boomed down the line.

The last surprise from my Dad I enjoyed was when I was seven. Ever since then his surprises just meant bad news for me. "That's nice," I said automatically.

"I'm only here until tomorrow evening so come have breakfast with me at my hotel. I'm staying at the Ritz-Carlton. You haven't bought your own apartment yet, have you?"

I ignored the question. "Why are you only here for one day?"

"I was in Puerto Rico, but I have ... business to handle in Moscow so I have to rush back. I stopped by to speak to you."

My heart sank. I knew then that there was something very wrong.

"What does this have to do with the Ivankovs?" I asked.

"Come to breakfast tomorrow at ten," he instructed, "I'll tell you everything then."

"I have something important to do tomorrow morning, Dad."

"That jewelry business you're launching? I told you to get people to handle it all for you. Why are you constantly involved?"

I clenched my fist. "Because I want to do it on my own."

"Hmm ... you always were a silly little thing. Well, you will just have to change your plans. I will see you at ten tomorrow morning. I will send a car for you. Ah, marvelous. My food has arrived. Goodnight."

"Goodnight, Dad," I said, but he had already hung up.

I went out then. I ate the noodles Britney had microwaved for me. I even put the finishing touches on the sample. When Britney talked to me I gave her all the right answers. But inside I was a seething mass of nerves. I felt it in my bones that tomorrow my life was going to change and there was not a damn thing I could do about it. At the usual time I said goodnight to Britney and I climbed into bed.

Sleep never came.

Chapter Four

FREYA

Curled up in my window seat, I watched the dawn arrive. It seemed magical. As if it was going to be taken away from me. Someone once told me the greatest luxury was freedom. Deep down I knew my father was about to snatch away my greatest luxury. How? I did not know yet. But in a few hours all would become crystal clear. For my father did not waste time mincing his words.

As life began in the street below I got into the shower. When I came back out wrapped in a towel, Britney was sitting on my bed, eating a bowl of cornflakes and chocolate milk.

"Morning," she said brightly.

"Morning," I said, matching her cheerfulness. I put my towel on the heater and naked went to open my underwear drawer. I took the first set I saw in it and began to dress.

"You never talk about your dad. Is he horrible?"

Horrible? Horrible was not a word I would use to describe him. My father was a repulsive sociopath. A man who was so utterly cold, he lived without compassion, remorse, or conscience. Only two things mattered in his life. The relentless insatiable acquisition of more and more power, and the pursuit of his own pleasure.

He didn't care about anyone or anything.

Once I went into his study and he was fucking a woman on his desk. I immediately tried to leave, but he wouldn't let me, but neither would he stop. I had to stand there with my gaze on the floor until he finished. As the woman passed by me, he said as casual as you please, "What did you want?" I've seen my father kill a man the way someone else would kill an ant.

I met Britney's eyes in the mirror. "My father is not ... horrible. We're just not close."

"Yet you're changing all our plans to go to have breakfast with him?"

I pulled on a white blouse and started buttoning it. "Yes. He is my father. Besides, he has to fly out again later today and this is the only time he has."

"Hmm ..." She eats another spoonful of cereal. "What do you think he wants to say to you?"

Tucking my blouse into a pair of comfortable black cargo pants, I picked up my hair brush. "I don't know."

"You mean, he didn't say at all?"

"Nope."

When I got out of my shabby apartment building in the Bronx it was 9:30. A glistening black town car with a dark suited chauffeur inside was waiting for me. It was the shiny statement of excessive wealth that did not belong in that neighborhood. Britney was hanging out of the window looking down on me. Her mouth was open in shock. A pair of dreadlocked twins playing guitar and smoking weed by the dirty graffiti wall in a corner of the street looked on curiously.

The chauffeur slid out of the car smoothly. "Miss Fedorov," he greeted, as he opened the door nearest the sidewalk for me.

Far from happy at the disruption from my wonderfully ordinary life, I got in and began to count the minutes when I would stand before my father.

The Ritz-Carlton was by Central Park. The moment I stepped into the sophistication of its world, far beyond the one I currently lived in, I felt the familiar chokehold of the old life that I had tried so hard to tear free of begin to reassert itself. I walked into the breakfast lounge. It featured an oriental color scheme. The high windows gave a picturesque view of the city's magnificent skyline. The exquisite furniture and paintings reminded me of our home back in Moscow. I could see my father's goons hanging around the lobby. They were trying to blend in with the other guests, but they stuck out like sore thumbs.

I made my way to the breakfast room.

It was expansive, filled with the scent of expensive coffee roast and the fragrance of flowers. Breakfasting in it were a smattering of people engaged in quiet conversations. I spotted my father in a corner table quite hidden by a gigantic plant that was so incredibly green it looked fake. Of course, it was not. As usual my father was on his phone.

"*Printsessa*," he called loudly the moment he noticed me. I cringed inwardly when people turned to look at us. My father had no use for customs or niceties. They were fools, he declared.

He ended his call and rose to receive me. Dutifully I walked into his large embrace. Shutting my eyes, I inhaled his familiar scent. The components of which were indecipherable as they had been carefully curated by a man who specialized in custom perfumes. Except, of course, for the jarring note from the cigars that he often had either in his mouth or dangling from his fingers.

For some strange reason, I suddenly thought of my mother.

"Sit," he said and I took the seat opposite him wondering why there was another by my side.

In his world everything was for a reason so I immediately called his attention to it. "Are you expecting someone else?"

He blatantly ignored the question and he regarded me critically. "You're thinner, *moya Printsessa*," he said. "Why are you living this way?"

"I'm fine, Papa." I smiled at the waitress as she came over, grateful for the interruption.

I didn't want him to know how nervous I was so I went all out and put in my order for eggs, a Belgian waffle, a bagel and cream cheese ensemble, and some yoghurt topped with berries and flax seed, and Assam tea.

When the waitress went away with our orders he watched me curiously. His black eyes unreadable.

"Your account remains untouched," he said. "And you're sharing an apartment in one of the worst neighborhoods. I also received reports that you now work in a low-class bar at night?"

My mouth felt dry and I wished I had ordered some orange juice. "I'm happy where I am."

"I disapprove," he said sternly.

In my mind, I muttered my response. *I don't care whether you approve or not.* Before he could keep going I quickly took my turn to ask the questions. "Why are you staying for such a short time?"

"This country does not welcome me." He laughed cynically. "It is better I leave before they tie me to some trouble. What about you? You've been finished with University a year. When are you planning to return to Moscow? Soon?"

"America is my home now."

His eyes flashed. "America is not for you. Your homeland is Russia."

I could have talked about the fact that my mother was American, which made me an American, but I knew that would only serve to encourage him to fly into a murderous rage. The last thing I needed was to make him feel the need to punish me. I played the only card powerful enough to reduce his interest in my return. "You know Moscow is dangerous for me at the moment, Papa."

'No one would dare touch you," he said, his face stone cold, but I had hit home. His enemies were plenty and vicious and not even the president of America is immune to assassination. Fortunately, his phone rang and he picked it up.

"Good. You are here," he said in Russian. It seemed the guest he'd been waiting for had arrived.

I looked down at the snow-white tablecloth and wondered why he was sharing our table with a guest. My suspicion went to the demon I had run into last night. Our families were bitter rivals so why then had he been the one tasked with asking me to call my father?

"Why did Maxim Ivankov come to see me yesterday?"

My father rose without responding, and with my heart suddenly hammering hard, I turned. As I had suspected, it was none other than the devil himself.

https://www.youtube.com/watch?v=VTsCZı_pHuM

She was impossible to miss, especially with that hair, a brazen auburn, wild and cascading in tousled waves all the way down to her waist. It was the first thing I'd noticed when I first laid eyes on her more than a decade ago. She was fifteen and I seventeen, and I had saved her from breaking a few bones in Moscow.

She had been hanging from one of the branches of an oak tree in my father's estate, mere seconds away from falling to the hard ground. I had stopped to watch her as she struggled vainly to keep her hold from slipping. I couldn't help wondering why she hadn't thought to call for any help whatsoever. I stood underneath her.

"Why are you not calling for help?" I asked curiously.

"I don't want to be found."

"So paralysis is a better option?" I was genuinely curious for her response.

She snapped at me then, "Get the hell away if you're not going to help."

My mood had been sour until then, but at her bark I had felt a smile stretch my lips and something warm fill my chest. So there we were, she struggling uselessly and I just watching the show. When she eventually fell, I had caught her in my arms.

The momentum of her fall sent us both toppling to the ground. It was strange to feel the warmth of her body on top of me. I remained in that state until she recovered enough to raise herself on her elbows and look down at me. The sun beyond seemed to create a fiery halo around her hair as she glared at me with the bright green eyes of a witch. They were nothing like mine. I knew mine were a cold, detached blue. Hers were alive with green fire.

For a few seconds neither of us moved. We just stared into each other's eyes. Then I felt my cock grow suddenly hard and press into her flesh. Color flooded her cheeks. She jumped up and raced away, her hair flying in the wind.

It was another three years before I saw her again.

Right now, she was glaring at me with those same bright green eyes that never failed to hold my attention. Scowling, she swept her gaze between me and her father. Clearly, she had not been filled in about what was going on.

As my three bodyguards scattered around the room, the other patrons sensed a rise in tension with the security detail that accompanied both me and Igor. No doubt they could sense from the severity of our profiles that we were not ordinary men who had come to eat half-a-teaspoon of Beluga caviar carefully balanced on a quail's egg.

I reached Igor Federov's table and I held out my hand to him. Many had heard about him and his brutal reputation, but few had ever seen him in person, or even knew what he looked like. He was a simple enough man, bald, with a strong nose, and dressed in a rust colored pin-striped suit. A gold necklace hung from his thick neck. He would have been a caricature of a Mafia don, a joke, if not for his gaze. It was ferocious.

At this moment though, he had a handshake and a smile for me, albeit a watchful one, full of effort.

I took my seat next to Freya. I could feel the hostility and antagonism coming from her in waves. I turned to look at her and our eyes clashed. Suddenly, it was as if we were back in my father's old estate. I was seventeen and she was fifteen, the air was warm, the sun was shining, and there was only us in the whole wide world.

Then her father said something.

I didn't catch it, but I felt it disturb the air around me, and I turned to look into his ferocious eyes. I was no longer seventeen, she was not fifteen, the air was not warm, the sun was not shining, and there was no erection in my pants. I cleared my throat. I only had a few minutes here before I had to move on to the next engagement for the day.

There was business to be done and the sooner we got down to it the better.

"What's going on?" Freya asked.

Totally ignoring his daughter, Igor addressed me. "It's been almost five years since I last saw you, Maxim. How are things?

I hear that you've taken over major parts of the country on behalf of your father."

My response was simple. "I heard that you've been well too, Mr. Fedorov." His chest bubbled with laughter at my elusiveness, but I could sense that the woman by our side was close to exploding.

She pushed her chair back and rose to her feet. "Since neither of you deem me important enough to receive a simple answer, I will excuse my meagre self from your highly-esteemed company."

She grabbed her bag and stormed off, but she had only gone a few steps when her father called to her.

His voice was like the crack of a whip and she came to a halt mid-stride. I turned to watch her rigid back. Slowly, stiffly, she turned. She had on one of those ridiculously baggy pair of black pants that women who don't want to be sexy wear. She had paired that with a loosely fitted white blouse. She wore no jewelry beyond a simple leather watch on her wrist, but I knew that it had originally belonged to her late mother.

"Sit," he ordered in Russian.

She hesitated only for a second, then she returned, sour and begrudging. To be honest it was quite troubling to see that this was what I would be getting my hands involved with. But then again I did like a little spirit in my women. And spirit she apparently had in spades.

Just then a nervous waitress arrived with a pot of coffee. I nodded at her, and she quickly filled my cup. I took a sip of my coffee and listened as Igor addressed his recalcitrant daughter.

"I really would have thought that you'd have thoroughly matured by now. How are you still so impatient and childish?"

She scowled outright at her father and I almost choked on my beverage. The look she gave the deadly don was more than enough to put someone on his hit list. What a privilege she enjoyed.

Her father turned to me. "Maxim," he said. "I have heard from your father, but not from you."

"I have accepted the agreement," I replied and turned to watch her at the same time that her eyes lifted to hold my gaze. She was waiting for an explanation for what I was referring to. I made it clear. "A Fedorov will be married into the Ivankov family.

All emotion disappeared from her face. Her father and I both waited for her response.

Neither of us expected her to burst into laughter. It was unbridled and humorless and loud. It made everyone in the room turn to look at us uncomfortably. Except me. I listened to the throaty sounds and felt my interest grow for the woman.

She turned to her father. "Is this why you're here? To sell me off so you can have more power to shove up your ass?"

It happened so fast she didn't see it coming.

The old bull lunged forward and struck a slap so hard across her face that she tumbled with the chair and fell to the ground. I heard gasps of shock and horror from around us as the other patrons reacted to the assault.

"She's yours," he said to me, as she lay sprawled on the

ground. "Better get your home in order. The sooner the better."

Her father stepped over her stunned body, and barked out rapid orders in Russian to his men. But before he could leave however, she grabbed his leg, and despite his anger he stopped.

"I'm sorry, Papa," she apologized in Russian.

I felt him draw in a deep breath. He bent down and easily pulled her up to her feet. He brushed her hair away from her white face, and placed a soft kiss on the cheek he had struck. With that he took his leave. When he was gone it was as if the air had been sucked out of the room. Just as I had expected, Freya glared murderously at me. I lifted my coffee to my lips and took another sip. She grabbed her backpack, and stormed out of the room.

With a sigh I finished my beverage, and thought of how I was going to handle this assignment. Moments later my cellphone lit up. It was the old bull.

"Do you have a way to convince her?" he asked. "She is my flesh and blood and I would prefer if it wasn't against her will."

"I will try my best," I replied.

Chapter Six

FREYA

"**F**reya!"

I jumped at the sudden call and looked up from the desktop screen I had been staring at.

"Are you done with the email?" Britney asked. "They're like waiting for a response."

"Uh ..." I looked towards the inbox open on my screen and moved to check it. "I'll do it now."

"What?" she groaned. "You've been staring at your screen since I sent it almost ten minutes ago. Where's your mind at?"

"Sorry. I'm on it." I quickly viewed the stone variations for the bracelet in our line and tried my best to focus.

Britney rose from her crowded desk and went over to the window overlooking the busy late afternoon Bronx Park. "I like the emerald, it gives an interesting addition to the charms but the cut of the crescent looks a little too clean, which makes it boring. How about ... What in God's name is going on down there?"

I looked up from the photos. "What is it?"

"Well, it looks like some celebrity is visiting the area ..."

I was immediately disinterested and went back to my analysis. "Britney, what if we just go with the sapphire set and—"

"There are men in suits downstairs waiting by two SUVs. They look so vicious. Oh, the door is opening ... It's not a celebrity!"

I looked up then and saw her mouth hanging open.

My heart began to race.

"I don't know who that is, but by God he looks fucking good. I need a closer look." I watched my business partner run from our office and begin her sprint down three flights of stairs in the old building to catch the sight of a man.

I jumped up from my chair and rushed over to the window, my heart pounding within my chest. I saw the two black SUV's she had been referring to and a few suited guards surrounding it, but no demon. My phone began to ring.

I turned and watched it warily as it rang to disconnection. Then I walked back to my desk and picked it up. It had been my father calling. I immediately called him back.

"*Printsessa*," he called as if he had not thoroughly humiliated me in a public place just a few hours ago.

"Papa," I replied, as I touched my cheek. "You haven't hit me since I was sixteen."

I could feel his smile. "I loosened my hold on you from then. You were becoming a woman."

"Then why are you tightening it once again?"

He chuckled softly. "I'm beginning to realize that adult or not you're still my baby girl. And I have to protect you."

"How can you then give me to an Ivankov? Have you forgotten what they did to Anna's family? And ours. They've tried to kill you so many times."

"Freya," he said to me. "I'm not going to be around forever, and your brother is no more. Beyond us no one else is as strong as they are. I need to be assured of your protection. We are enemies, but with our goals aligned and simple courtesy we will be able to exist just fine. We will be formidable. And there's no one else in the world beyond Maxim that can even come close to being worthy of you."

"I want nothing to do with that demon."

"He is a powerful man. You need a man like that to keep you in line. You are too independent and headstrong."

"He is a ruthless killer," I shot back.

"He is dependable," my father said. "As long as you become his, he will ensure your survival through thick and thin. His sense of honor is without compare."

"Fuck honor," I muttered, the tears falling from my eyes.

"I hate it when you talk like a whore in the gutter."

"I'm upset, Papa."

"Well, I have to go. I'll talk to you later, angel."

But I couldn't let him go. "Papa, wait ... please."

"It's for your own good, *Printsessa*. I'll call when I get to Moscow," he said and ended the call. I held the phone to my ears as I stared out of the window at the ugly apartment block across the street. It felt like the very ground had been kicked from under me or a giant vampire squid had wrapped its muscular tentacles around me and was irresistibly dragging me down into the dark deep ocean floor where there would be nothing but the bones of all the poor dead sea creatures. I shivered at the depressing image.

Just then the door to the office swung open and I immediately wiped my face clean of all emotion and turned around to face the man who was playing with my world.

At first all I could do was gaze at him but then Britney's flailing arms from behind him drew my gaze away from his.

"You freaking know him?" she mouthed shamelessly, her eyes widened with shock, and awe and fright all in one. Pretending to fan herself, she held onto to the door frame for support.

"Here she is," she finally recovered enough to say. "We work together here. I apologize for the mess, we're a little short on space. Please go in."

I immediately declared my stance. "You're not welcome here," I said. "Get out."

Britney stared at me in shock, her gaze moving from mine to his.

Maxim turned around and spoke to her. "Give us a moment, Miss Steans," he said.

Britney's mouth hung open. "You know my last name?"

He swung the creaky door shut on her, and turned back around to face me.

I still couldn't believe he was standing in my office. Neither could I believe that I was about to be tied to him in a way that would be my worst nightmare. No matter what, I was going to bring an end to this. I watched him, breathless with some strange emotion, as he moved across the room over to a waiting chair beside a messy pile of packages that we were yet to get to.

Nothing could ever be between us especially after Anna. I decided to appeal to him directly. If Maxim hated the idea of this union too, there was hope we could somehow hatch a plan to thwart my father. He was known to be hard-headed and even his father was unable to move him when Maxim was not in agreement.

"Maxim," I began. "Please call this marriage off. It's an absolutely insane idea. We both know that you and I will never be able to get along ... so unless you want a miserable life wouldn't it be better to call this madness off right now?"

"We don't need to get along," he drawled.

His words brought me too close to despair. If he however was on board ...

"You want this?" I asked, shocked.

He studied me with eyes that were like blue gems. So beautiful and electrifying they enticed you with the promise of being able to see into the man's soul, but at the same time it frightened you at what destruction and danger lay in the cold, deadly depths.

"This union," he said with an elegant shrug, "will make our

families a formidable force. What's there not to want about it?"

His answer disappointed me, but it shouldn't have surprised me. Of course, he would want it. He was like my father. What he already had was not enough. His whole existence was dedicated to acquiring more power and wealth.

"Don't you want to be happy? Is controlling the horrid underworld the only thing that you truly want?"

"What I want," he answered, "is protection. We were both born into a world of many sins, so the best we can do is keep those sins from eventually coming back at us."

Temper blazed in my stomach. "Well I'd rather be happy for one day than protected and miserable for a hundred."

He cocked his head then to study me. "Is there someone you... care for?"

"Why? So you can go and kill him?" I almost screamed.

He sighed. "Not at all. I was trying to establish the fact that you have no reason for your objection to this union. After we're married you'll be able to carry on with your... plans. There will be no restrictions to your activities."

I had been about to speak but at his words, my mouth shut back closed. "What? You're proposing an open marriage?"

He frowned. "I meant your business plans." He waved his hand around the room. "Whatever this is. Our marriage will not be open."

Burning hot tears of anger stung my eyes. Living in New York and making plans for my future, I thought I had left the past behind for good. I couldn't believe this was the life I was going to be resigned to. I had to make him see things my way. Appeal to his sense of fairness, if he had one.

"Maxim," I began, my voice soft and pleading. "I don't want the same life you want. I don't want power or millions in the bank or bodyguards everywhere I go. I want an ordinary life. I want to fall in love for real. I want to have a family of my own. I want to have picnics in Central Park with them. I want to take my kids to school and not worry about whether they will be snatched on the way home. Surely you understand this."

His phone began to ring then and without taking his eyes off me, he pulled it out of his suit jacket and pressed it to his ear. He didn't say a word and instead listened.

"What time?" he asked in Russian finally. I'll be there." Then he put his phone away and refocused his attention on me. "This must have all come as a shock to you. I'll give you a few days to mull over it so that—"

"There's nothing to mull over," I interrupted. Passing by him I marched over to the door and pulled it open. It sent Britney flying into the room almost landing on her face.

"Oh," she said lamely from the middle of the room. Her face was bright red.

I frowned at her and she immediately hurried away. I turned back to Maxim.

"I am not marrying you, Maxim, and that's my final response."

"I'll be at Tribeca Piers on Friday afternoon at exactly noon. We will conclude this arrangement then."

Chapter Seven

FREYA

"Have you decided what you're going to do?" Britney asked, as she came into our tiny kitchen where I was cooking dinner for us.

"Nope." I left the tomato sauce I'd been stirring and headed over to the bottom shelf of the cupboard to get a packet of pasta. The whole time I was aware of Britney's worried eyes following me across the room. She had been trying her best to pry my situation out of me, but I was actually too upset to even speak about it. The last person I ever wanted to speak about, or even think about was Maxim Ivankov.

"Um …," she said cautiously, "after you left I received a call from the top buyer at Delaneys. He said, fingers crossed if all goes well then he'll be able to have us in their branch on Madison Avenue."

"That's great news," I said, but I felt nothing. So I said it again, and this time I put more emotion into it. "That is great news."

"Yeah, he seemed pretty hot about it," Britney said, but her voice reflected no real happiness, which made me feel bad because this was our big dream and I was trampling all over it. But I couldn't help it. How could I be happy about being in Delaneys when my whole life was being turned upside down?

"I need to call my dad, could you please help me watch the water so it doesn't boil over?"

"Sure," she said, moving towards the pot.

I went into my room, shut the door, sank to the floor, and thought of how I could make my stance clear to my father. A call would do nothing. He would simply refuse to discuss the matter. I decided to send him a message. It would make it clear that I was willing to fight till the end.

I drafted the letter. It was a long one. I swore to him that I would denounce him as my father if he forced me into a union that I wanted no part of, but after I was done, a solitary tear ran down my face. I knew there was absolutely no point in sending it. I had more chance of changing the mind of a brick wall than my father. Any hope I had of changing my situation did not lie with my father. I had to work on Maxim. There had to be some way for me to convince him that this was a terrible idea not just for me, but for him as well.

I was sure he did not want to be saddled with me. A couple of times when we had ended up at the same parties he was with drop dead gorgeous models. Both those women clung to his every word like he was God. He would never be happy with an independent spirited woman like me. I would never cling to him like that even if my life depended on it. In fact, I believe we would end up killing each other. Maybe that is the way I should go about this. Convince him how bad a marriage with me would be.

A quiet knock came on my door. "Coming," I said, wiping away the solitary tear. I went back out and saw that she had already placed both of our meals on the coffee table. She had also lit a candle and opened the bottle of champagne we had been saving for the day that a big store agreed to carry our products. Squaring my shoulder, I went and took a seat on the carpet next to her.

"I made it spicy," she said.

That little consideration made me smile. "You plan to spend the night on the toilet seat?"

"Oh no, I took mine out before I *doused* yours in chili and pepper," she said pouring champagne into coffee mugs. If my father could see what she was doing... champagne in coffee mugs.

I smiled and we toasted to our first success. I tried my best to push aside my anxiety enough to eat something. Perhaps things would become clearer to me when I did. We ate quietly, with Britney sneaking looks at me until I couldn't take it anymore.

"My father wants me to get married," I blurted.

She was careful with her response. "To the guy that came to the office today?"

"Yeah." I put my fork down. "Please don't say he's hot."

She bit her lips to hide her smile, but nothing about this situation could even mildly amuse me. "Is there a reason why you're so against him?"

I took a deep breath. I knew that it would be best for me to be cautious with my words just as I had always been, but today, and at this moment I cared very little about holding my tongue. "He killed my best friend, about eight years ago."

She froze. "What?"

"He pretended to be in love with her and she trusted him and gave him information lethal enough to get her and her family killed."

"Jesus Christ, Freya. You're speaking about death as though it were normal. Who are these people?"

Really, she wanted to say who are you? "I never speak about it, but you must have guessed by now my family is involved with the Russian mafia."

Her eyes widened. "Actually, I did not guess any such thing. If you're from... such a family, what on earth are you doing here in this cockroach infested apartment with me? Why are you trying to sell bits of jewelry when you could be dripping in the stuff?"

"That's because until now I have done my best to steer myself away from that life."

"Okay. The worrying part is when you said until now."

"Well, marrying this ... man will shoot all of that to hell. It will keep me a prisoner for the rest of my life. Not to mention that I just might end up killing him myself. Then I'd really be finished." Even thinking about him made my stomach recoil. I rose with my half-eaten meal and headed into the kitchen. I scraped the food into the bin and began to do the dishes. I needed to keep my hands busy.

Britney followed me into the kitchen. "Any plans to stop this arrangement?"

"Ah, Britney. You have no idea. I cannot cross my father."

"Why not? You're not a child."

"You know how there are fathers in parts of Asia and the middle east who will kill their daughters because they have dishonored them by not wanting to marry the men they have chosen for them? Well, my father was cut from the same cloth."

"Then let us get this fiancé of yours to call the whole marriage thing off. Surely, he's not on board with this crazy plan."

I turned off the faucet and focused my attention on her. "As a matter of fact, he is."

"Why? He seems like he could have any woman he wants. Er ... no insult to you, of course. You're beautiful, but why can't he find his own?"

"They are doing it to bind the family together. To ensure there are no more turf wars between us."

"Right. So what happens next?"

"He told me to meet with him in a few days at Tribeca. To state my terms..."

"Well, how about you make them as outlandish as possible. Ask for things that you know he will never agree to, so that there's no way in hell he will even consider this arrangement."

"And if he still does despite all of this?"

She opened her mouth, then closed it again because what could she say?

Chapter Eight

MAXIM

I waited for her at a table aboard the restaurant's ship, docked at Tribeca Piers. In the distance was the city's skyline and the lit Statue of Liberty. On my table was a glass of Japanese malt whisky.

Just as I'd expected, she was deliberately late so I quashed the irritation inside me and ordered a refill. I'd give her ten more minutes. Even she wouldn't dare be later than that. The drink arrived almost instantly and I decided to take the opportunity to relax. The simple rest was unusual for me. I took in the gentle rise and fall of the waters, separated from my table by only the wooden edge of the boat.

Then I lifted my gaze to the sight of passing boats, yachts, ferries filled with excited tourists taking in as much of the city's sights as they could. Further in the distance the infamously tall buildings stood majestic, scraping the skies.

Excited chatter pulled my attention towards a party of exquisitely dressed girls heading towards the bar. They reminded me of a flock of flamingos, decorative and showy. Freya on the other hand was a mustang. Wild and fierce. My phone began to ring and as I picked it up, the flock moved to reveal my flame-colored mustang dressed in all in black. How very dramatic of her.

"Maxim," I said into the receiver, as our eyes locked.

I listened to my call, while she marched up, slammed a document on the table, and glared at me as she waited for me to round up my phone call.

"Call me back in an hour," I said into the phone.

"I agree to the marriage. Here are my terms," she stated defiantly.

I picked up the one page document and glanced down it. There were ten items on it. None of them would be agreeable, of course, but one stood out more than the others. I flung the sheet away and it floated up into the air. I watched as her gaze followed the early afternoon wind catch her list of purposely unreasonable demands and carry it to its watery death.

She smiled and returned her gaze to me. "That's okay, because I brought another copy ... just in case you accidentally lost the other one. And there's plenty more where this came from too." She placed another paper on the table and secured it with my phone.

I held her gaze. Her animosity towards me was impressively fierce. I wondered if a day would come when I would see something soft in those emerald eyes when they settled on me.

I looked briefly away from her and got my thoughts together. "We cannot have an open marriage ... and you *definitely* cannot have a child with any man you please."

Her eyebrows rose. "This is a marriage of convenience. Surely you're not expecting me to sleep with you?"

I leaned back against the chair. "Sit down, Freya."

For a split second she hesitated. It was clear she hated being told what to do, even if it was something as simple as sitting down in a restaurant. With a tightly clenched jaw she complied.

"What do you want to drink?" I murmured.

"I'm not thirsty," she muttered. "Can you please answer my question?"

"Not only do I expect you to sleep with me, I expect absolute loyalty from you. Any man who touches you will find himself in the same place as your list of ridiculous terms."

"You expect loyalty while you fuck around to your heart's content?" she snapped.

I frowned. "Of course not. I will honor our marriage vows."

She exhaled sharply. "Look. I'm going to be honest with you. I don't want to marry you, Maxim. There is no way any union with us in it will work. Anyway what kind of man would want to marry a woman who doesn't want him? Can't you see what a terrible mistake it would be?"

"The terrible mistake would be if we did not get married because of your childish and ridiculous insistence that you want to have the ability to go to the zoo without bodyguards.

People who are born without limbs learn to paint with a brush held between their teeth. You will simply have to learn to work within the boundaries you have been born into, which mean bodyguards at the zoo."

She straightened her shoulders. "Fine. In that case. It must be a marriage in name only. I do not ever want our marriage to be consummated."

"I'm afraid that will not be possible."

"Why not? If people without limbs can learn to paint why can't you learn to live without sex? I'm ready to do it."

I reached for my whisky and took a sip. "For two reasons. A: People without limbs have no choice. I do. And B: You will be required to produce heirs."

She held my gaze without blinking. "Can you hear yourself? Can you hear what you sound like? We're not in the dark ages of arranged marriages anymore, to any normal person what you are suggesting would sound insane."

I shrugged. "I agree it is not conventional in this day and age, but since my motto is Never Follow, Never Explain, I have no problem with being outside the acceptable norm."

"I can't believe you would force me to be your wife," she gasped.

"All you have to do is say no," I told her quietly.

Her lips trembled. "You know very well I can't, my father would kill me."

For a split second, I thought of Igor's ferocious eyes. Indeed, that would be her fate. It would have been so easy for me to walk away from this union. No one, not even my father would dare question my decision, but then an image of Freya flashed into my mind. Her legs open, her body arched, her head thrown back with ecstasy, and words formed of their accord and slipped out of my mouth.

"That is not my problem."

Chapter Nine

FREYA

I stared at him in shock. I couldn't believe he'd just told me he wouldn't help me even if it meant my father would kill me. Maxim's cold, unfeeling eyes stared right back and suddenly the whole world fell away. The air between us crackled with the tension.

Then his gaze dropped to my mouth.

And suddenly my heart stopped beating. Something else began to infect my blood, running through my veins like poison. It was not hate, fury, or disgust, it was... pure insanity. I stayed frozen as something deep inside my belly woke up and opened its eyes. No, it can't be. Not for him. He was the enemy. It would be an unthinkable betrayal of Anna. He was her killer. A monster. I felt as if I was suffocating. Without thinking, I was on my feet and running. My head told me I was making a scene, but I couldn't stay.

"Freya," I heard him call out as I weaved through the crowd, but I didn't respond.

A big hand grabbed a hold of me and in annoyance I jerked my hand from the grasp.

"Let me go!" I screamed, as I kept moving, but I was grabbed again and this time so firmly, I couldn't dislodge it. I whirled around. At first I was so wired I didn't feel the steel of the blade lodge itself into my back. Those few seconds before the pain could get past the haze of fury and adrenaline gave my attacker those precious seconds to slip into the crowd. I opened my mouth to tell Maxim, who was only a few steps away, to fuck off. Instead a shocked gasp came out.

Maxim's eyes widened. "What is it?" His voice was urgent.

My knees gave way and I felt myself falling. His reaction was lightning quick. He caught me and pulled me towards his body. He must have felt my blood flowing like a river over his hands, because his eyes changed as his gaze left mine and lifted up into the crowd.

"Get him!" he roared.

A flurry of panicked movement began around me as people began to notice what had just happened. I tried to push his hand away but the tears had already gathered in my eyes, as the pain reverberated through me. I felt his hand press against my wound.

"You'll be fine," I heard him say, but my gaze had rolled up towards the sky. It began to dim quite rapidly before me, and then his face came into sight again.

His eyes... struck me. They were just as vibrant as the sky had been just a moment ago. Something caught in my chest as I stared at him making it impossible for me to breathe. I felt the tears roll down my face just as I registered my hand rising. It was all his fault. All of it. I wanted to hit him, but he instead grabbed my hand as my world... was lost.

Chapter Ten

MAXIM

https://www.youtube.com/watch?v=OWl9p3oFKgg

*S**he had nearly died in my arms.***

If that blade had punctured an organ, or my men had not been carrying a bleed kit she would have fucking died on that boat. I stopped pacing the room restlessly and stood for a moment in the center of it. My nerves felt frazzled. I wanted to kill someone, but what I needed to do was to calm the fuck down.

I took a seat next to her and watched the light dusting of freckles across her nose. She had been stitched up and bandaged and now her arm was strung with an IV. There were wires hooked up from her chest to the machine that monitored her heartbeat.

At first, the damp squid of a doctor expressed the opinion 'that level of care is quite unnecessary' but I took a step forward into his personal space and quietly told him if anything happened to her I would hold him personally responsible. I can't imagine he knew who I was so it must have been the tone of my voice, or the look in my eyes, because he did the usual. Turned as white as a sheet and dedicated himself to his own survival in the short-term.

Her hair was tangled, silky strands spread out over the pillowcase like rivers of red, lit ablaze by the early morning sun filtering in through the window blinds. I couldn't stop myself. I reached out and touched the fiery silk. I let the soft wavy strands slide through my fingers.

She was unconscious to the world, but she sighed softly, as if something deep inside her, that even she had not yet recognized, felt my touch. At the sound I exhaled my first proper breath in the last twenty hours.

Her eyelids fluttered and I immediately leaned away. Giving her a heart attack the moment she awakened was not one of my goals for that day. I felt my phone vibrate and I pulled it out of my pocket. It was my brother, Levan. Her chest was rising and falling peacefully so I quickly slipped out of the room into the corridor to take the call.

"Is everything alright?" I asked.

"I should be the one asking you that. I just heard from Makhail. He can't understand why they tried to get to her now."

"Instead of tattling about it, Makhail should be unravelling it," I growled.

He sighed. "Let him be, man. He told me because he knew I'd be worried. Any ideas why this happened?"

"About a thousand," I said dryly.

"I can't believe Fedorov lets her live alone and without protection in that city."

"Do you really believe that Fedorov would let his daughter go about without protection?"

"Then where were they when all this happened?"

"They would have shown themselves if I was not there. They could see my men had everything under control almost instantly."

"How is she doing now?" he asked.

"About to come awake."

"I'll let you go then."

"Yeah. Watch your back," I reminded him. "Your wedding is just around the corner."

"You too," he responded. "From what I hear you might be tying the knot before me."

"Well she's just received a hole through her back. So I doubt that."

"Take care, Maxim."

I wasn't done with the call. "Before you go, I heard there was trouble at Brighton last night."

His sigh was heavy. "Yeah, I'm handling that now. I have a meeting with a detective in forty-five minutes. Otari and his idiots got into a brawl with some Armenian gang. Unfortunately for them some rookie uniforms arrived on the scene and they found their stash of weapons and ice. I'm of the mind to just throw them to the authorities for at least a decade. That should be enough to reset their brains."

That made me smile. "You don't have the heart to."

"You'll be surprised. Anyway, we'll talk some more after I've had my meeting. I'll leave you with your new bride. One day in your company and she's already had a knife through her. I fear for what the future holds."

"With this girl, weapons of steel are currently the least of my concern."

He chuckled. "Exciting days ahead, Maxim. I have great faith in her."

I put the phone back into my pocket and went back to the room. As if on cue, her eyelids began to flutter restlessly. I realized then that she must have already been awake for at least a few minutes.

Her eyes opened. They were strained from the pain, the corners crinkling as she tried to reposition herself. She dragged her gaze away from mine and looked down at the IV needle in her hand.

"Why are you here?" she asked, her tone clearly hostile.

I wasn't in the mood to fight so I decided to take my leave. She was awake, and alive and that was all that mattered... at least for now. Just as I reached the door it was abruptly pushed forward.

I met the furious eyes of the don himself.

"You bastard," he swore. "Is this how you protect her?"

"Technically she is still under your protection," after a tiny pause I added, "Sir."

He was a reasonable man. He noted the truth in the statement and courtesy in which it was expressed and continued on his way to visit his daughter.

Chapter Eleven

FREYA

My father hurried to my side and placed his hand over mine. "Freya," he called.

I sucked in my breath at his use of the name my mother had given me. He hated it and when it appeared on his tongue it meant the situation was grave and he was trying to comfort me. I felt certain it was grave, but at that moment little, beyond the pain and anger I felt at the demon, had sunk in, so I felt quite numb.

The scenes leading up to the second I was stabbed played in my head. They were fresh and hurtful. The cold, unfeeling demon had completely refused to help me even if it meant I would end up dead. I focused my eyes on my father. I must have looked pale and pathetic lying in that hospital bed, because he seemed disturbed. Even in that reduced state I knew right away this might be my only chance to reason with him. I willed the tears to come, but they wouldn't. I brought back the image of the mangled body of my pet, Pasha, after he ran out in front of a car when I was nine. Soon enough my eyes misted over.

"Papa," I called out pitifully, keeping my gaze lowered.

"Yes, my dear daughter," he replied quite sincerely, placing dry kisses on my hand.

My, my, kisses on my hand! He must be feeling especially guilty, or I looked especially wretched. I let even more crocodile tears pour down my face.

"There, there," my father consoled.

With the drama of a black and white movie, I lifted my eyes brimming over with tears and gazed tragically at him. "Papa, I cannot marry Maxim."

For a few seconds his cold eyes regarded me expressionlessly. It was almost like looking into a reptile's eyes. Then he patted the back of my hand affectionately. "Not now, Printsessa," he said softly. "Just focus on recovering first."

I knew then that it was pointless. My head flopped back against the pillows.

"Did you see the man who attacked you?" he asked, his voice business-like and brisk again.

I shook my head wearily. Then I shut my eyes, and suddenly felt very, very, very exhausted.

~

The flowers came as I returned from the bathroom. Tracy, a cute Japanese intern, rolled me into the room and there it was. A massive bouquet of about two dozen sunflowers, their faces as big as children's heads was sitting next to the bed. At first I was confused. How could he have known? Then I realized how and it instantly destroyed my mood.

As Tracy helped me to get back into bed, I barely registered the pain that came with the movements because my chest was aching, aching even more for the friend I had loved, the girl I had found hanging from the ceiling fan, with a rope she had bought at the hardware store around her neck. Her tongue was swollen and protruding from her mouth, and her blouse was wet with saliva.

"Are you alright?" Tracy had noted my changed demeanor.

I found a smile for her. "I'm fine."

She wanted to help me lie on my back, but I refused. "It's alright. I'll just sit for a little while."

"Okay," she said with a smile and turned to leave. "Let me know if you need anything."

"Thank you," I responded, and watched her leave. My gaze remained on the door, but I saw nothing. My mind was filled with Anna. How I had cut the rope down with a kitchen knife that day and held her in my arms sobbing, until finally the police arrived and pried her away from my clawed hands.

It was a long time before I turned to look at the flowers.

It made my heart ache in a way that immediately choked me with tears. She must have told him that sunflowers were my favorite flower. Why did he send them to me? Was it a threat, that perhaps I could also end up like Anna? Or was he just plain dumb?

I wanted to pick up the phone to call him, to vent my fury, but all the raw emotion made my chest feel tight and constricted, so I focused on breathing evenly. Ever since he came into my life again my insides were constantly boiling.

I stared at them, at how ugly they had become simply because he had sent them. How dare he? Viciously, I swung my hand out and it hit the tall glass vase. It flew from the table and crashed to the floor, shattering into sharp shards, water rushing out, and the flowers scattering on the plain gray floor.

A few seconds later there was hurried footsteps and Tracy burst into the room.

I turned to meet her eyes, first filled with concern, then confusion, as she looked from the chaos of shattered glass and strewn flowers at my feet, to the dead look in my eyes.

"Are you alright?" she asked.

"I'm fine," I replied. "Please get someone to clean it up and take it away. I hate sunflowers."

Then I lay down on my bed, drew the covers over me, and shut my eyes to find peace.

Chapter Twelve

MAXIM

"**S**he destroyed the flowers?" Levan repeated.

Otari nodded. He was afraid to meet my eyes, so it was a relief to keep them on my brother.

"Why?" Levan asked.

"I don't know, Sir."

"Leave," I said, and Otari immediately exited the office.

Levan turned to me. "Do you know why she would do that?"

"Apart from the fact that she hates me, you mean?"

I returned back to the Belarus factory acquisition report I'd been studying before Otari came in, but the words on the page could have as well not been there. Nothing registered beyond what Otari had told us. I shouldn't be surprised, but did she truly hate me that much? Not that it put me off. In fact, the opposite was true. Her intense hate invigorated and intrigued me. The idea of conquest always did that to me.

Making her mine was going to be an extremely enjoyable task.

"Why did you send her sunflowers?"

I could feel his gaze burning through me as he waited for an answer to my question. I shrugged. "I was told they are her favorite flowers."

He looked at me speculatively. "Ahh, so you do have a thing for her."

I shrugged. "You are wandering into territories you shouldn't little brother."

"Hmm ... so who told you about the flowers?" he asked, refusing to drop the topic.

"Anna Petrovska."

"Anna Petrovska? Wow! I almost forgot about her."

There was a very long silence that followed as both of us revisited memories from the very skinny, blonde girl. When Levan spoke again his voice was small with grave concern.

"Do you really want to marry Freya? You might end up being miserable. I mean I know you're not particularly looking to marry for love, but there is a certain satisfaction you can get from being with someone you can at least be civil with. Freya is like a wild..." he searched for the right word.

"Horse?" I supplied.

"Yes, like a wild horse. She will not let anyone tame her enough for her to be ridden on."

"I think I can ride," I said with a grin.

Levan sucked in a breath. "You know, I actually think she would be perfect for you if she didn't hate you so much. Having said that hate is the other side of the coin. If you play your cards right she would come to love just as fiercely as she hates you now. Come to think of it, she almost reminds me of Bianca in that way, but Bianca only goes after trouble when it comes looking for her. Freya seems the kind to stir up storms even while she's aslee—"

"Don't you have work to do?"

His eyes sparkled with amusement at my irritation. "My flight to Macau is in an hour."

"Well then get going. The airport is not exactly next door."

His grin grew even wider as he rose to his feet. "I'm excited," he said. "Very excited to see how it goes down with you and the wild mustang. You never lose and she doesn't seem like one who gives in easily either."

An idea occurred to me. "Perhaps your fiancée could pay her a visit?"

Levan frowned. "Why?"

I shrugged. "To drop off your wedding invitation."

"Maybe, but I don't want her to go alone. We'll go together when I get back to town."

"I don't want you there. You'll just remind her of me," I said.

"We don't look that much alike so I very much doubt Freya will mistake me for you."

My gaze turned hard, but my brother was his own man and he didn't budge.

"I've never been enemies with Freya and we've all known each other for a long time. Bianca is a stranger to her, and I don't see Freya as someone who will open up to a stranger just because they're both women."

I said nothing even though I agreed with him on his assessment of Freya.

"Besides, no way in hell am I letting Bianca go alone to meet Fedorov's daughter. One wrong word from Bianca and she could have a gun at her head. I'm not taking any chances."

"Forget I asked then."

"Too late," he replied coolly and walked out of my office.

Chapter Thirteen

FREYA

"Who was it?" I asked looking up from the vintage earring drawings we had been studying on the kitchen counter before the doorbell rang and Britney went to hang her head out of the window to see who it was.

"Some Russian panty-melter called Levan." She pulled a face. "He's with a woman though. Why are all the good-looking ones always taken, and why do they keep coming to find you recently?"

"He's Maxim's younger brother," I replied shortly.

Her eyebrows shot up. "Ah ... the plot thickens. Do you want to see him?"

"I've never had any problems with him."

"What about the woman? Is she with him?" she asks hopefully.

"I have no idea who she is, but there are no females in their family."

"Then perhaps I have a shot then? Let's let him in."

The sudden shrill ring of my phone made me jump. There was no caller ID, which gave me a pretty good idea as to whom it was. These mafia folks were all so damn intrusive. I was never one to cower, and from what I knew of Levan neither was he so I might as well face this head-on. I picked up the phone and answered the call.

"Yes," I barked frostily.

It was not Levan who answered. It was a woman. "Hey,' she said in a friendly tone. "I'm Bianca Russet ... Levan's fiancée. We heard about what happened to you and decided to come visit you. Levan says he's known you from when you were both children, and we'd love to see you, and we also brought our wedding invitation and some homemade cake. Actually, I made it myself. It's a new recipe so you must tell me if you like it."

She must have been nervous, because she spoke very fast and stopped abruptly as if she'd suddenly realized she was babbling. I took a moment to digest all she had said.

"Who is it?" Britney mouthed.

I hit the mute button. "His fiancée."

"The woman is his fiancée?"

"Sorry."

Britney's face fell and it somewhat amused me. "Trust me, you're not missing out on anything. The worst fate in the world is to get involved with that miserable family."

"Let's let them in," she said, brightening immediately. "I'd love to see how an engaged mafia couple interact with each other. Especially since it doesn't seem likely I'll ever get to see that from you."

I gave her a hard look, but unfazed she grinned and skipped away to let them in. I stood up and followed her into the living room. While we waited for them to come up the stairs, Britney looked at me.

"Well, isn't this exciting?"

"Actually, it's not," I said sourly.

"You grew up with this, but I didn't so it is pretty freaking exciting to me."

At that moment there was a knock on the door and Britney rushed to open it.

First in was Bianca Russet. She was beautiful and quite... normal.

I looked from her to Levan and wondered what the hell was going on. Did she not know of his world, and the darkness that it came with?

She smiled brightly at Britney, then walked straight up to me and held out the box in her hand. "This is for you, Freya."

"Bianca is a baker," Levan explained, his watchful gaze on me. "She has a little bakery not far from here, on Allen street."

Levan, I was surprised to note was being quite chatty. My recollection of his childhood personality was completely different. Maxim was dour and said nothing at all and Levan was reserved and watchful. I wondered at the brightness of his new persona.

"Levan said you were allergic to cinnamon, but there is no

cinnamon in chocolate cakes," Bianca said nervously, still holding the package out to me.

Britney walked up to me and nudged me hard enough to make me stumble. I glared at her then turned towards Bianca.

"Thank you," I said, and received the homemade chocolate cake that she had apparently baked herself using a new recipe. I shouldn't be horrible to her. It was not her fault I was being forced to marry the demon. If anything, she was to be pitied.

Bianca took a step back and turned to Levan. I could have sworn I saw his eyes sparkle as their gazes met. He wasn't even touching her, both his hands were in his pockets, but they stood as though they were one. She moved again and let herself rest against him as though that was all she'd ever known, and he ... he towered over her protectively, as though the world needed his permission to even approach. Suddenly, I understood the light in his life. He had found his soulmate. And suddenly, I had never felt more jealous in my life of another woman.

"Thank you," I said again, and walked away with the cake. Britney stepped in and led them towards our small living room, apologizing for how cramped everything was because we had to store our stock in our living room.

Bianca laughed and told her our apartment was charming.

I put the cake on the kitchen table. From my position I could see right into the living room and I watched them jealously and saw how when they sat down, Levan's arm automatically slid around her waist while her hand rested intimately on his thigh. They were *so* in love. Something inside me felt bereft. If I married Maxim I would never have that. Ever.

"When are you getting married?" Britney asked.

As I watched they turned to gaze into each other's eyes. "In five weeks. November 23rd," she answered.

"Wow, that's close," Britney commented, her eyes wide and full of curiosity.

"Not close enough for me. I can't wait to get my ring on her finger so the whole world will know she's mine. And only mine," Levan stated proudly.

Bianca tightened her lips to hide her blush and looked away from him, but he couldn't take his eyes off her.

I brought out a knife, and began to slice up the cake to serve, my movements were jerky. I had to ask. "How did the two of you meet?"

"At my bakery," Bianca answered. "Levan was a..." she stopped, and tilted her head while she thought of the appropriate word, and he laughed out loud. I wanted to hear the story behind that look.

"Well at the time I thought... well he told me he was a Masters student at NYU where I was attending too. But later found out that was not the case at all."

He lowered his head to hide his smile and she gave him a playfully sour look. "Anyway, I had a crush on him, and being the naïve fool I was, I told him about it, which made him disappear for two years."

The shock on Britney's face was amusing. "Why?"

I had a good enough guess as it most definitely had to do with someone's death, perhaps even almost his.

"Well some family issues made him leave the country," she said, her voice still haunted by that old pain. "But he came to his senses and came back to me, and we got together again."

I scoffed at the explanation as I lifted the tray to take it to them.

Levan heard me. "Why the sneer?"

"Britney is not a stranger, and neither is Bianca. You can say what *actually* happened."

Rather than taking offense she turned to me with an excited surprise. "What do you think happened, or are you aware?"

"Wait," Britney suddenly said. "I'm just realizing that you seem a bit familiar," she said to Levan. "Have I seen you somewhere before?"

He shrugged. "Perhaps."

She looked away to dig into her memory bank, while I placed the cake on the coffee table. I winced at the slight pain from the effort and Bianca immediately sprung up to help me.

"I'm so sorry," she said. "We're meant to be the ones helping out."

"It's fine," I said. "What do you all want to drink?"

"I'll come with you and we'll do it together," she said decisively.

"Thank you," I said, and we headed back into the kitchen. I smiled at her as I opened the fridge and took out some orange juice. "Is this alright?" I asked.

She nodded. "It's fine for me, but Levan hates orange juice so some water will be fine." She retrieved a glass from our drying rack and filled it with tap water for her fiancé, which she then put on the tray with the other glasses and the jug. She insisted on carrying the tray too.

"Thank you," Levan said, taking a sip from the glass of water she handed to him.

"You're not afraid I might have poisoned it?" I asked.

Britney looked shocked at my question, and even Bianca looked slightly worried, but Levan only laughed.

"You never came anywhere near it. Bianca fetched it not you," he said.

I realized the error in my thinking. Levan was friendly and sweet because he had Bianca, but inside he was still the same watchful man.

"Plus, you wouldn't dare," the new and improved Levan added. "We used to be friends."

"Yeah, until your brother went ahead and murdered my best friend's family."

My tone was bitter and cast a weighty silence across the room. "Bianca, I'm sorry if I'm making you uncomfortable. You've just walked into a minefield and you don't understand what is going on, but Levan's family and I don't exactly have the best of relationships. Which makes me wonder why he's here." I turned on him aggressively. "Did your brother send you? What exactly did he ask you to check on?"

"If you were doing well," he answered easily.

I smiled tightly. "I happen to know it wouldn't spoil his day if I fell into a ravine tomorrow, but if we're all going to pretend to play this game, then please let him know that I'm doing just great. And that he should please stay away from me so that I can continue to do even better."

"Why do you hate Maxim so much?' Levan asked.

"Are you seriously asking me that? Don't you know?"

"I am asking exactly that," he said.

"He killed Anna," I screamed.

"He didn't kill Anna, she took her own life," he said calmly.

I could feel my anger begin to take over. "And whose fault was that? Your brother wiped out her family."

"Have you ever stopped to find out why, or what actually happened?"

"The whole of fucking Russia knew what happened. He did it to prove himself to your father. Anna's father was challenging your father with some lawsuit and Maxim took him out to prove that he was qualified to join his father's army of demons."

"Your father's business is not any smaller or less violent than ours, Freya."

"Perhaps, but no one is as evil as Maxim. How else could a fucking nineteen-year old kid kill a man and his wife in cold blood. All for some accolade?"

The room was deadly silent.

Levan frowned. "Is that what you were told?"

"It is what I know," I argued.

He rose to his feet and held out his hand to his fiancée. "Let's go, Bianca."

"Of course, you'll always be on his side."

He didn't say a word and began to walk. Bianca looked torn, apologetic towards me and yet understanding of Levan. Britney was just confused.

I felt hurt and wasn't satisfied enough with my taunt. "Oh, and for old time's sake, since you said that we were 'friends' could you let me know what your family's plan is with this whole marriage situation? Is Maxim trying to go grand this time? Get married to me, then take out my whole family? Just let me know, *friend.*"

Levan smiled, and when I saw that it wasn't in offense but mockery, it made me very uncomfortable. "You've always been really cocky, Freya," he said "and I understand that it's because you've wanted to always be on guard. But you need to sometimes put your pride down so you can figure out the truth. You knew Maxim before Anna met him. Tell me, when you heard what he had supposedly done to her family, were you shocked or unsurprised? Did he seem like the kind to so heartlessly do something like that?"

"Maxim is lethal."

"And so are you, perhaps even more so than he will ever be. Otherwise, how else can you so easily accuse him of all that you just have without knowing the actual truth?"

"Truth. What do you know about the truth? Anna told me this herself, a few days before she committed suicide."

I was shaking. How dare he? How dare any of them even come close to me.

"Someday, ask Maxim what really happened and why he did what he did. I know you enough to know that after hearing it you definitely will not feel as you do now. You will understand. I hope you can come to our wedding, *friend*. Take care."

He took his fiancée's hand and walked out of our house.

Chapter Fourteen

FREYA

I couldn't sleep.

It had been two days and I still couldn't sleep. It was not so much the pain of the wound on my back but Levan's words that haunted me.

"You need to sometimes put your pride down so you can figure out the truth... after hearing it you definitely will not feel as you do now."

My back hurt, so I got out of bed carefully, and headed out to the kitchen. I pulled the fridge open and looked at the contents. A few minutes later I was still standing there deep in thought. I brought myself back to the present and wondered why I had opened it in the first place. I couldn't recall why. I certainly wasn't hungry. So I shut it and was thrown into the darkness of the kitchen.

"You knew Maxim before Anna did. Tell me, when you heard about what he had supposedly done to her family, were you shocked, or unsurprised? Did he seem like the kind to so heartlessly do something like that?"

The truth was I had been shocked out of my skin.

For that whole day I had walked around in a distraught daze. Maxim had intrigued me from the first moment I had fallen on him from the tree on his estate. Thereafter, I had watched him when he wasn't looking, but acted like he didn't exist when he was around. Even so, I was irrevocably and irresistibly drawn to that strangely intense boy who stared people into the ground and hardly ever said a word. That secret dream or fantasy of him being my dark prince shattered into a million pieces with Anna's words.

It was as if a switch flipped in my head. And I began to hate him with every fiber in my being... but now according to Levan, perhaps without reason.

Was Levan right? Was... I wrong? Was there actually something more? Something I had missed? Then I remembered Anna's white face. No, she was not lying. How could I even doubt her? It was Levan who did not know the truth. Angry with myself for being so easily convinced I turned and made my way back to my room. I found my phone and for a moment thought to wait for courtesy's sake given the time of the night, but I decided against it. I needed him to know that I had absolutely no respect for him whatsoever.

He didn't pick up. I threw the phone on the bed in annoyance especially at the way my stupid heart was pounding and then moved to lay down. A few more minutes passed before I reached for my phone and tried again.

He picked up on the third ring.

"Yes," he said brusquely.

Ripples of awareness rushed through me at the hard, sure tone of his voice. "It's Freya."

"I know."

My fingers clenched around my phone. Of course he would. He could never ever be taken unawares and always had way too many tricks up his sleeve. I wondered then why I was even bothering when he would probably at the end of the day just make me believe exactly what he wanted me to. "You know what, no need," I said and ended the call. Bastard didn't call back and after an hour I slipped into an uneasy sleep.

$\sim$

"*A*re you okay?" Britney asked.

"Yeah why?"

"Well, you've been staring at that brick wall outside the window for the last ten minutes."

I blinked and returned my gaze back to our company's website that I was supposed to be updating. I didn't see a thing but my mind was running, until I just had to speak.

"Your dad wouldn't marry you off to someone... someone abusive, would he?"

She looked at me with an incredulous expression. "What are you talking about? Of course he wouldn't?"

"Hmm," I said, and slinked back into my head.

"What are you thinking of now?"

"If my father were to think that Maxim was abusive towards me, perhaps he would call this ridiculous marriage thing off."

Britney, rightly, looked incredulous. I understood how she felt because I was entertaining thoughts that no sane person would or should, but I was getting desperate.

"And how do you want to pull that off?" she asked sarcastically. "Provoke him into throwing you down a high-rise building?"

"A flight of stairs might do the trick."

"Freya!" she cried, her expression horrified.

"Fine!" I groaned and returned my gaze back to my computer.

"Fine what exactly, Freya?"

"Fine, I'll stop trying to save myself from a lifetime of pain and bitterness."

She sighed. "Have you even spoken to Maxim?"

I reacted defensively as the question hit too close to home. "Spoken to him about what?"

"About what his brother mentioned the other day."

I scowled at her.

"Hear me out, Freya. I know I don't ... I know I can't fully grasp the gravity of what happened with your friend—"

'No, you can't," I cut her off.

She ignored the interruption and kept going. "I can't, but perhaps it's time to revisit it. Perhaps it's time to ask Maxim what happened, you know, from his point of view."

"He would just lie and she can't defend herself."

"Okay, so you want to be true to her memory, but what if there is something more... something Anna didn't get?"

I stared at her for the longest time without knowing what to say, but I did know how I felt. *Suffocated,* by everyone... by a possible scenario that they insisted I hear... but I wanted to keep believing in Anna. I had to. I couldn't betray her. I was the only one she trusted. If her spirit was watching I wanted her to know I was faithful to her to the very end. A mere man couldn't turn me against her.

"I don't want to talk about this anymore."

"Alright," she said and turned back to her computer screen.

I, however, couldn't take my mind off any of it. I rose from my desk with the pretense of going for a smoothie and the moment I got to the bottom floor of our building's entrance, I pulled out my phone and called Maxim. He picked up on the second ring.

"Maxim."

There it was again, that tingle of awareness and fury that always stole my breath. "I have some questions to ask you. When can we meet?"

"When is good for you?" His voice was smooth, suave.

"Tonight?"

"I'll be in Belarus. I won't be back till next week."

I sighed. "Then when?"

"Lunch in an hour."

I sighed heavily again. "Sure."

"I'll send a car ov—"

"No need," I cut him off. "I'll find my own way. Where?"

"My office," he replied.

"Your office? Why?" I asked suspiciously.

"Because I'm busy. I can't leave. We'll talk while we eat."

"Whatever," I said and ended the call.

Chapter Fifteen

MAXIM

"You're going to Belarus for a week? Since when?" Tom, my old friend and lawyer asked, a deep frown on his forehead.

I returned the phone to my pocket and glanced at him as we rode the elevator together. I felt like I was burying myself slowly, and I didn't understand why I was doing it. It was almost a compulsion. "Relax. I'm not going anywhere."

"Good, because you owe me a game of poker tonight. I need a chance to win back the fifteen grand you stole from me last week."

Our gazes met on the shiny surface of the elevator doors. "I didn't steal it, I fucking won it from you."

"You're an asshole, you know," he muttered.

"Someday, Tom, you're going to lose your head for talking to me like that."

He laughed. "That'll be the day. Now, the real question is: who is important enough to make you tell porkies? In the ten years I've known you I've never once seen you tell a lie, not even in the face of death. You're too much of a proud fucker for that, so who the hell was on the phone?"

The elevator dinged, then swished open as we arrived on the eighth floor for our conference meeting. Ignoring him, I stepped out of the confinement. I wanted desperately to loosen up my tie, which felt like it was suffocating me, but we were both heading to a meeting with some investors from Venezuela to discuss an oil drilling project. Every one of them was a badly disguised piranha in a suit. I didn't plan on being on the menu.

As soon as the pleasantries were done with the meeting began.

But I couldn't focus. I lied. Because I wanted to see her. No, that was a lie. I needed to see her again. And I was not prepared to wait until tonight. Ever since I saw her in the hospital, I had been plagued by thoughts of her: her untamed curls, the defiance in her gaze, the fire from her tongue. Everything about her burned me, in a bitter, sweet way... and I couldn't fucking wait.

Hell, I wanted to taste her so bad, my cock ached.

Chapter Sixteen

FREYA

https://www.youtube.com/watch?v=Dkk9gvTmCXY

I rolled into Ivankov Industries in my wheelchair.

Of course, I didn't need it. I hadn't used it since the day I had left the hospital, but I needed to take a stand and clearly remind him that I'd gotten hurt because of him. To also clearly remind him how dangerous he was to me, and how much of a misfortune it was for me to marry him.

When I reached the exquisite reception of the sky-high (okay seventy-six floors) of glistening glass and chrome lobby I looked around me with reluctant awe. Yes, the Ivankovs were truly the most powerful Russian mob group in this country, and definitely the most extravagant. New York was their turf. My father ruled in Europe and the United Kingdom.

What particularly caught my attention was the at least thirty feet tall palm trees that were dotted around the lobby. It made me wonder how they had been able to get them into the building.

The receptionist, a beautiful, bored, blonde wearing a nametag that said Melanie, looked quite confused by my appearance at her station. She turned to glance at her male colleague.

"Can I help you?" her male colleague, wearing a nametag that said Daniel, asked, as he ran his condescending eyes down my wild unruly hair, my unmade face, my baggy t-shirt tucked into the loose pants that he assumed covered my crippled legs.

"I'm here to see Maxim."

His eyebrows rose to incredible heights. "As in Mr. Maxim Ivankov?"

"Do you know of any other Maxim in this building?" I asked tartly.

They shared a look, probably wondering what on earth a rude, disheveled woman in a wheelchair could possibly want with their high and mighty boss.

"And who should I say you are?" he asked in a crisp, no nonsense tone. He had decided I had no right to be there.

I shouldn't have, but I couldn't help it, I decided to mess with them. They deserved it for judging me based purely on my appearance. "His fiancée," I said smugly.

The female receptionist snorted with disbelief at what she considered a preposterous idea. I looked down to hide my smile.

"Ma'am," her male colleague said sternly. "What's your name, please?"

"Freya."

He waited for a last name, but when I didn't provide any, he went on with barely controlled irritation. "Well ...uh, Miss Freya, to see Mr. Ivankov, you'll need an appointment."

"Well, I just told you that I'm engaged to him. Do I still need an appointment to see my fiancé?"

The girl spoke up, her tone sneering. "With all due respect ma'am, if you are engaged to him why don't you just... call him?"

Someone else, obviously far more important, appeared beside me, and Daniel gave Melanie a look as if to say can you handle this on your own. She nodded and as he moved on to serve the newcomer, she turned to me with hard eyes.

But I was done playing games with Maxim's snooty staff. With a sigh, I pulled my phone out of my pocket, and was about to dial his number when he emerged from the bank of elevators. He was with a group of sharply-suited, swarthy men. He was easily head and shoulders taller than all of them except one, a man I vaguely recognized. Maxim's face remained stoic as he listened to one of them speaking.

My plan was to wait until they moved away from him, but they all began to walk towards the revolving doors. Surely the asshole didn't intend to stand me up.

"Maxim!" I yelled.

My voice rang through the lobby, echoing and magnifying when it hit all the hard surfaces in that vast space. People stopped their civilized murmurings and looked around in surprise. Their gazes settled on an unkempt tramp in a wheelchair.

I felt no shame.

But to my surprise, there was no embarrassment or shame in Maxim's face either as his eyes found mine. He didn't care that I was in his workplace looking like something the cat dragged in and screaming his name like a lunatic. His face was expressionless, but his eyes never left mine as he approached me. The expression in them made me suddenly feel small, defenseless, and unsure of myself. Ironically, I even felt an almost crippling urge to stand.

My heart warmed at the fact that I hadn't been thrown out or worse, ignored. Instead he was coming towards me and for the first time, I needed his covering and protection, craved it almost- against the mocking eyes of the world.

He stopped before me.

"You were about to leave," I explained.

"You could have called me," he said.

I looked away, my breath quickening at the smoldering gaze of his icy-blue eyes. It chilled me and set me ablaze all at the same time.

"I'll go wait somewhere," I said and started to turn around but he grabbed the handles of my chair and started to push me towards his associates.

"Tom, would you please round up on my behalf," he said as we got closer. Then he addressed the group as a whole. "Great meeting again. Thanks guys."

We were still the focus of attention when Maxim began to push me through the security checkpoint of the building. The uniformed guards instantly granted us access and he pushed me into his empire. I couldn't resist turning to search out the receptionists' faces.

Melanie's mouth was dropped open in shock and Daniel was staring at us in disbelief with his hands on his hips. I knew it was childish to gloat, but I couldn't help myself from smiling triumphantly and giving them a little wave. Both were incredibly quick to respond with their own little waves to the boss's new fiancée. That should teach them not to be so shallow and condescending again.

As we headed towards the elevators though I began to wonder at my odd behavior. I wasn't one to seek attention, but it seemed as if I almost relished going out of my way to make Maxim uncomfortable. If what I felt for him was just pure hate then why was I so preoccupied with getting a reaction out of him?

We stopped by his private elevator and as he leaned over me to press the button for the car's arrival, I took the opportunity to watch him through the reflection on the highly polished doors.

I had always thought that a man in a well-cut suit had the same effect on a woman that a woman in a bikini had on a man. In an exquisite charcoal suit, pale gray tie, and white shirt Maxim was impeccable in a way that made me shift uncomfortably with sexual awareness.

What was even more disconcerting was the fact that I obviously had no such effect on him.

In fact, the jerk didn't even bother looking at me while we

waited for the elevator car to arrive. Instead, he pulled out his phone from his pocket and began to go through what I assumed were messages. When the elevator dinged its arrival, he pushed me in and we were on our way up to the topmost floor. When the doors swished open again, we were in a large waiting room. He pushed me right past his secretary, a short, scraggly haired man that bore an uncanny resemblance to Daniel Radcliffe, gave the impression his boss wheeling in a disheveled woman towards him was an ordinary everyday occurrence. He smiled politely at me as he stood and went ahead to open the double doors to what must be Maxim's office.

Chapter Seventeen

FREYA

"Whathat do you want to eat?" Maxim asked as we got through the wide doors.

I was stunned by Maxim's office. It was one seamless glass cube, and almost made me feel as though I was suspended in the sky, the landscape of the entire city almost seemed like an unreal painting that he had no doubt spent a fortune to have access to.

"Whoa, this is awesome. You must feel like God up here," I said in awe.

When I didn't hear a response, I turned to see him watching me as he stood behind his desk, all regal and powerful, his phone in hand.

"There are loads of high-rises in the city. Go rent the top floor of one of them," he suggested.

"I'm a struggling jewelry designer. I can barely afford a sublet in the Bronx."

"You're richer than you think," he said softly.

"My dad's money is not mine and I refuse to get blood on my hands so I can have an office in the sky."

It was water off a duck's back. "What do you want to eat?" he repeated.

"Let me see ... what's the most expensive lunch that money can buy?"

"I wouldn't know."

"Well, that's what I want."

We gazed at each other and for a moment I wondered if he would someday just get fed up with me and put a bullet in my head. Then he pressed the intercom to his phone and I heard his secretary's voice come through. "Gary, come in,"

A few minutes later, he walked in, a fixed smile on his face. "Yes, Sir."

"Tell him what you want," Maxim said and took his seat. He picked up a folder before him and began to flip through the documents inside.

"What's the most expensive lunch money can buy in this city?" I asked him.

"Ah, uh... I guess I have to look that up."

"Well that's what I want, except if it's a clam or oysters dish. In that case, then skip it and get me the next most expensive option."

"Yes, Miss Federov," he responded. Well, well, he knew who I was. He turned his gaze to his boss. "The usual for you, Sir?"

Maxim nodded and his secretary walked away. I rolled my

chair towards his polished walnut desk, and stopped at a reasonable distance away. "So are we going to talk?"

"You were the one who asked for this meeting," he said, lifting those piercing eyes up to meet mine. "Have your say, I have another meeting in thirty minutes."

I rolled my eyes at his air of arrogance and got straight to the point. "Levan insinuated that what I have always believed about your role in Anna's death is incorrect. Is that true?"

"What do you know about my involvement?"

"The same thing as the rest of Russia. You 'handled' her father, a good man, I might add, to prove yourself to your father."

"That is true," he admitted.

Something painful hit me right in the middle of my chest. I had come here with some secret hope in my heart. All traces of civility towards him immediately disappeared and once again we were like vipers, staring each other down.

"So what then am I doing here?"

"I don't know. What *are* you doing here?"

I couldn't believe him. *Oh, how I hated him.* I turned around with my chair and began to head towards his exit. Just then the door was pushed open and his secretary came in holding a notepad and a pen in his hands. For some reason, I stopped in my tracks.

"Miss Fedorov, the most expensive grilled cheese sandwich is from Serendipity 3. It costs $214 dollars."

It took my next question for me to understand that I didn't want to leave just yet. "Why is it so expensive?" I asked.

He referred to his notepad. "The bread itself is baked with Dom Perignon champagne. The filling is *caciocavallo podolico*, which is a special cheese imported from southern Italy. The rare breed of cows that produce this cheese are bred on the Apennines where they feed on upland grasses and mountain plants like wild fennel, nettles, blueberries, liquorice and myrtle.

Apparently, this causes the cheese to carry vegetal notes of smoke, herbs, toast, and barnyard that are balanced by an intense fruitiness and lactic tang." He bobbed his head comically and shrugged as if he had no idea what he had just said, but it didn't matter anyway because it was all just a bit of pompous nonsense.

I couldn't stop my smile. I liked Gary. How strange that he would work with a cold, heartless monster like Maxim.

"There is more…" he added with deliberately widened eyes. "The… uh… bread is brushed with a mixture of white truffle oil and twenty-three karat gold flakes, which adds extra crisp, Then the sides are encrusted with sheets of edible 23-karat gold and it is served with a tomato sauce, which is basically a luxe version of tomato bisque filled with juicy chunks of lobster."

He lifted his head and looked at me inquiringly. "Does it sound like something you would like to consume?"

"Get it for me. I'll take it to go."

Betraying no emotion at my request for take away, he exited the office. I turned around to face Maxim. His focus was still completely on the document he was reading almost as though I didn't even exist. I knew the document was not all that absorbing. He was deliberately trying to make me feel insignificant.

"Do you ever feel bad? For what happened?"

His reply was curt and instantaneous. "No."

"I don't believe you," I said.

He raised his gaze to mine. "Why?"

"You're a horrible person," I said truthfully, "but you're also human. You can't not have felt any remorse. That was a whole family you wiped out and for what?"

He stared into my eyes for the longest time and I waited, praying that he would say something that would redeem him. For those few seconds it seemed as if there had never been anything I wanted more than for him to show me he was not the monster I thought he was.

"What do you recall about my mother's death?" he asked.

My brain was temporarily scrambled. The question had popped out of nowhere. "Uh..." I decided to play it safe. "Not much."

"Well, she was my family, and Anna's father wiped her out."

I was even more confused. "What?"

"I didn't go after Anna, or her mom. They were collateral damage as much as I was when they killed my mother. I went after her dad because I wanted to ruin him. His case with our company at the time was minor, but I took it for the chance to ruin him. My only regret is that Anna's mother came in just as I was about to pull the trigger..."

He paused and I stared at him in amazement.

"Do you want to know what that good man did in the face of death?" he asked quietly.

"What?" I gasped, suddenly breathless.

"He used his wife, and the mother of his own child, as a fucking shield." His mouth curled with the disgust he felt for the man.

"You're lying," I whispered automatically, even as I knew in my gut he was telling the truth.

He shrugged carelessly. "Believe what you want. I am not here to convince you."

"So you shot them both?" I asked incredulous.

"What choice did I have?"

"Why did you want him dead so badly?"

He leaned back in his chair and looked away from me, his eyes on some distant point in the sky. "It takes a very strong woman to be an Ivankov and my mother was not strong. She couldn't cope with being the wife of a man who sat and supped with death every day. When I was ten, her deep unhappiness made her turn to drink ... and eventually into a desperate affair with Anna's father."

He swung his gaze back towards me. "But he had a different agenda. He wanted to hurt my father. At first he tried to turn her against my father, but she refused, so he sent some compromising pictures of her to my father. I think he expected him to turn on her, but my father is an unusual man. He can watch a man being flayed to death without flinching, but he could not harm a hair on my mother's head. He remembered her as she had been... when he first found her in a little village in Russia, carrying firewood, her golden hair wild, her cheeks red with cold. Even after he lost her to confusion, sorrow and drink that was how she remained in his heart. He was about to burn the pictures in the fireplace when my mother came into the room and saw them. Seeing the pictures of her own betrayal in his hands completely destroyed her. Her guilt was the straw that broke the camel's back. In less than a month she was dead from an overdose. Levan found her body. He was only seven at the time."

"But you got involved with Anna at nineteen. How was he able to get away with it until then?"

"Because he made sure that he remained in the dark. Even in the photos he sent my father he never showed his face. I only found out about him because she left a two by two photo of him in one of my books and a note asking for forgiveness. I never told anyone, not even my father, until I had put the bullet into his head."

"Why?" I asked. "Why did you want to handle it yourself?"

"Because she left the note for me. It was not forgiveness she wanted. It was revenge."

"But Anna," I breathed. "She didn't deserve this."

He watched me. "What about Levan?" Did he deserve to lose his mother in such a gruesome and humiliating way? Levan and my father and I were forced to live with our loss, Anna chose to take the easy way out. I'm sorry she took her life but this was never about her."

"You used her."

"I saw my chance and took it."

I didn't know how I felt. Part of me was numb. I still *hated* him, of course, but I also didn't feel I had the right to. What he did was wrong, but at the same time, to a certain extent, I could now understand why he did what he did. Anna wasn't faultless either for taking her life in that way. Neither was her father for destroying his mother and hurting his family the way he did. While I was staring at him, there was a knock on the door and Gary came in. He had my sandwich to go.

"I'm not hungry. You have it, Gary," I said, wheeling myself quickly out of Maxim's office in the sky.

Chapter Eighteen

FREYA

"**Y**ou left without the gold sandwich?" Britney asked in disbelief.

I looked up from my computer screen. "Yeah, so?"

"Hell, Freya! Where's your mind? The bread was baked with 23-karat gold. You know how much I love gold. You could have brought the sandwich back for me. Now I will have to wonder about it for the rest of my life."

"Daylight is dying and we need to send those photos first thing tomorrow morning," I reminded.

"I know, I know," she said, and went back to snapping photos of our range of white gold rings, and half-moon charm bracelets inside the makeshift studio she had set up on her table with a cardboard box, rolls of white paper, and some spotlights."

"When are you resuming at the bar?" she asked strategically placing one of the rings on a strawberry that she had misted with a spray bottle.

"Today," I sighed. "We need the money and pronto."

She looked back, her face concerned. "We don't need it that badly. Your wound ..."

"I'll be fine,"

"Just don't get into any fights," she cautioned.

I laughed. "I'm Igor Fedorov's daughter. It's going to take more than a one week old stab wound to stop me from defending myself."

"I meant don't *start* one." She rolled her eyes and went back to clicking away on her camera.

"I'll be as good as gold."

"Don't remind me of that sandwich."

I laughed.

"Anyway, you still haven't told me why you got so mad and stormed out of Maxim's office."

"He told me that he went after Anna because her father was responsible for his mother committing suicide."

The camera almost fell from her hands. "Good God! You guys seem very casual about taking your own lives, or killing other people. Is it a Russian thing?"

"Not a Russian thing," I said. "But it's our reality, my family's and Maxim's."

My phone began to ring then, so I quickly searched for it under the clutter of files and photos on my desk.

"Hold on," I said to her when I found the phone and saw that it was my father.

"Papa," I answered, my stomach in knots.

His cool voice came through. "How do you feel Printsessa?"

I immediately weakened my voice. "Still very weak, but I'm getting better."

"Yes, I heard you went to see Maxim in a wheelchair." There was amusement in his voice.

"I was feeling particularly bad that day."

"Well, come home then. So you can recuperate in a nice house instead of that flea infested place you live in."

"Uh..." The strength came back into my voice. "I'm a little busy right now, papa, so I can't. But don't worry, I'll be fine here, and—"

"There'll be a plane waiting for you this evening. You can return next week."

He ended the call and I was left staring ahead and seeing nothing. There was so much to do, but nothing was more important than somehow getting him to change his mind.

"You alright?" Britney asked.

I blinked and turned to her. "Want to go to Russia for a week?"

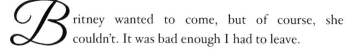

ritney wanted to come, but of course, she couldn't. It was bad enough I had to leave.

That evening I was picked up in a town car in front of my apartment building and driven to the private charter grounds of Teterboro airport.

I didn't recognize the jet but what I did recognize was Nikita, my father's secretary of fifteen years. She greeted me with her gorgeously fruity voice. I embraced her. It had been too long.

"Doing okay love?" she asked, her blonde curls bobbing around her cheeks.

"Yeah," I replied. "Dad wants to ruin it, though."

She laughed out loud and it was contagious and I joined her.

After a while I settled into a truly wonderful menu of steaming cabbage soup and beef stroganoff that my father's cook used to cook from the time of my childhood. I had to admit her food still tasted the best. With my stomach full, I dozed off for the remaining eight-and-a-half hours until we landed in Moscow.

For the sake of caution, my father always sent me what I could recognize truly came from him, be it a person like Nikita, or his familiar Soviet limo Gaz-13 with his special number plate that was waiting for me a little distance away from the plane. I got in and didn't recognize the driver or the guard in front but I did instantly recognize my father's scent of Ghurka Black dragon cigars.

When I was a young girl I could remember wishing he would stop smoking because I was worried about what something that smelt that foul would do internally to him. How silly I was. I should have worried about what he could do to the poor cigars.

When we arrived at the house, I got out and took in the white mansion I had called home for most of my life. Now my home was a cramped two-bedroom in a neighborhood that Britney called the ass end of the big apple. Nevertheless, I knew which one I preferred.

I was greeted by Elena, my father's housekeeper. She was a good woman and I had great affection for her, but she only nodded formally. After rejecting her offer of a meal or a drink I headed straight up the golden balustrade and red-carpeted flight of stairs to my room. I crossed the massive gilded space and jumped into my old king size bed with its silk sheets and goose down pillows. Compared to the bed I had in my apartment it was like falling into clouds.

I was asleep in minutes.

Chapter Nineteen

FREYA

I came awake to the sense of a presence by my side. It was my father and he was seated comfortably on my bed as he watched me sleep.

"Papa," I mumbled sleepily.

He chuckled affectionately. "Why did you not eat?" he asked in Russian.

"I wasn't hungry. I had a massive meal on the plane," I replied.

He placed a palm against my cheek. I didn't move. This hand that could caress so gently could just as easily slap so hard I would feel the vibration in the bones of my neck. This time his fingers moved to caress. At that moment I felt an old tug in my heart. This was my father. All said and done he had fed, clothed, sheltered, and protected me for most of my life. I felt sad at the reminder of his insistence that I marry Maxim. That was the only thing right now that threatened to pull us apart. I looked into his eyes. If I was ever going to reason with him now was the moment.

But as if he understood what I was about to say, he placed a kiss on my forehead and rose to his feet. "We are going out to dinner. Put on a dress and maybe," he leaned forward and brushed his fingers through my crazy hair, "tie your hair back? There are four new dresses for you to try."

I nodded dumbly and looked past him to the coffee table in my lounge area. There were four large boxes tied with peach ribbons awaiting me.

"Take your pick tonight and keep the rest," he threw over his shoulder as he exited my room.

I unboxed the dresses, at first without interest, but they were so extraordinarily beautiful I couldn't help but be seduced by how gorgeous they all were. I chose a white silk dress with spaghetti straps and a slit that shot all the way to the middle of my thighs. It was one of those dresses that was so simple and classic you knew the moment you saw it, it must have cost the earth itself. A stylist would have recommended peach or apricot lipstick, but I went for bold red. I pulled my hair back into a high ponytail on my head and finished off the look with an emerald choker that had been my mother's. Then I closed my safe, and quickly slipped into a pair of white strappy sandals.

As I came down the stairs I knew I looked the part, but when I saw Elena's eyes widen with surprise, I realized I must look better than what I thought.

"You look like your mother," she whispered.

"Thank you," I whispered back. Tears threatened to choke me. Elena couldn't have paid me a higher compliment. My mother was a great beauty queen. She had been crowned Miss America in her time.

"Your father is in his study." I went to his door and knocked softly. He called me to come. I opened the door and I entered.

"Beautiful," he declared with a nod of satisfaction. Then he moved forward and took my arm.

"How severe is the pain?"

"It's much better now. It can be ignored, so no need to worry," I said as we slipped into the back of his limo.

As the car slid smoothly out of the tall black and gold gates our conversation moved to his last trip to Peru. Cocooned in the comfortable interior of the car I began to relax. When my father decided to charm someone, there was no way they were not going to be charmed. I was charmed. I listened eagerly to his adventures and laughed at his stories until the car came to a stop and my father said, "Ah, we are here."

I thought we would be going to one of my father's usual super expensive haunts in the heart of Moscow, but we had pulled up in front of a set of iron cast gates I was all too familiar with. I turned to my father with a look of betrayal.

"What are we doing here?"

"Having dinner."

I turned my face away. "I'm taking a taxi home."

He didn't say a word and that was worse than if he had bothered to tell me off. I sat stiffly, fuming inwardly, my face turned away from him until we arrived at the front of the splendid Ivankov mansion. The door was pulled open for me, but it was not by the Ivankov's butler, but Bianca herself. She was grinning widely and seemed filled with a child-like excitement to see me.

"Freya," she called out merrily, and for a moment I was so stumped to see her I forgot I was meant to be furious at my father's deception. The next thing I knew, I was being pulled into the house by the hand. Bianca pulled me through the house right into the kitchen where there was a flurry of activity. She pulled me through it all towards a long table filled with too much food. She picked up a tiny square of toast with caviar on it.

"Do you love caviar?" she asked excitedly.

I was too bemused to tell her caviar was not special to me. I could have eaten it for breakfast every day of my childhood and I had always chosen cereal instead. I took the tiny toast offering and popped it into my mouth. Bianca snagged two flutes of champagne from the tray of a passing manservant and held one out to me.

Her eyes were sparkling almost as much as the golden liquid in our glasses when she clinked her glass with mine and said, "To us."

I echoed her words and took a sip of cold bubbles.

"You look really beautiful," she said.

"So do you," I said sincerely. Her hair was pulled back just like mine, with golden stray strands framing her lovely face. Her silver dress was superbly cut, sleeveless, and hugged her body exquisitely.

"What's the occasion?" I asked.

"Maxim's father is in town, which apparently hardly ever happens so they wanted this to be a sort of introductory dinner between the two families."

"Hmm…" I mused sarcastically. "An introductory dinner, for a marriage I have countless times said I am not interested in."

Her happy smile broke and I felt sorry for always pulling her into the midst of my anger with the Ivankovs. I actually liked her, and given different circumstances, we might have even become friends.

There was something I did wonder about though, and couldn't hold it back any longer. "You love Levan a lot, don't you?"

Her eyes softened and she smiled. "I do."

I concluded then she wasn't well versed in the horrors of being married into a Russian mafia family, especially one as dangerous as our two families. I drained my glass and chose not to say anything. Who knew? Maybe I was wrong and she was right. Her love would be strong enough to weather all the storms coming their way.

She however knew exactly what I didn't want to say. She reached for my hand, held it in hers, and said, "I owe everything to Levan. He and I came together out of tragedy. It's a long story which I will tell you in detail someday, but basically, I was kidnapped by a madman and everyone around me suffered and nearly even lost their lives trying to get me out. My father, my best friend, Levan … and Maxim."

My brows shot up in surprise at the mention of the last person.

She nodded. "Yes, Maxim. Secretly he might have wanted to kill me for all this trouble I was causing. Levan was almost given a life sentence because of me." She smiled. "But he saw that his brother was in love with me and he helped. Repeatedly."

"Wait, what? Maxim helped repeatedly?"

She nodded.

"Are you sure we are talking about the same person?"

She laughed. "Yup."

I frowned. I couldn't imagine Maxim being moved by love.

"So, Freya, I *have* experienced the dangers of being involved with this family and the mafia in general in the most brutal, first hand way, but I couldn't let Levan go and neither could he, so we found a way to make it work. After our wedding, he will be leaving the conglomerate for good. We're moving to South Africa, and he's going to become a brewer there. It's been his dream to make the finest craft beer ever made, but he's always had to put it aside because of the family.

"What?" I gazed at her in disbelief. Levan was leaving the family? His father was letting him? How the hell was that even possible?

"Yeah," she nodded. "Obviously, I'm not saying that Maxim's going to do the same. He's more... well... involved and important to the business, but all I'm saying is that I was very surprised when Levan told me that Maxim was willing to marry you."

She suddenly realized how her words must have sounded, and

her hand went to her mouth in apology. "That's not what I meant to—"

"Relax, it's okay," I said and patted her on the shoulder in amusement.

"No, no, I have to explain what I really meant. What I was trying to say was, Maxim is very much his own man so I had a very hard time ever picturing him agreeing to marry a woman he has no interest in. Even after a short time of knowing him I can see just a request from his father for him to marry you would not have been enough to get Maxim to do anything. Yes, he works closely with his father and according to Levan will take instructions from his father where the older man has more experience, but never on anything Maxim does not personally agree with. Anyway, what I'm trying to say is underneath that distant, aloof exterior he is a great guy. He is just as fiercely loyal and intensely passionate as Levan." She wrinkled her brown eyes. "Maybe even more. You know what they say about the silent ones. So, why not give him a chance, eh? He might not be as bad as you think."

"What are you two cooking up?"

We both looked up then, startled by the sudden bass voice. It was Levan. Then my gaze fell on the person that stood beside him, and my heart jumped in my chest.

Every single time I laid eyes on him, I was stunned all over again by how handsome he was. How regal... how imposing. It stirred things in me that, God's truth, made my toes curl. Especially now. He was dressed quite casually which was as rare as sights went. His crisp white dress shirt was unbuttoned at the collar. The sleeves folded to just below his elbows, revealing strongly-veined, tattooed skin that belonged to a man from another world.

Bianca meant well, but there was just too much bad blood between us. It wasn't just the man I was against, but his world and everything it represented.

As much as he made my blood race he was not the man for me.

Chapter Twenty

MAXIM

S
he was here!

When my father requested all of us fly in for the dinner, I was certain she wouldn't show up but here she was, dressed like a bride.

Her white dress fit her like a glove, curving and dipping in all the right places and the neckline was low enough to reveal the gentle swell of her milky-white breasts. Her hair had been pulled back from her face and I missed the wildness of her hair, but it did make her look even more delicate and fragile. Her skin was like fine porcelain and her eyes, effervescent as they stared at me defiantly. Her lips were plump and painted the kind of sinful red that made me almost willing to swim across a few seas just so I could suck them into my mouth. To *taste* her... to have her body pressed hard against mine, and those slender fingers fisting my shirt as she fought to hold on to her sanity.

Suddenly, it was hard to breathe as I felt myself harden. Not to cause embarrassment that would be too hard to come back from, I gave her a hard look and walked away.

"Maxim," Levan called, but I continued towards the study. I needed a drink. But as I passed the lounge, I heard my father call my name. I retraced my steps and entered the lounge room to see that my father had opened his best bottle of whisky, drinking it with Freya's father.

It was a sight to behold indeed, given that for the latter part of the last two decades they hated each other so much they couldn't even bear to be in the same room together. I slipped my hands in my pockets and stood before both of them.

"How are the wedding arrangements coming?" her father asked.

"I believe that question will be more suited for your daughter, Sir," I answered. "She seems to have a mind of her own."

"A mere woman with a mind of her own?" my father scoffed.

"She is no mere woman, she probably has a stronger mind than any of us here."

There was a sour look on Igor's face. "My daughter is like a highly-strung horse. She just needs a firm hand."

"What exactly is the problem here?" my father asked with a frown.

"I think it's best if you hear from her yourself," was my response. "No one speaks for Freya."

Then I continued on my way towards the study where I poured myself a generous amount of whisky. It calmed my nerves, but did very little to take my mind off the girl in the kitchen. She wanted absolutely nothing to do with me and that alone made her unique.

I went to stand by the window. Outside the garden was lit with many lights. The water drops from the waterfall sparkled like diamonds.

At that moment I wanted her so badly I could feel it burning inside me. The fire inside of me I wanted to burn inside her too, but then I thought of my bad-tempered father coming face to face with the tigress he had called a mere woman.

I downed the rest of my drink and frowned. If I was not careful there was a very real possibility this marriage would be called off before the night was over.

Chapter Twenty-One

FREYA

"So what date have you and Maxim decided to set for the wedding?"

I choked on the honey cake that had been sliding down my throat, and had to hit my chest for some relief before I lifted my gaze to meet the hard, cold eyes of Mr. Ivankov.

Say what now, or something else equally irreverent sounded in my head, but I noted the watchful, cautious gaze of my father, and decided to tread carefully.

"I ... uh." I looked at Maxim who had his eyes fixed on me as though in a dare. So, of course, I said exactly what I wanted to. "As a matter of fact I have no plans on marrying Maxim. I've relayed this to my father and Maxim, very clearly."

"Freya!" my father called menacingly.

I dropped my fork and stared my father down. "What? What do you expect from me? You didn't even have the kindness to tell me that you were bringing me here to make marriage arrangements for me. I thought you wanted me in Moscow to recuperate, after being stabbed just for being seen with Maxim. And now you all want me to marry him?"

"What exactly about my son do you object to?" his father asked.

I looked the Don right in his fierce eyes and felt a sliver of concern at how this would affect my father and his plans, but he hadn't thought how this would affect my life and my plans so that was his problem to handle. I took a deep breath.

"Your son is a wonderful man. Any woman who gets him should consider herself very lucky, but I just don't want to get married," I replied, "to anyone."

"Every woman must get married," he said, a perplexed frown on his broad forehead. "Every woman must have a man by her side, to provide for her, to protect her—"

"Well, I was right in front of Maxim when I was attacked and he couldn't do anything about it. I could have died that day!"

At my accusation everyone and everything stopped moving. Even the manservant who had been serving us had to remind himself to resume after my fiery accusation that the family's top dog was inadequate.

I glanced at Bianca. She had her head down. Levan looked as if he was amused by my outburst. Maxim's father just stared at me as though I had horns on my head. But my father looked like he wanted to burn me alive.

My eyes moved reluctantly to Maxim. He was expressionless.

I began to suspect then that I might be burying myself into

some sort of grave here so I quickly rose to my feet to take my leave.

"Sit down!" my father roared furiously. The whole room seemed to shake.

Out of respect for him and a gnawing fear that I had gone too far, I did as I was asked, but I folded my arms across my chest defiantly and waited for him to try to threaten me. For the first time in my life I was ready to defy him. What was he going to do to me? I was dependent on him for absolutely nothing so short of tying a noose around my neck and dragging me to the altar, how was he going to get me to do what he wanted?

"Your marriage will take place in two weeks. You can have your ceremony, after Levan and his fiancée have celebrated theirs."

"With all due respect father," I said, "no, thank you."

"You will obey me in this," he said very softly.

"No, I won't. The only way I'm marrying is if you literally shoot me dead and drag my corpse to the altar. Short of that, no one is going to force me to marry anyone against my will."

With that, I rose from the table and in the tense silence in the room, made my way out. I would have called myself some mode of transportation, but I knew there was no way any vehicle was getting into this compound. Also, I had left my phone at home. I would have to wait until my father was ready to leave. More than anything I hated feeling like a spoiled brat, but brat or not, no one was going to encroach on the life I had been trying all my life to carve out for myself.

My stomach was churning as I headed towards the Ivankov's

famous garden. It was called Morning Calm and had been personally tended to and planted by Maxim's mother. After her death it had been scrupulously maintained by a team of gardeners. Now that I knew the sorry story surrounding her death, I couldn't find it in my heart to appreciate the place as a green paradise filled with the most beautiful flowers from all over the world. The fern-leaf peony, royal azaleas, and schrenck's tulips felt as if they had been watered by her tears.

To those she had left behind, this place was probably hell.

Chapter Twenty-Two

MAXIM

E very eye was on me the moment Freya left the room, and for the first time in a very long time the urge to laugh came over me. She was something else and I was filled with reluctant admiration for her courage.

"Maxim," my father said, his voice heavy. "What are you going to do about this?"

I took my time. "You heard her," I said. "She doesn't want to get married."

"Yes, but what are you going to do about this?" my father asked, a hint of irritation showing.

"I can do many things, father," I replied, "but forcing a woman to the altar against her will is not one of them."

My father looked almost lost. He turned to Freya's father whose face was red with anger. "What does your daughter want? Why is she so against this?"

"She wants her freedom," Levan answered.

Like a drowning man suddenly spying a bit of flotsam my father turned to him desperately. "And that she will have. Maxim is not going to restrain her."

"She might also be scared," Bianca added gently. "About having to live a life of worry about Maxim's safety. I know I was terrified for Levan."

"Well that does not make any sense," Freya's father interjected impatiently. "This is her life. She was born into it."

"But she didn't choose it and she is doing that right now. Choosing something different for herself."

"Bianca," her father said. "It is not her fate to choose. She must accept Maxim. There is too much at stake. New players have entered the field and I will not be here forever to protect her. The only person who can make sure she will always be safe is Maxim. Do you have any idea how we can get her to accept Maxim?"

I watched as Levan turned to her with interest, his hand braced under his chin as he waited for her answer.

She looked first to Levan, then back to Freya's father. "She needs to fall in love with Maxim."

Her words were not music to either of our fathers' ears. They leaned back heavily in their chairs.

Chapter Twenty-Three

FREYA

I sensed Maxim before I heard him.

The nerves in my body were tingling, the way a deer will twitch when it smells something harmful in the air, but in the mix of that alertness was also an excited buzz that made the tiny hairs on my body stand to attention. I tried not to notice or care but when he was so close to me that I could feel the heat from his body and smell his wildly expensive custom after-shave, I gritted my teeth and whirled around.

It turned out that he wasn't in fact as close to me as I had imagined, but he did have two glasses of red wine in his hands. He offered one to me.

I stared at it for the longest time, wondering whether to take it.

"Yes, it's poisoned," he said, his lips twisting into a wry smile, and my hand immediately reached for it.

I sipped my wine as we both kept our eyes on the massive fountain of the garden. It seemed as though it would have been just perfect for us both to remain there forever. I didn't like the thought, so I turned around to face him.

"I should leave," I said.

He nodded without even looking at me. "Go ahead."

His words hurt and I sank my teeth into my lower lip with fury at my own weakness. How appealing he looked in that moment under the star lit night. If only, in another life, under different circumstances.

Before I could stop myself, I found my lips moving. "Do you want to marry me? Or are you just doing this because it is a request from your father?"

"It is a request ..." he began, then trailed away, his gaze fluttering down to my lips.

All of a sudden, my mouth felt dry. I pulled my gaze up to his. His eyes bore into mine. He knew. He knew about the sizzling attraction that existed inside me for him. I felt exposed and almost mocked.

"It is a request... that I do not mind," he finished softly.

"Why?" I asked. "We don't even like each other."

"*You* do not like me," he corrected. "*I* don't have a problem with you."

"Oh."

Suddenly I couldn't bear it anymore. The scent of the flowers mixed with his luxurious cologne, the nearness of his body, the look in his eyes, the way my body was responding to that look. I felt as if I was a mouse being hypnotized by a massive, highly colored snake. I was being drawn into his lethal spell. A spell from which I could never recover.

With a shake of my head I took a long backwards step away from him.

His mouth opened to say something, but I didn't wait to hear it. I couldn't. He was too dangerous to my sanity. I fled as if the hounds of hell itself were chasing me. I arrived back at the dining room to see that my dad had risen to his feet and seemed like he was ready to leave. He gave me a look of extreme disappointment, but he did not say anything. I'd never felt more relieved. We didn't speak, but I did politely say my goodbyes to Maxim's father, Levan, and Bianca.

"Let me know if you need any help with your wedding," I said to her.

"Actually," she said sweetly. "I will. I want to wear your jewelry on my big day. I saw a really gorgeous necklace when we were at your place. Perhaps I can pick out that piece for me and some other stuff for my bridesmaids?"

"Really?" I breathed.

"Yes," she said. "I'll come to your office and we can go from there."

I tried to get myself together. "That would be awesome."

"And we'll try to get them photographed and carried in some publication."

I was so shocked I looked from Bianca to Levan. "Are you guys trying to bribe me?"

"I'm not," Levan replied. "Bianca just likes supporting everyone."

"Take my phone number," Bianca said.

In a daze I took her phone number, accepted her embrace, and soon we were on our way. The ride back with my father was not at all comfortable. Not one word left his lips. It would be much better if he had screamed and condemned me. The complete silence made me feel horrible. From the time I was a child I always knew, in our world, every minute with each other could be our last. That I should never squander it.

I hated feeling that one day I could be regretting this car ride.

"The plane is ready," he said to me, as we arrived at the house. "You can leave when you want."

I got down from the car and he was driven away into the night. Where I did not know.

Chapter Twenty-Four

FREYA

T he moment the taxi pulled up in front of my apartment, I experienced a feeling of relief. I had escaped my father's tentacles in one piece.

I had survived and made it back, still unmarried and with my freedom intact. I was extremely exhausted but I knew Britney needed assistance. We had scored rooftop access at a residential property in Soho, and she was supposed to be managing a quick photo shoot with some model friends she had managed to convince to work for free. Really, she needed me there so I thanked the driver and hurried on to the house with my luggage. If I was quick I could be with her in less than an hour.

I put the key to the lock and the door pushed open. The door had been left unlocked. Or more accurately, as I looked closer, the door had been *broken* open. I listened. There were no sounds at all.

Dropping my bag on the floor, I reached into our storage basket by the door and grabbed an umbrella. Then I began to walk as quietly as I could into our apartment. My heart was pounding in my chest. My entire system was alert to the possibility that whomever had broken in might still be there. Perhaps even have a gun. No matter how fast I was, I couldn't outrun a bullet so I shouldn't be taking one more step forward, but I couldn't stop myself because I was an idiot who wanted to see my enemies.

There were very few places to hide in our small apartment. I ran my gaze across the one couch and armchair we had in the middle, and the hideous bright red hanging chair that Britney had bought from the flea market.

There was no one there, so I headed towards the two bedrooms. Mine was empty, and so was Britney's, so I returned to the living room to think.

Fortunately for me, I had found no one, but with the passing of danger I began to shake. I'd never been haunted like this despite all the enemies my father had managed to accumulate throughout the years. Anyway, where were the guards that I knew my father had on me?

I pulled out my phone to call him, but given the cold way we had parted, the last thing I wanted was to give him a reason to reiterate his point that I needed a man to protect me.

I needed to tell someone about this, and it had been instilled in me from a very young age that you never call the police. No matter what you didn't call them. There only one person I could think of. It was all his fault anyway. Until he came into my life, everything had been normal. I knew he'd already be back in town so I pulled out my phone and called him.

I got straight to the point as soon as he answered. "Someone broke into my apartment."

"Are you alright?" he asked, his voice calm and sure.

Something warm broke open inside me, and began to spread through my veins. I cleared my throat to rein in my focus. "Sure, I just thought to let you know, and to find out if you can think of a way to quickly bring this harassment to an end."

"I'll be there in five minutes," he said.

Before I could protest or agree, the line went dead. I rose in a moment of instinctive panic. The apartment had been trashed, but then I sat my ass back down, refusing to be bothered by the complete mess.

I went into my room and busied myself with unpacking and putting away the clothes I took to Moscow and the four new dresses I brought back. Then I gathered all my underwear that had obviously been rifled through and dumped them in the washing machine. Bastards!

"Freya," I heard my name called.

I walked out to see Maxim in the most casual form I'd ever seen him in. He had on a dark polo shirt and dark slacks. Suddenly, the most irrational and stupid thought crossed my mind. I wanted him to pin me against the wall and take me. Against my will.

My gaze moved restlessly over his body. I couldn't stop staring at him.

The bulge of his thick biceps against the material and the way it molded to the ridges of his chest made me feel hazy. He rested his icy blue gaze on me, and I had to blink twice to clear my head.

"Are you alright?" he asked, his voice seductively velvety.

"I'm fine," I replied, my body tingling with awareness of him. "You didn't have to come over."

He turned around to inspect my broken lock. I watched him as he dialed a number and issued out the instructions in Russian to fix my lock immediately. His voice was brusque, but the language had never sounded so sexy to my ears.

I needed to sit down, I was losing my mind. I didn't want him. I wanted a career. I wanted a normal man. A normal life.

He turned to me, concern in his blue eyes. "Are you sure you're alright? You look dazed."

That snapped me right back to reason. "Um, I most definitely am not dazed, and I need to leave right now. Britney needs my help at a shoot." All of a sudden fear gripped my heart. *Britney.* Was she actually safe?

In my state of shock I hadn't even called to find out if she was actually okay and not been kidnapped or something. I scrambled for my phone and dialed her, but she didn't pick up. I shot to my feet, terrified out of my mind.

"Pick up, pick up, Brit," I muttered through gritted teeth, as I paced the ground.

"Is there a problem?" Maxim asked.

I spun around to face him. "Britney, my roommate. I need to find out if she is okay."

"Do you know where she is supposed to be?"

"I'm not even sure. On some freaking rooftop somewhere." I sounded hysterical. I turned my back on him and choked out, "Pick up, Brit!" The panic was so real, I felt as if I was being suffocated.

Maxim took the phone from me.

I spun around ready to fight him.

Chapter Twenty-Five

FREYA

"Calm down!" he said, his eyes narrowed.

The blood seemed to be rushing through my ears, my chest was heaving, and my hands were trembling. My chest felt so tight simply breathing was a feat. My vision blurred.

"Freya," he called and shook me. "Look at me," he said, his chest pressed hard against mine. "She's fine," he said to me. "She's fine. She has no value to them. They have no interest in her."

I stared into his hard eyes and felt a cold calm begin to wash over me. Even when my phone rang it sounded like it was coming from a great distance and of no urgency.

It was only when Maxim held it out to me that I came to my senses and grabbed at it, my heart nearly gave out when I saw it was Britney.

"Where are you?" I almost screamed.

"I'm still at the shoot. What's the matter with you?"

Thank God, she was on a rooftop. I could hear the bustle of streets and the honk of vehicles that nearly overpowered her voice. "Nothing's the matter with me."

"Good. When are you going to get here?"

"I'll be there as soon as I can," I said to her. "Be careful."

I heard Maxim's phone vibrate and I turned around to see his watchful gaze on me as he listened.

"Yes," he responded and I wondered whom he was answering to. "She's alright." He ended his call. "A man was spotted leaving through the fire escape in your bathroom."

"Oh shit," I cursed and immediately began to hurry towards it, but he caught me and for a second my feet actually left the ground as he pulled me back. Setting me on the ground, he went ahead. I was left staring dumbfounded at him. Eventually, I followed, and watched as he inspected the open window and poked his head out to look down at the street beyond. He pulled his head back in a few seconds later, secured the latch, and turned around to face me.

"It's not safe for you to be here," he muttered.

"Well, it only started becoming dangerous since you came into my life," I retorted, unable to hold myself back.

I needed to sit down, so I exited the bathroom and collapsed on the sofa. He followed and stood in front of me, his hands jammed into his pockets.

"Was it one of your guys on the phone?"

He nodded.

"Why didn't they stop the break-in in the first place?"

He sighed and folded his hand across his chest, which was mighty distracting and not good for what was left of my energy. I was trembling in a way I hadn't since my mom died.

"Because they have been told to stand down. Your father keeps a vigilant team on you, day and night."

I groaned. "My question is why do I keep getting attacked if there are people guarding me?"

He shrugged. "It could be something to do with the fact that you weren't in town."

I chewed my lip. "Look, until all this blows over would it be possible for you to send someone over to guard Britney?"

He nodded. "Of course."

I quickly gave him the address where Britney was shooting. He immediately called someone and gave him instructions to get there.

"Oh, and please don't tell my father about this," I said when he looked up from his phone call.

"About what exactly," he asked quietly.

I met his gaze. "That you're involved. It's just going to make everything even more complicated."

His mouth twisted at the corners. "I'm pretty sure he's already heard. It would have already been reported that I am here."

"Does this mean I'm going to have full-time, never-out-of-my-sight bodyguards before midnight strikes?"

"That's exactly my intention," he said, his voice hard and determined.

I looked at him with irritation. "I don't need that. What you really need to do is figure out why I am being haunted. I am very sure all this has absolutely nothing to do with me."

"Both you and Britney will require full-on security from now on."

Suddenly, I wanted him gone. He was beginning to overwhelm me. Every time we met it was the same thing. After a little while in his presence I started to feel as if I was being drawn to him, as helpless as an iron filing to a giant magnet. "Thank you for stepping in, I really appreciate it."

"I'm not leaving until they fix your door."

He went over to the armchair by the corner then, and lowered himself into it. Ignoring me he read something off his phone. I rose and escaped to my bedroom. I closed the door and leaned against it. I took deep breaths to calm my heart. It was beating so fast it was almost fluttering. Just as I had expected, I could do nothing but stand by the door and calm my over excited body. I needed to call Britney.

I pulled the phone out of my pocket and got through to her. After apologizing that I wouldn't be able to make it because of the intrusion.

"Oh my God," she gasped and I felt sorry for her. She had not signed up for any of this. "Don't worry everything will be fine," I assured her. "All this will pass." As soon as I get Maxim out of my life.

"Are you alright?" she asked breathlessly.

"Yeah, I'm fine."

"What's going on, Freya?"

I sighed. "I'm almost certain it has something to do with Maxim. I was living in relative peace until he showed up."

"Hmm ..."

"Anyway, someone is going to arrive soon to protect you so when he comes, please call me so I can confirm with Maxim that he is the one. We need to be extra careful."

"Uh, what do you know? I think he just arrived," she said.

"Describe him," I commanded tightly.

"Well, he's in a badly cut suit, bald, brick wall broad, and very vicious looking. He just came onto the rooftop and is standing by the door all military like, but silent. Should I go over to him?"

"Just a second," I replied and hurried out of the room.

"Maxim," I called and he looked up from his phone. "Who's the guy ..." A better idea occurred to me. "Britney, send a picture of him real quick."

I waited and had to look away to avoid meting his gaze. I could feel his eyes on me. It made me so self-conscious I wanted to scratch my skin off. The bud between my thighs throbbed so painfully that I kept shifting my weight from one leg to the other.

When she sent the picture I stood at a safe distance from him and turned the phone towards him. "Is this your guy?"

He got out of his chair and without warning reached for my hand. My grip instantly loosened and the phone fell to the ground.

I stared at my wrist in wonder. His touch had burned me. I

didn't move to pick the phone up, so he leaned over, retrieved it, and looked at the image. "Yes, that's Viktor," he confirmed. "He'll keep her safe."

"Thank you," I replied and he handed the phone back to me.

I was extra careful not to make any sort of contact with him, but after I ended the call I suddenly felt hot and bothered. "Do you want something to drink? Tea, coffee, water?"

"Coffee would be good."

Britney had brewed some that morning, but it would be yuck by now so I walked stiffly towards the kitchen to make some more.

Chapter Twenty-Six
MAXIM

I was intensely aware of her, but I knew she was watching me so I didn't raise my head and let her know how much satisfaction just being in the same room with her gave me. Hell, I could have spent the whole day with her. And considering the waspish mood she was in, it was some feat for me. I have never had time for other people's dramas.

"Does love mean nothing to you?" she demanded suddenly.

I lifted my head. "Excuse me?"

She swept her hand towards me. "You said that you were willing to marry me because the request wasn't too bothersome. Don't you want to be with someone you're in love with?"

"I'm not in love with anyone," I replied and returned my gaze to my phone but she had my rapt attention.

"Well don't you ever want to be?" she insisted.

I felt the impatience in her voice and almost smiled. It was too easy to bait her. I lifted my gaze to watch her. "What does being in love mean?" I asked.

That got her attention. "You really don't know or are you just taunting me?"

"I've never been in love," I answered honestly. "And since I have a suspicion it makes fools of men, I'm more than willing to settle for mutual respect and responsibility."

"That sounds dull," she said.

I didn't have a response.

She folded her arms under her breasts, drawing my eyes to them. "Actually, you also seem pretty dull."

I lifted my gaze to her and knew that was just what she wanted; my attention.

"Did you always want to be a mafia don, or did you have some other dream? Bianca told me Levan's was always to be a brewer."

"Yes, I have a dream," I said just as my phone buzzed with a message. I looked at it. The locksmith was coming up the stairs.

"What is it?" she asked.

I rose to my feet. "It's to keep those dearest to me, safe. Now I have to go. The locksmith should be here any moment now and I have people watching you, so you can rest easy."

Both of us heard the tread of the locksmith in the corridor. As I passed her I wanted to reach out and stroke her cheek. The impulse was so strong I had to clench my fist to stop myself.

Chapter Twenty-Seven

FREYA

I watched him leave and felt my heart drop into my stomach. *The cold bastard.* How could he be such a block of ice? Did nothing affect him? I had wanted a chance to at least come close to him again... To perhaps elicit a kiss from him, but of course nothing like that was possible with him. Anyway, why the hell was I thinking such thoughts about him? I hated his guts. Confused, I thought of Levan and how deeply he cared for Bianca. Why couldn't he be like that?

"I'm here to replace a broken lock," the locksmith said. He had a mop of curly hair and his hands were blackened and dusty.

I nodded and pointed to the front door.

"Righto," he said, putting his bag down.

"Would you like some coffee?" I asked.

He grinned. "That would be awesome."

I went back into the kitchen and stood next my freshly

brewed coffee. I tried to stop replaying everything about him in my mind. From the soundless way he moved, to the way that he had held me in the midst of my panic attack, or the way that he spoke, but especially what he'd just said.

My dream is to keep the people dearest to me safe.

He may have been severely lacking in the romance gene department, but even I had to admit those words sounded genuine, unpretentious and pure-hearted. I felt my heart soften and realized immediately that I was playing a dangerous game. By the time I left the kitchen with the locksmith's coffee I had hardened my heart again.

Britney sent me some of the shots she'd taken and I began to curate them. The locksmith left, I began to put everything back into place again, and life as I knew it kicked back into motion, but all day long my mind kept straying into the forbidden territory that was Maxim.

I couldn't stop thinking of him.

Even when I forced myself to remember the hate I had for him over Anna, that too had seemingly faded in intensity in light of his explanation.

Britney came back. The night stretched intolerably. The next day was long. I kept looking at my phone. I wanted to call him, see him, touch him. Way too many times the sudden urge for him to touch me again completely overwhelmed me. At night, I thought of him and touched myself. The orgasm was so intense I nearly cried out. When daylight broke, I felt like a junkie. Even Britney commented on my appearance at breakfast. We worked together in silence. Then I left for my evening job for the first time since my injury.

I was nearing the end of my shift when my heart nearly stopped.

I saw *Maxim*... or at least I imagined I had. I had just delivered an order when it seemed as though his icy blue gaze had caught me from across the crowd. But someone took a seat before me and I was forced to drag my attention away from searching the crowd for him to my customer.

Monsieur Antoine was seated in front of me.

I sucked in my breath and tried to work up an honest smile, but it was hard to, especially with the almost-faded bruise by his temple. He damn well deserved it though.

"Good evening, Monsieur," I greeted evenly.

The look he gave me made my blood run cold. "Is it?"

I neither wanted to provoke or be provoked by anyone tonight. I needed this job. I swallowed down my pride. "I'm sorry about what happened that night. I hope we can move past it."

He gave me a bitter look. Just then my floor manager Ryan called out to me. "A moment, Freya?"

I was more than grateful for the save. "Excuse me," I said and hurried over to Ryan. I gave him a smile and hoped whatever errand he wanted to send me on would take me away from the bar for more than a little while.

"So," he began, looking more uncomfortable than I'd ever seen him.

"What's wrong?"

"It's so fucking hard for me to say this. This world's a fucking disgusting place and you haven't done anything wrong. You are also one of my best workers but... my hands are tied. I'm going to have to let you go, Freya."

That was completely unexpected. I blinked so rapidly the room flashed before my eyes. Did I hear wrong or was he joking? He did sometimes have a weird sense of humor. "What?"

"It's that French bastard. He insisted on it. I'm so sorry, Freya, but he spends a fuck load in here and I can't lose him. I'll give you a glowing reference. You should have no problem finding another job. You're one of the best."

I felt hurt, so hurt that for the first few moments, I couldn't say a word, or move. Then I straightened my spine.

"Sure," I said nonchalantly. I turned around and looked directly at the pathetic bastard. He had a sick smile on his face.

He raised his tumbler to me in salutation. "See you around, Princess!"

Everyone around me seemed to for some reason call me Princess, and the title was seriously beginning to piss me off.

I wouldn't give him the satisfaction of looking hurt. "Be careful in the alleyways," I called.

His face changed.

I winked at him then. Turning around I marched into the staff room and grabbed my belongings. Fuck him. Fuck this bar, Fuck Ryan. I didn't need any of them.

Chapter Twenty-Eight

MAXIM

I saw her the moment she came out of the bar.

Which was a bit surprising as there was twenty minutes left on the clock before her shift was over, so it made me wonder what was wrong. Was she ill, hurt? Had something happened. I hated knowing there was very little I could do about anything that affected her. So I just watched her. I expected her to go down towards the subway, or hail a taxi home, but she just kept walking away from the subway, her head bowed.

I felt anger stir inside me. Did she not know how dangerous that kind of behavior was, especially *now*, to be so damn inattentive? Hell, for a smart girl she was acting like a kid. Look at her. She was not alert at all. Not an ounce of caution toward her surroundings. To the point where she could be shot dead at any moment and not even see it coming.

And this after she had been stabbed. Un-fucking-believable!

I was so furious I wanted to get out of the car, and grab her by the shoulders and shake her. But that was not an option.

Gripping the steering wheel, I watched her for a few minutes more. When I could bear it no more I drove away. I pressed down on the gas pedal. Thank God I had put Roman on her. He was my best man. What Roman didn't know about surveillance and protection could be written on a stamp.

I got to the next traffic lights. I glanced up into the rear mirror. There was only one car behind me. When the lights changed I made a screeching U-turn. The driver blared his horn angrily, but minutes later I pulled up next to Freya. She was so deep in thought I actually startled her. At first she just looked at my car blankly, then bent down to look at me through the window.

"Are you hungry?" I asked.

"Yes," she replied frostily. "I'm starving."

Chapter Twenty-Nine

FREYA

He took me to a place called Sylvia's on Malcolm X Boulevard. It had just what I needed. I ordered chicken and waffles and threw in some shrimp salad and buttered corn. I didn't bother explaining myself to Maxim. A man like him wouldn't have a clue about the concept of comfort eating. As I suspected, he ordered a salmon sandwich and we sat down by the window to wait.

Today, he was dressed as though he had been on his way from work in an impeccable charcoal striped waist coat, the white dress shirt folded up the sleeves, and a dark intricately patterned tie in place.

His hair was low, as usual, skin supple and golden from the reflection of the light in the room, but his eyes were brimming with annoyance. As if he didn't want me to see his true state of his mind, he turned towards the view of the vibrant street, but his fist clenched and unclenched on the table. That was the most restless I'd ever seen him.

"Is everything okay?"

He turned his head toward me and stared into my eyes. I felt my belly start to quake. God, how could this man have such an effect on me? Just one look and I felt like jelly. I swear, I just couldn't move, and certainly couldn't look away. Thank God, our food arrived. I tore my gaze away from him and immediately dove right in, but my appetite was gone.

He spoke then. "I don't want you to work at that bar anymore."

I stopped. If he had worded that in any other way I would have responded politely and told him I had been fired but something in his authoritative tone provoked me.

"Um... okay," I said, the same way an irritating teenager would say to its parent.

"I'm serious," he said, through gritted teeth. "You cannot remain there. There is absolutely no way to guarantee your security. You are way too exposed when you're in the bar, you come out at ungodly hours, and then you proceed to roam the streets aimlessly."

I knew he was right, but I couldn't stop myself from acting like a brat. "I said okay."

He frowned. "I hope we won't have to have this conversation again."

"I hope so too," I snapped. "*I,* decide where I work, but thank you for your concern."

"I'll give you a job," he said. "You studied fashion merchandising did you not? I'll refer you to a design firm in my building. They should be able to find you a position there that you-"

"I don't need your help, Maxim," I cut him off, and rose from my seat. Then, I felt bad. He had just fed me and was just looking out for my safety. I begrudgingly corrected myself. "Look, I don't need your help in figuring out my livelihood, but thanks for dinner and thanks for... caring."

Something flashed in his eyes. I wanted to bend down and kiss his mouth then. The urge was so strong it shocked me. He watched me from his window seat as I ran out to the street and grabbed a taxi.

Chapter Thirty

MAXIM

I watched her leave, then got into my car and headed home.

As I parked my car in the underground car park, my phone began to ring. It was Levan.

"You okay?" he asked.

"Yeah. Where are you?"

"At your place."

I disembarked and slammed the door shut. "I'll be right in."

I headed towards the private lift that carried me all the way up to my penthouse. The doors swished open. "What are you doing here?" I asked throwing my car key on the side table.

"I heard from Mikhail," he began.

I stopped, mildly annoyed. This thing with Freya had me on edge and I was finding it more and more difficult to keep my temper. "Why are my movements being fucking reported to you?"

He frowned. "Will you relax? Nobody is keeping tabs on you, but this is a difficult time and while I'm leaving, you're still my brother, and I need to be sure that you're safe."

"Then don't leave," I said, unbuttoning my shirt, and heading towards the curving marble stairs.

We took the stairs two at a time. I turned around to catch the smile on his face. "You're full of bullshit, you know, Maxim. The truth is you're completely fine with me leaving. You're even relieved, I'm sure."

I walked into my massive bedroom. All the curtains were open and the light from the stars shone in through the doomed glass ceiling. Behind me Levan hit the light switch making yellow light flood into the room. He was not wrong. I was going to keep an eye on him in the new life he was embarking with Bianca, and I had absolutely no complaints. He would no longer be in the direct line of fire of our world.

I sat on my bed and Levan came to sit next to me. "I'm really worried about Freya.

I stopped midway through pulling off my shoe. "Why?"

"Her father has enemies too but they've not exactly been going after her. These attacks only began after you came into the picture."

I turned to look at him. "I've been thinking that too, but if they wanted to get to me then why not target me directly?"

"Maybe whomever it is has been waiting for the right moment. It's not exactly easy getting to you." I could hear the sadness in his tone as he spoke. "Maybe the point is not to just hurt you directly, but to hurt the entire conglomerate. Any harm coming to Freya on your watch will literally turn everything upside down and set off a war between our two fathers. Our two families being joined together is a terrifying prospect for many. It doubles your power and reach ... unthinkably."

"Hmm.... That narrows down the possible suspects to everyone we know."

"It could also be for revenge," he said. "Maybe you hurt someone's family member along the way and now they're coming for yours through her."

"Then why don't they come after you too?"

"Again, it won't be as bloody. Painful for you but, turns little upside down. Freya's father however will burn us to the ground, or at least try. We could both destroy each other. Imagine what a vacuum we would leave then."

"They want to hurt me with someone else's sword. Perhaps this person doesn't have enough resources."

"Yes, that's what I would think. Anyway, I came here to tell you that this is exactly the reason why it has to be solely Freya's choice to get with you. Not as a duty, or favor to anyone because it is definitely not going to be a rosy path. I understand why she is so against it and I don't blame her at all."

"I'm not forcing her."

"Her father is."

"I can't do anything about that. That's between them."

"Do you want her, Maxim? Not a means for growing the business, but as a woman."

I looked away from his probing eyes. "Yes," I admitted.

"Good. That's all I wanted to hear. We'll talk more tomorrow. Now you better get to bed and I better get back home. I had to sneak out after Bianca fell asleep. It will not be a good morning for me if she wakes to find me gone. No surprises! That's the rule of our relationship."

That made me smile despite myself and as he left, I found myself gazing after him with just the twinge of envy. If only, Freya... A pair of defiant green eyes and a tumble of wild fiery hair crashed into my mind and I couldn't stop the excitement that coursed through my system.

No woman had ever been able to rent even the least bit of space in my mind before, but Freya Fedorov seemed to very easily find her way in and out at will. I didn't much care for the vulnerability and frivolities of love, but perhaps a woman who made my cock jump with just one look would not be too bad of an acquisition.

Chapter Thirty-One

I was walking down the subway stairs when the call came in.

"Hey, Freya, it's Bianca."

My heart began to beat faster and I knew it was because of her close relation to a pair of piercing blue eyes that haunted my dreams.

"Hey, Bianca," I answered as casually as I could.

"I was thinking of checking out some jewelry today. Would you be available anytime today?"

I was suddenly even more excited. "I'm yours."

"Great," she responded. "I'm just waiting on an early afternoon appointment for our wedding venue. So after that I'll be right over to you. Let's say about 2.00 p.m."

"Perfect," I responded.

As soon as the call was over I phoned Britney and told her about the proposition.

"Oh my God! That is freaking amazing," she cried excitedly. "Their wedding will be full of paparazzi and the crème de la crème of society so our jewelry on her is going to get a ton of exposure. Is their wedding sponsored in a magazine or something, do you know?"

"I doubt that very much," I replied. "It is elite, but a completely private affair, I imagine. If anything, the Ivankovs shy away from publicity."

"Hmm, either way it's a good opportunity for us."

"Yes, it is," I agreed happily, as the subway car arrived.

~

*A*t about a quarter to two Bianca called again.

"I'm so sorry, Freya, but I have to push our appointment. I just got the call to come inspect the venue now. But I'm having a dessert tasting this evening at our apartment. Perhaps you could come by and eat with us while we look at jewelry."

"Oh, uh sure," I replied and wanted so badly to ask... about him... but I didn't dare. Almost. Before she cut the call though, I grew some balls. "You ... er ... you're having some friends over?"

"Oh, just my best friend Aldie, and Levan if he's back by then."

"Oh, okay," I said, and couldn't help feeling disappointed. "Sure, I'll be there. As well as some pieces that I think you may like, I'll bring our new catalogue as well. There are designs in there that no one has seen yet."

"Oh yes, definitely do," she replied.

Chapter Thirty-Two

MAXIM

I t was just a little bit after eight in the evening when Levan popped his head through my office door. "On my way home," he said.

I wondered why he was informing me.

"Bianca's having a dessert tasting tonight. For the wedding. Want to come?"

I returned my gaze back to my computer without a word and he laughed in response. "Of course you don't. At least I offered. She invited Aldie, and Freya's also coming over to show her some jewelry. I'll have fun alone with them then."

Bastard, I swore silently at the way he had slipped her name into the fray, but I didn't dare give him the satisfaction of my sudden interest. So I held myself back as he shut the door. I tried to return to my work but even the words on my computer had blurred. I sprang to my feet and grabbed my suit jacket.

I called him as he waited for the elevator doors to open. "I sent Otari and Viktor on an errand so you'll have to give me a ride home. "

"That's not happening," he said. "I'm already late, and last I checked you knew how to drive."

Fucking bastard.

"If you leave without me I'm going to hurt you," I said and his mocking laughter haunted me to the depths of my being.

His town car pulled up in front of the building and I got in the passenger seat. "So am I driving you to your house or mine?"

"Fuck you, Levan."

He laughed.

As we neared his apartment my palms grew sweaty, and the blood in my veins began to simmer in anticipation. Before we could even arrive at the door Bianca had already opened it. She gazed at me with a secret smile, as though she had expected to see me and I felt more exposed than I ever had.

"Maxim," she said in her best hostess voice, as Levan's arms enveloped her. A second later they were lost in a kiss.

I passed them both and headed into the apartment. I prepared myself as I walked through the foyer for the moment I arrived at the open layout home and saw her. I thought I was prepared, but it was like a blow to the solar plexus to see her again. This time her hair was loose. The way I had always dreamed it. There was a white ribbon in it. It looked old-fashioned. Girls didn't wear ribbon anymore, but it made her look as if she belonged in another world, a forgotten, special world, where milky white women like her were worshipped on an altar.

Aldie rose when she saw me. "Hello, Maxim. It's been a while, how are things with you?" she said almost shyly. They were seated at the long dining table, an assortment of desserts laid out on it.

The last time I had seen her had been at our place in Spain a few months earlier, just before Levan had been sentenced to life in prison and thrown into jail. "Great," I responded.

She nodded and sat back down. Then I turned to Freya.

"Hello," she greeted politely, and suddenly I couldn't speak. I was only able to give a nod in response. I turned around and headed towards Levan's study. If I had not I would have been exposed.

Chapter Thirty-Three

FREYA

*T**he arrogant bastard.*

My mouth was hanging open. I couldn't believe how rude he had just been.

"What is it?" Aldie asked.

"Did he just ignore me?"

"Uh, I think he nodded," she placated.

"Is that good enough? Do you just nod to a fully worded salutation?"

She snickered and I tried to feel amused too, but I just could not. I was actually hurt. I had never stopped thinking of him and all the while he couldn't give a shit. Hell, he couldn't even say hello.

"Don't mind it too much," Aldie said, "that's how he is. He barely says anything."

"Oh no, he speaks," I corrected bitterly. "Just not to people that he feels are beneath him. Isn't that just plain arrogance?"

"Uh," her eyebrows furrowed and I realize that I was ranting to someone I'd just met for the first time a few minutes earlier.

"Ignore me," I said with a forced smile. "I've known him a while and I was just being touchy. Rough day."

"Perfectly fine," she said with a genuine smile as Levan and Bianca returned to the room.

The dessert tasting soon began, but Maxim didn't join us. "He's not one for sweets," Levan explained.

I resisted the impulse to roll my eyes. He definitely needed some with all the bitterness he carried in his twisted cold heart.

Bianca's assortment of desserts for her wedding were exquisite. The stars of the show were mini cannoli, golden cupcakes, blended mochas in shot glasses, and the cutest caramel apples dressed in tuxedos. Almost an hour later, the tasting came to an end and the final choices had been made.

"I need to run," Aldie said, rising up. "Early morning tomorrow."

"We'll walk you out," Levan said and he and Bianca stood.

Looking around at the loads of used plates, I decided to help them get a head start on the cleaning. I was pretty sure they had some help, but it was my habit not to leave a mess for the morning. I began to gather the small dessert plates and forks we had used and took them over to the sink. They had a dish-washer, and I was about to give them a rinse when Maxim emerged from wherever he had crawled into.

I completely ignored him as he came over with a used cup of

coffee and placed it on the counter. I glared at the dirty cup as he turned to leave and couldn't hold back any more.

"Why are you so impolite to me?" I asked. "Is it because you see me as beneath you?"

He turned and gave me his full attention. "Excuse me?" he asked, and just like that my brain was scrambled again, at his gaze, at the melody of his voice, and most definitely at the fine specimen of a man he looked clothed in his charcoal suit, black shirt and white tie.

I turned away before I embarrassed myself. "Forget it."

Out of nowhere his hand closed around my arm.

My heart gave a nervous jump I whirled around like a cut snake. Hissing with aggression. "What the hell do you think you're doing?"

"Why do you always want to provoke me?" he asked softly.

I stopped breathing. He was too close, his scent of musk and lemon, twirling all around me, and those eyes on mine... and then on my lips. My knees became jelly.

"Let me go!" I tried to pull my hand away but he wouldn't let go.

"Are you attracted to me?" he asked.

My mouth dropped open with incredulity. The next few moments were of me puffing air and unable to form a coherent sentence to defend myself. I settled on an outraged insult. "Get over your fucking self, Maxim."

"Kiss me," he ordered, his gaze fluttering down to my lips.

I felt my cheeks burn.

"Let's see if this attraction between us is really as potent as it seems."

His gaze lifted to mine with the challenge and I wanted to defy him. By God that was all that I swore to myself I wanted, but the truth was a whole different matter. I wanted something even more.

My voice weakened but I gave it my best shot. "Let me go," I croaked, like a helpless Victorian damsel. I tried again to pull away, but by now my willpower was feeble, reduced to nothing in the presence of the beast.

He let go, but then his hand slid around my waist and in the next breath, his lips were on mine.

I felt a zap!

A painful jarring sensation shot straight to my core and awoke every single nerve in my body. He kissed me softly, gently, and I felt myself begin to crumble to the floor. His taste was like a drug, released into me to completely unravel me, and it was so sweet that it stole my breath away.

His tongue teased mine, stroking and withdrawing and at the hard suck of my lips I almost felt liquid hot desire begin to drip from my thighs.

"*Maxim*," I held onto his shirt, desperate not to fall ... desperate to hold on to what remained of my sanity. This was wrong... he was wrong. I was supposed to loathe him. That was all I knew for so long.

Somewhere in the distance, I heard laughter and was instantly jerked back to my senses. Maxim did not hear or did not care.

I tried to pull away, but he held on tightly to me and slipped his tongue even deeper into my mouth. I couldn't help it. All I could do was suck on his tongue. He tightened his grip around my waist and I was so lost in him that for the next few seconds I did little to protest. But then I felt everything go silent and that was more than enough to jar me back to reason. I grabbed uselessly at his hand around my waist.

"Maxim!" I heard a call from the distance, and his grip loosened.

Our parting made the sweetest, softest, sucking sound. I knew that punctuation to the end of how much he had just made the world spin under my feet would haunt me in the days to come. He let go of me and turned away, not giving any of us a chance to see just how much he had unraveled. I watched him, his chest rising and falling with every harsh breath. I turned around to meet Levan and Bianca watching us. Levan had a very thoughtful gaze on his face while Bianca couldn't hide her smile.

"We're so sorry for interrupting you both," she apologized, and grabbed onto her fiancé's hand. "Let's give them some privacy."

"No need!" I almost yelled. "I'm leaving." I began to look madly around for my purse until she reminded me that it was in the foyer. I almost sprinted towards it. She came after me to see me out, but I barely heard a single thing she said.

I was out of the door in a flash. My whole world had just turned upside down.

Chapter Thirty-Four

MAXIM

https://www.youtube.com/watch?v=qgy7vEje5-w

I couldn't go home.

With that one kiss, it felt as though my entire belief system had come crashing down, and I needed to finish what I started. I went and got my car and found myself arriving at her apartment building and parking on the opposite side of the street.

They lived on the third floor of an old Bronx apartment building and although the blinds were open all I could see was a glimpse of their living room. But there were no movements whatsoever.

But I couldn't leave. I had to see her again. One look, and I promised myself I would go. Just one look.

I felt cursed, put under a spell that I couldn't understand. Even the crippling dose of self-loathing that filled me was not enough to make me pull away. I sat there like a fool. For one little glimpse.

I knew not to call her. She wouldn't respond. She was probably as shaken as I was, but had an ego that was bigger than any man's. It aggravated me, but at the same time heightened my excitement for her.

I saw a car pull up in front of her building and stop. A few seconds passed and no one came out of it. I sat up, all my senses on high alert. Then a man came out of the front passenger door. He was dressed in a t-shirt and jeans, and had a baseball cap worn low enough to hide his face. He had a pizza box in hand, but he looked around cautiously. The way a hitman does.

I could be just paranoid, but no harm in being safe. I immediately grabbed my gun and got out of the car.

I began to approach the car. As I got closer the car jerked to a start, and I immediately pointed my gun at it. It screeched away and I knew then that I only had a few seconds before Freya would be in trouble.

I pulled my phone out of my pocket and made a quick call as I ran up the stairs.

"Follow the car!" I said to the men watching.

"Already on it," came Nikolai's response.

"How many of them are in the car?"

"Just one," he responded. "The driver."

That meant he would be too preoccupied to warn his colleague who had gone into Freya's apartment.

I arrived at her door and knocked hard, twice. It took a while, but soon it was opened and Freya appeared at the door looking more annoyed than anything else. I looked beyond her into the room, my gaze searched and saw no one except Britney, sitting on their couch.

The expression on Freya's face shocked me. "Maxim sweet- heart," she sang out.

I knew then he was already in there.

"What are you doing here, darling? It's already too late and Britney and I are just about to go to bed, but I'll see you tomorrow?"

"I forgot my tie here," I said, and when she still refused to step aside I gently pushed her out of the way.

All seemed well, but I knew that was not the case. Her friend looked terrified while Freya had fear written all over her face as she looked from me to the counter. I turned around and found myself staring down the barrel of a gun.

Chapter Thirty-Five

FREYA

I hated with all of my heart that Maxim was here.

My shock at seeing him at the door had been immeasurable, then relief, and then the fear that he would get hurt had swamped me. I didn't want him here.

"Put down your gun," the idiot that had posed as a pizza delivery man ordered.

He was skinny and had the weirdest looking face and flattened bangs I had ever seen. I couldn't place his ethnicity but he had the protruded facial structure of a dog or wolf. I liked wolves and dogs, but it was not a good look on him.

"Drop your fucking gun!" he yelled, and I could see that his fully tattooed hand was now shaking, where it had previously not been when he had been faced with just myself and Britney. I could see then that he feared Maxim. He probably even knew him.

I breathed easier, but we were still in the midst of a madman and possibly mere seconds from life and death if he got spooked and began firing. Britney was the one whom I pitied the most. She was trembling so hard in her flea market red chair I could almost hear it rattling under the pressure. I swore then that I would find a way to get her out of all this.

Maxim lowered the gun and gently placed it on the ground as per the instruction given. When he rose back up, he asked a question that we all wanted to know the answer to. "Who sent you?"

"Shut up!" The madman barked nervously. "Step away from the gun. Far, far away. Or else I will blow her fucking head off right now."

He pointed the gun towards me and my heart almost jumped out of my chest. I needed to sit down but I couldn't move an inch from my position against the door.

"Tell me who sent you," Maxim repeated, "I'll let you go. I'm a man of my word."

He began to approach him and suddenly a bullet was fired. Britney screamed as even the walls seemed to shake with the explosion. My hands went to my ringing ears. For a few seconds, I was in shock. I felt sick to my stomach and was almost too afraid to open my eyes, but when I did, I saw that Maxim was alright and Britney who had her head buried between her knees was completely still. She might have passed out.

"Don't you fucking move!" the gunman screamed. It was clear he felt he'd lost control of the situation and was in panic mode.

Everything in the room stilled as we waited along with the madman for what Maxim would do.

Maxim took another step forward.

I found my voice. "Uh, I don't think that's the best approach, Maxim."

"I will blow your head off!" the madman promised, his eyes wild, but when that didn't seem to faze Maxim he turned the gun towards me. "I will blow her fucking head off."

Maxim raised his hands in the air. "You know who I am. If you kill me or her, you will be hunted down like a dog and made to suffer for days. Your skin will be torn off you. Your dick will be cut off and fed to you. Your mother will die. If you have children they will die too. If you have a wife or girl, pity her for what she will suffer."

The man began to shake uncontrollably.

"I'll let you go," he said. "I'll count to three, and you can leave."

I suddenly wasn't sure who was more out of their mind. Maxim or the madman, but I kept my mouth shut, but I did notice the intense way Maxim was studying him. Perhaps he knew something that I did not.

He backed away then and the man seemed to be considering what he had just said.

Maxim turned to me and I was more freaked out than anything that he had actually taken his eyes off the guy.

"What are you doing?" I whispered.

"Move!" he ordered. "Move away from the door right now."

I looked towards the madman and saw that he didn't seem to have any problems with Maxim's request. So I took one step to the side, and when I saw that he didn't react, I hurried over to Britney's side.

Maxim moved away too, and to my surprise, stood as a shield in front of me and Britney. I cradled poor blameless Britney and prayed for this nightmare to quickly come to an end.

The madman began to move, slowly and carefully and soon he was at the door.

"You can leave. I won't do anything to you," Maxim said.

The man stood there uncertainly. Then he lifted his gun and pointed it directly at Maxim.

Suddenly, I knew then that things were going to go sour.

"Move out of the way!" the man yelled. "I didn't come for you, Ivankov. I have my orders."

So he did know who Maxim was.

"Well you're not getting to her unless you go through me."

"I will shoot you!" he roared.

"Do it. You know the consequences," Maxim replied. I had never seen anyone look as torn as the gunman. With a heart-breaking look at us, at his failure, he turned and ran for his life. Maxim picked up his gun and was out of the apartment in a flash, after him.

The life was nearly squeezed out of me. "Come back!" I yelled to him. "Why the fuck are you going after him?"

I ran to the door but before I could leave Britney cried for my return.

"Please don't leave me," she begged and I instantly went back to her. I sat by her side and rocked the both of us. I was terrified for Maxim. I felt as if I would die if anything happened to him.

Chapter Thirty-Six

MAXIM

"**Y**ou're not staying here," I declared, the moment I returned. "Pack what you need, you're coming to my house."

I thought she would argue against the idea, but hoped she would have been scared enough not to. I was grateful when all she said was, "I'm not going without Britney."

"You can bring her," I said, relieved.

They grabbed the things they needed and in a short trip later we were back at my home. They were shown different rooms by our housekeeper Mariah, but Mariah said both girls decided to stay in the same room. I realized they were both gravely shaken and it made me even more furious at the attack. I was about to enter the meeting with my head of security when Levan called me.

"I just heard," he said, his voice muted, probably so as not to alert Bianca.

"Everyone's alright," I quickly established.

"*Fuck*," he swore. "It must have been so hard on them. It was just a few months ago that I was in deep shit, and now this? Why does this stuff keep happening?"

"The common variable is women," I pointed out sarcastically.

He laughed. "I don't even know what to say to that."

His laughter unwound me a little bit and I began to look at the situation with a little less heat. "I've got to go, but I'll give you the details tomorrow."

"Sure, but why did you go over to Freya's place? I was told that you were already there. Did you know something was going to go down?"

"Goodnight," I responded, and put an end to the call.

Then I walked into the study and listened to my men brief me about how they let the gunman disappear into thin air. As for the driver, he had apparently crashed his car during their pursuit of him and been injured and knocked unconscious. My men couldn't do anything but drive on as a police car arrived almost immediately on the scene.

"We took his photo. Through that we should be able to find out more."

I felt irritated, angry and disappointed. What would have happened tonight if I had not been there? Was this what I was paying top dollar for? And what about Igor's men? Were they asleep on the job as well, or had they relaxed because my men were on the job? Were both teams slacking off because they assumed the other team was on it? I decided then to tell Igor to pull his men off. I knew my men were better. They just needed a damn good kick in the ass.

Then I let my team see my extreme displeasure. Roman was white-faced by the time I was finished. More security devices were put in place and the meeting came to an end.

Restless and disturbed I went upstairs. I stopped outside the room Freya and Britney were sleeping. There were no sounds coming from inside and no strip of light under the door so it was safe to assume they were sleeping. I didn't want to knock in case I woke them up, but I needed to see that everything was okay. Quietly I pushed the door open, no more than a crack, and in the darkened interior saw the shapes of their still bodies on the bed.

Satisfied that they were both safe I shut the door and headed to my room.

I had just arrived in my room when a message arrived on my phone.

Can you talk? Is it too late?

It was Freya, and my response was immediate.

Yes.

Her reply came quickly.

At the bottom of the stairs? Five minutes?

I thought about it for an instant.

No. Kitchen. We can make some tea or something.

The moment I hit send, I reread the message and couldn't

believe those words had come out of my head, more so
because I couldn't remember the last time I'd even touched
a kitchen appliance. Putting the phone back into my
pocket, I hurried immediately to the kitchen. All was dark
and quiet, the staff having finished for the day. I opened a
few cupboards and found the cabinet where the coffee pods
and tea were kept. I pulled out a box of Chamomile tea
infusion. Then I filled the kettle with water and flicked the
switch on.

I sensed the moment she arrived, but didn't turn around. For
some reason I wasn't yet ready to face her. A corner of me
even felt dread that perhaps she would again blame this all on
me and it would drive us even further apart. Not after
tonight. I shut my eyes and hoped.

When the water boiled I retrieved the kettle and brought it
over to the counter where I had already laid out the flowers
in tea cups. I couldn't believe how domesticated I was being.
If any of my men saw me now, they would be in shock.

"This will calm you," I said to her.

"I'm already calm," she replied quietly. "My question is why
were you so calm when he was pointing the gun at you?"

I looked up then, and met her gaze. Only one lamp lit the
massive kitchen, but it was more than enough for me to
clearly see the accusation in her eyes. "What are you saying?"

"I know that you're usually calm, but we were in a very
volatile and dangerous situation. At any moment things could
have gone from bad to tragic, and you let him point a gun at
you like that. What made you so sure that he wouldn't
shoot?"

I felt a surge of anger, but I kept my voice even. "Are you insinuating that I am behind all of these attacks?"

Silence. We stared at each other.

"What made you so sure that he wouldn't shoot?" she repeated.

I tried my best to put aside my ego and I had a strange feeling of hurt she could think so lowly of me. What was important now was her safety and to assure her that I was not her enemy.

"If he had wanted to shoot me he would have done so from the moment I came in. I realized as I studied him that he was afraid of me. He knew exactly who I was and that his family's lives would be destroyed if he dared to hurt me. My father is not a very forgiving person. He was sent there for you, not me, and if he had overstepped his bounds he would have been the one to end up dead."

She blinked and for a moment seemed confused. "So he came to kill or kidnap me and your arrival saved me?" she asked cynically.

"I agree with you that something feels off. I can't put my finger on it yet, but what on earth would make you think I would be behind any of this?" I asked, swallowing my pride.

"Trust is not exactly a cheap commodity in the world we come from, Maxim."

"So what would I gain from getting someone to kill you?"

"It doesn't have to happen now. Perhaps it's all an act leading up to when you're able to get me to willingly marry you. And then one of these thugs finally gets lucky and finishes the job.

No one would say my death was your fault. You can play the grieving husband for a while."

"And what would I get in return?"

She faced me bravely in semi-dark space. "Two empires for the price of nothing."

I watched her, more impressed than furious. Even I hadn't thought of that. She was definitely her father's daughter.

"Sure, if that's what you choose to believe."

"It's not the truth?" she asked.

"Would you believe me if I told you it wasn't?"

"No," she replied, "but still I'd like to hear your response."

"It's not," I replied, and I heard her release a shuddering breath.

"I have more questions," she said, taking a step towards me. "Why did you respond so fast? You couldn't possibly have been informed and been able to appear in front of my door that quickly."

"I followed you home," I replied.

Her eyes widened slightly at the admission. "Why?"

I could have lied, but I told her the truth. "Because I couldn't stop thinking about our kiss."

Her chest heaved at the reminder.

"Britney and I will get out of your hair tomorrow."

That instantly brought back my annoyance. "Where are you going to go?"

"We'll figure it out."

"You're not leaving."

Her response was a deeply burrowed frown. "What? Are you going to stop me?"

"As you've rightly pointed out, if anything happens to you I might be blamed. Therefore, to protect my interest, and until these problems are resolved, you'll remain here with your friend where you can be more easily protected at all times."

She opened her mouth to argue, but then shut it. "My head is a mess. I have to think about this. Let's talk about this tomorrow."

I nodded. "Fine."

She hesitated. "Goodnight." Then she turned around, and exited the room.

I picked up my mug of chamomile tea and took a sip. It tasted of nothing and it fucking burned my tongue. But I didn't care. She was under my roof now.

There was fresh cream cheese, bread, and bagels for breakfast. It immediately brightened my morning, but Britney was still quite shaken and silent. She picked at the crust of her bread, and barely touched the aromatic drip coffee Mariah had made for us.

"He's really rich, isn't he?" Britney eventually lifted her head and said.

I was just so happy that she was speaking. She had been too quiet, and for too long. "Yes," I said as I took a look at the regal dining room we were in. The walls were lined with famous modern artworks. The priceless old master paintings were all locked away in safes. Lalique lights illuminated the room.

"I mean look at that kitchen," she said in an awed voice.

Through the door, we had an almost picturesque view of the bright, exquisite kitchen. From the granite workspace to the beautifully sleek appliances, imported marble walls, and hardwood floor. It was a space that was so different from our own apartment that it was impossible not to marvel at its grandiosity.

"Yeah, a great kitchen is a wonderful thing. When my mom was alive we lived in a different house than the one we have now in Moscow, and you should have seen what she did with the kitchen. My dad was horrified for a bit and then he just let her do her own thing. It was pink and emerald green with a bit of white granite here and there. I loved it, but after she passed my dad didn't want to remain in the house anymore."

"You never told me how your mom died," Britney said quietly.

I brought my gaze to her despondent, brown eyes. Now was probably not the best time to tell her about it, but I didn't want to ignore her either.

"She was poisoned," I answered shortly.

She looked shocked, then her eyes began to mist. "I'm so sorry. I shouldn't have asked."

"No, it's alright." I put my hand on her shoulder. "It was a long time ago. My father found out who was responsible and let's just say he died a terribly painful death."

Britney went quiet again. "I finally figured out why Levan looked so familiar."

"You did?"

She nodded. "His family was involved in a huge case with the former acting DA, Sarah Dale. She accused Levan of kidnapping her grandson and he was thrown in jail for a little bit.

But then she later changed her testimony, and said that her grandson was kidnapped by some mafia guy. He was never found, but his minions were, and thrown in jail."

"Oh," I said.

"Yeah, it was big news then, but we didn't care," she laughed sadly. "We were still bartending at The Dead Rabbit."

I smiled, and realized this must be the case Bianca referred to when she told me how she and Levan had reconnected.

"We have to send $800 for the rustic ring sample by noon. The stackable one with the green stone," Britney said, bringing me back to the present.

"I thought we found a cheaper supplier for the rustic sample. You said he agreed to $450."

"Well I haven't heard from him in three days so I think it's safe to assume that he's bailed on us. $800 is the cheapest we can get so far. The design is quite intricate."

"Yeah," I responded.

She bit her lower lip. "And the rent is due this week. $750."

I could feel my face dropping. The rent was my responsibility, but without my bartending job I only had a tiny amount saved in the bank. I needed a job like yesterday. No matter what happened I was going to find myself a job today."

"I have some savings," she said to me. "About $600. Not much but it'll help. Perhaps I should get a job too."

"Nah," I refused. "Wasn't our agreement. If we both work, the business will be even slower. You handle sales and media and everything else in between while I handle the bills. Has Barneys reported any sales yet?"

"Nothing yet."

I found a smile for her and squeezed her shoulder in assurance. "I'll get the money," I promised her. "Even if I have to ask my dad for it."

She smiled sadly, and I knew then that she was not okay. She knew how much I hated the idea and how hard I'd tried to be independent. In the past she would have instantly rebuked me and steered me away from that path. But now it was almost as though she didn't even hear me.

She rose to her feet then. "I'll go get ready to head to the office."

"You can't go back to the apartment," I said gently. "Just stay here. You need the rest."

"What are you going to do?"

"I have an interview at Milano's bar soon so I'll head out there about ten. I'll text you when I have the money."

"Alright," she said, and headed off lifelessly back to her bedroom.

I watched her leave and felt a heaviness settle in my heart. I couldn't shake off the feeling that everything we had worked so hard for was turning into sand that was escaping between my fingers, and the harder I tried to hold on the faster it was running out.

I tried to finish my breakfast, but I had long lost my appetite. I needed to talk to Maxim about security, and about getting us the fuck out of being prisoners in his house. I could stand the pressure, but Britney... I was sure she was about to break.

Maxim had left before either of us woke, and I was quite relieved at the news, especially after the way I had accused him last night. A lot had happened within the space of a very short time, but now I couldn't avoid him anymore.

We had very grave matters to settle.

Chapter Thirty-Eight

MAXIM

I was at lunch when I received the call from her. Two of my contacts from Wall Street were with me.

"I need to speak with you," she said to me. "Can I come to the office?"

"I'm at lunch," I replied. "Can you come to 11 Madison park in about forty minutes?"

"Sure," she answered and ended the call.

I put my phone away and tried my best to hide the excitement that filled my body at the thought of seeing her again. I quickly ended my meeting. They were both surprised as we had just sat down and ordered our meal, but they stood and left immediately.

I dialed Roman. "What has she been up to today?"

"She's been to the bank and two bars. One in Williamsburg, and the other in Greenwich Village."

I looked away in thought. No doubt she had gone in search of a job, but those were not very attractive areas. She needed a job and one where I had some semblance of control, I quickly made the call. Now all I had to do was find a way to present it to her in a way that she would find easy to accept it.

She came in, wild-haired and dressed more provocatively than usual. She was in a pair of black shorts that showed her flawless porcelain skin. Her lips painted a deliciously sinful red. The strappy black top she wore drew my eyes to her firm breasts.

I shifted uncomfortably in my chair at the painful blast of arousal that made my cock feel heavy and hot between my legs. What was it about her that enraptured me so much?

She took her seat and asked for a drink of water.

I signaled to the waiter, and soon enough a glass was brought to her which she consumed quickly. Then she set the empty glass down and met my gaze like a soldier now readied for battle. It was endearing as fuck.

"You want something to eat?" I asked.

"No need," she replied.

"They have *Pelmeni* and *barabulka* here," I said. As I recalled from her behavior at functions we were forced to attend by our fathers as young adults, she had a great fondness for the traditional dumplings and red mullet dishes.

She swallowed, her appetite wetted.

"Lunch is on me." I called the waiter over to take her order.

She picked up the menu and looked at it. "I also want the celeriac and hazelnut soup, and the blueberry pancakes."

"Any drinks, ma'am?" the waiter asked.

"A glass of Sancerre, please," she said and he went on his way.

She returned her gaze to mine. "We need to uh … talk about my current living arrangements, and some other things. But let's start with that."

"Okay," I agreed, and leaned into the chair to watch her, my gaze on her plump, red lips. How I wanted them around my cock.

"We can't stay with you for much longer, so by tomorrow we should be out of your hair, but we will need to leave with security. I don't want to ask my father for it, and neither do I necessarily want to ask you, but I think we can both agree that the attacks are somewhat linked to you so you should take responsibility for what happens."

Time to make my stance. "You'll only have my protection under my own terms. You'll have to live in my house, where security can be thorough until this situation is sorted out. You left today against instructions. My people tried to reason with you to allow them drive you but—"

"*Maxim,*" she stopped me. "I cannot live like this. I have a life and responsibilities."

"It is a temporary situation that will all be sorted out soon enough."

"Well until then I'm not about to leech off you. We will return home, and you will provide us with the needed security there."

"No." I reiterated. I would not allow any negotiation on this point. "Full protection or nothing at all. Maybe you can weather the pressure of knowing you can be attacked at any time, but I saw what last night's episode did to Britney. You want to take that risk?"

She glared at me, but I was not backing down, and since she cared enough for her friend, it wouldn't be as easy for her not to do so.

At that moment someone stopped by our table. We both turned to see the striking blonde standing next to us. Holly Tudor. She was the youngest daughter of a multi-millionaire hedge fund manager. A diamond choker encircled her neck, and her dress, a silky champagne rose number with spaghetti straps, hugged her hips and flowed down her thighs.

"Maxim," she called in the breathy voice I was quite familiar with.

She proceeded to rest her hand on my shoulder, and the unnecessary contact earned her an irritated expression. Her hand dropped away. We slept together on occasion when we met at different parties, but it was an unspoken agreement that it came with no strings. It was an agreement she had adhered to thus far. I turned to the ball of fire before me and understood what had threatened little Holly Tudor.

"This is?" she asked, her tone as condescending as was humanly possible.

"No one," Freya answered and rose to her feet.

I knew just how to sit her back down. "Running away so quickly? Don't you want you *Pelmeni* and *barabulka*, your soup, your blueberry pancakes?"

She pulled the strap of her purse off her shoulder and returned to her seat, a blindingly fake smile plastered on her face. "You're right, but I have better things to do so I'll take it to go."

"That's true," I said and took a sip from my glass of Scotch. "How's the job search going?"

She turned a murderous gaze on me, but the woman standing next to me looked particularly amused, as she confirmed that Freya was truly no one, at least financially.

"Maxim," she called, in her breathy voice. "When am I seeing you? How does this weekend sound? I'll be all yours."

"Not this weekend, but thanks for dropping by, Holly," I said to her.

She responded with a sultry smile while she somehow managed to make sour when she turned it on Freya. She slinked away and I didn't bother looking back, my gaze fully on the seething woman before me.

Freya cocked her head dramatically as she watched her leave. "She looks like a prostitute. I suppose you pay her well."

"Why, are you interested in applying for the position?" I mocked.

She turned a very shocked gaze towards me. Too taken aback to respond, she let out a snort. "Excuse me?"

I got straight to the point. "You need money, don't you, and I'm willing to pay to fuck you."

She leaned back into the chair, and folded her hands across her chest, her eyes were glittering with a strange expression. "How much are we talking?"

"Name your price," I replied coolly.

"How about a million," she responded without blinking.

"Deal," I murmured, my gaze never leaving her.

I saw the moment when she realized just how deadly serious I was, and for a moment I saw the terror flash in her eyes. She opened her mouth to speak, but no words came out. She jumped to her feet so quickly, her hair flew around her face like a halo. She was so furious her next words shot out of her like bullets.

"*Fuck you,* Maxim."

"I wish you would," I responded. "You're driving me out of my *fucking* mind."

She gasped in shock, but she was so taken aback by my words she couldn't find a suitable response. Giving me a confused and angry look she stormed out of the restaurant.

Chapter Thirty-Nine

FREYA

I couldn't breathe.

I lurched out of the restaurant onto the sidewalk. The autumn breeze I had enjoyed earlier now seemed way too hot for survival.

Parched, I found myself walking into the nearest 7/11 and grabbing a can of coke. I paid for it and leaned against the counter for support as I downed more than half the can. When I came up for air, I felt my brain begin to restart.

What the hell just happened?

Sure, we'd established some kind of lust between us, but never had I expected him to become so blunt and vocal about it. There had been absolutely no trace of amusement in his eyes. He wanted to *fuck* me... and truthfully, I'd be damned if I didn't want the exact same thing too.

But he was Maxim, and I wanted nothing to do with him. Nothing could be between us. I wanted no part of the kind of life he lived.

I finished my coke and left the store then walked around blindly for at least an hour. I knew I should stay away from Maxim. He was dangerous to my sanity.

When I got back to his house I hurried up to Britney's room and found her in the shower.

"I got the $800 for the sample," I informed her happily. "I was able to get the cash out of my abandoned college account."

She shut the faucet off and came out of the shower. "What about the rent?" she asked quietly as she tied her towel around her and faced the massive vanity mirror.

"I'll figure it out," I replied. "I didn't like the bars I interviewed at today. The areas were kind of dingy, and that's just cutting it too close for safety. But I have another interview in Manhattan tomorrow so hopefully that goes well, and then we'll be back on track."

I watched her nod quietly without meeting my eyes, and then begin to apply her skin care products on her face.

She was still so affected by the previous evening's incident that I felt terrible.

"Guess what happened at lunch today? I had lunch with Maxim and he asked me to... I can't even say it."

She looked at me curiously. "What?"

I took a deep breath. "He asked me to sleep with him... for a million dollars."

She shrugged. "He was probably joking, Freya. It's just sex. Nobody pays a million for a bit of pussy."

I noted her careless shrug, and became officially worried about her state. She should have been jumping and screaming. She was always more excited and expressive than I was. I hated to think of what that incident had truly done to her.

"Britney, are you alright?"

She met my gaze through the mirror, and then turned around to face me. "I think... I'm going to go to my mom's place in Atlanta for a little while. I need a break."

My stomach did a very painful somersault. "Uh," I began in my smallest voice. "Sure, of course... whatever you need."

She nodded. "I'm going to leave tonight. I've booked a flight."

"Sure, um, some of the guards will accompany you to the airport, and perhaps even to Georgia, just for a bit of safety. I'll get in touch with my dad."

Her face seemed to fall even further. "Do I need that? I'm not connected to any of this, am I?"

Guilt barraged me. "Well, uh... you're not, but just for a little while, just to be completely safe, just until they're sure that everything is fine. I don't want to take any chances."

"Okay," she said to me. "I'm sorry, Freya,"

"Don't be," I said. "You have absolutely nothing to be sorry for. I'm the one who's sorry."

She walked out of the bathroom and I felt my eyes mist with tears. My legs gave way under me and I collapsed to the tiled floor. After two years of struggle, it felt as though I was back to square one, completely alone and without help... and trying to take on the mountain that was my father. The life I wanted to create for myself seemed so far away.

The truth was I needed Britney. We perfectly complemented each other.

She handled and did all I couldn't, and I did everything that she was weak at. We both understood that from the day we met as co-bartenders a year earlier. She had fallen in love with my vision to start my own jewelry company, I felt like the heavens had finally crossed over to my side and blessed me with someone who could run the administrative side of things. I was solely in charge of design and finance, and she did everything else. Photography, marketing, admin, branding.

There was no one like her. If she didn't return soon, I would be screwed a thousand ways to hell.

Knowing that I needed to be strong now more than ever, I cleaned the tears off my face and rose to my feet. Pulling my phone out of my pocket, I dialed my father and waited as it began to ring. When he picked up I got straight to the point.

"Papa, I need some security for my friend. She needs to head back home for a bit. I want your men to make sure that she is not being followed, and be ready to help her and her mother if they are attacked."

"What are you saying?" My father asked.

"You know about what happened at our house last night, do you not?"

"Of course I do. You are with Maxim. That is perfect."

I rolled my eyes and went on. "I'm leaving too, papa. I was only concerned because of Britney, but since she's leaving I do not want to be here at all."

"Where are you leaving to? I have told him to keep you safe."

I took a deep breath to suppress my irritation. "Papa," I said as patiently as I could. "I am not going to remain in Maxim's house. I don't want to be under obligation to him so please send some men to protect both my friend and me."

"Remember what I have always told you," he said to me. "You either follow my orders or you take your own road. There will be no men for you. If you need protection ask Maxim."

With that he ended the call, and I was left staring at the phone in my hand in shock until I felt a surge of hatred and anger begin in my belly at the way I was being treated by these two men. God, how I wished I had money and I did not need them at all.

I dialed Maxim's number and waited, but he did not pick up. I tried again and again, and near smashed the phone against the wall with frustration when Britney came into the bathroom fully dressed, and holding her duffel bag that we had quickly brought along with us.

"You ready?" I asked.

She nodded and I led her out of the bathroom. I dialed Maxim's number again and when I still couldn't reach him, I called Bianca.

"Can you help me reach Levan or Maxim?" I asked. "It's urgent."

"Sure," she said, "I'll call Levan immediately."

She ended the call and a few minutes later, Levan called me back.

I told him what I needed for Britney and the request was instantly granted.

"But, Freya," he said to me, "I can only allow them to take Britney. Maxim is solely in charge of you. I can't allow you to leave until he returns and gives his personal approval.

I couldn't believe what I was hearing. "What? When did I lose all power over myself and become Maxim's prisoner?"

"Stop being childish, Freya. You are there as much for your own protection as his," Levan said. "If anything happens to you, your father will not stop until we're all six feet in the ground."

With a furious sigh, and with the need for Britney to be on her way as soon as possible, I agreed. "Please tell your men to please protect her in every way they can. She is very, very precious to me," I begged.

Chapter Forty

MAXIM

https://www.youtube.com/watch?v=RnBT9uUYbɪw

I came home to find her drunk... as a skunk in a beer barrel.

She was waiting on the stairs for me, and I noted the almost empty $58,000 bottle of Dalmore Highland Malt Scotch clutched in her hand. Well, at least she had taste.

I'd had one of the worst days, and I wasn't looking forward to a tantrum from her tonight.

Pretending not to see her, I shut the door behind me and began to walk down the foyer towards my study.

"Maxim," she yelled out, but I didn't stop. I kept walking. Taking my phone from my pocket I was about to call Mariah to take care of her when she began to race towards me. For someone that inebriated she could move fast.

It was only instinct that caused me to turn my head and catch the glint of glass from the corner of my eye. I swerved just in time, and saved a nasty bump on my head. The bottle smashed against the wall, spilling its precious liquid and flinging sharp shards all over the place.

I looked at the disaster, my brows furrowed, then turned impatiently towards her. She really was too much.

"You're fucking ruining my life," she screamed as she flew towards me. "And that's what you always do. You fucking ruin everything for everybody."

She attacked me like a small but feral cat, nails extended, fur flying, teeth bared, legs kicking. I caught her clawed hands, but she only got even more crazed. I shook her to bring some sense back into her. When she threw her head backwards to try and somehow head butt my chest, I saw her reddened, swollen eyes. They were swimming with tears, and her cheeks were wet.

I knew what had happened. She had lost her friend and partner, but I'd assumed it was a temporary separation, and not too big a deal, but perhaps it was more serious than I'd thought.

I sighed. *"Freya,"* I called and she struggled to pull her hands out of my grip.

"Let me go! Let me fucking go, you animal!"

I let her go and she fell to the floor, landing on her ass.

"Ow ..." she cried.

It made my heart hurt to see her like that.

"Fuck," she cursed, her hands flailing around on the floor.

My heart lurched when I saw the broken glass pieces that surrounded her. She was going to fucking hurt herself. I went to her, but at my approach she immediately began to try to scramble up to her feet. I caught her in my arms and despite her swearing and thrashing, threw her over my shoulder and moved her away from the hazardous glass shards on the lounge floor.

I set her on her feet a distance away, and of course, she proceeded to attack me. Tonight she was out for blood. She fought with me with the techniques she'd been taught from her father's best fighters and they were not a joke. She was too drunk to even stand properly, but she was more than a handful. Even though she was small, she had the technique and strength of some of the better men I'd combatted with. While that was impressive it was time to end the skirmish.

I tripped her up, caught her falling body, and slammed her against the wall. The breath was knocked out of her and I hoped it would cause just enough pain to calm down, but when that didn't do a blind bit of good, I slammed my body against her and imprisoned her tightly against the wall.

She was heaving and panting, but so was I, our chests rising and falling to meet the rhythm of our breathing,

"Let me go!" she gasped.

"Freya," I said. "You need to calm down or else you're going to hurt yourself."

"You're the one who's hurting me," she shouted, and the tears began rolling down her eyes.

I stilled.

"Do you know how fucking hard it is?" she asked, her voice

breaking. "Do you know how fucking hard it has been? I wanted a different life. My own life." She sobbed. "I was all alone, but I found help, and you took it away. How the fuck am I supposed to keep going now?"

I couldn't speak. Her pain did something strange to me. It wrenched my heart.

Suddenly she began to laugh bitterly. "You offered me money earlier," she said. "That's more than enough for a looooong while." She leaned forward to whisper into my ear. "I'd rather take that than a dime from my father. I will never let him own me."

"I have another secret," she said and then leaned so close, her lips touched the side of my neck. I felt my cock harden when she whispered against my skin. "I'm going to enjoy earning that money from you. A million you said? You can fuck me in every way that you want, Maxim Ivanov. I'll enjoy it because... even though I hate you... hate you so much... for some reason... I want to fuck you so bad my pussy is throbbing for you. I'll make sure I get as much out of this sick need as I can. While you'll get nothing more than a memory that you will never have the chance to relive again."

I looked at her twisted face, and felt such hurt for this woman before me. She appeared so strong to the world, but was so fragile. If only she knew that nothing she could request from me would be worth more than having her... even if I would only get to experience it once. I would near do anything for it.

Before I could stop myself, I moved and crushed my lips to hers... and I was *lost*.

I was already painfully aroused from our tussle, but as I drew her taste into my mouth, I felt everything inside of me begin to *unravel.*

She fought me, her teeth biting down on my lips. I felt pain and tasted blood, but I couldn't stop.

It intertwined with the taste of us, raw, and vicious, and sickly sweet.

It melted her, and I couldn't help the primal feeling of satisfaction that flowed through my body. I let go of her arms and she threw them around me. She slanted her head and shoved her tongue into my mouth. I relished the urgent, intoxicating assault.

Our kiss was hard, and almost vindictive in its intensity. It was mind blowing. I grabbed her ass, lifting both her feet clear of the floor and I ground her crotch into the thickened swell of mine. The thrill of being able to do that to her was exhilarating, incredible.

Never in my life had I lusted over or needed someone the way I did her. I almost couldn't breathe as I ravaged her with everything I had. The frustrations of the enmity between us seemed to fan the fire even more fiercely. My hands went to the button on her jeans. It melted away, her zip flowed down like a knife through butter. I could already smell her arousal. I was like a man possessed.

My hand touched the warm silk of her panties.

I felt like a man who had walked for miles without shoes to reach a place of pilgrimage. Finally, I was at the entrance. The priest had opened the wooden door guarded by fierce dragons. Soon I would see the face of my God. The God who had hidden his face from me.

My finger hooked into the silky scrap of material and I felt her wetness, her delicious sweetness.

Suddenly, she tore herself from me with a gasp, and slipped sideways. I felt such loss that a strange snarl rolled out of my throat. Like a heat-seeking missile, I went after her. In the next moment, I had my lips back on her mouth.

She tasted pure, of unadulterated, heady pleasure, the kind that could only be dreamt about. God, I could not get enough.

She placed both her hands on my chest and pushed me away. "Get off me!" she yelled.

I was so gone I almost couldn't find my sense of reason to pull away. She shoved at my chest again, this time with all her strength, and I felt myself moving.

I saw my reflection in her eyes, and it was one that brought me shame. It was the image of a weakened man ... almost broken and completely tamed ... *by her*.

The realization struck me with more fear.

Chapter Forty-One

MAXIM

"How dare you touch me?" she panted.

"You fucking loved it too. I'm not the only one who's intoxicated. You're as maddened by it as I am."

"I have an excuse. I'm drunk. What's yours?" Then she turned away from me and ran from the room.

I punched the wall and welcomed the pain. My breath was coming fast and hard. I tried to calm myself down, but nothing could bring me back down from the high that had just exploded in my brain. I wanted her, with a ferocity that felt as if it would sooner or later drive me insane.

I couldn't tell how long I remained there, but then suddenly I heard her steps rushing back down from the stairs. I closed my eyes and prayed for strength. She was playing with me like a cat does with a mouse. *Here freedom, sorry nope. Here pleasure, sorry nope. Here heaven, sorry nope.*

A few moments later I heard her close to me. Much too close.

I opened my eyes and found myself staring into the barrel of a 9mm Glock.

Her request was simple. "Tell your men to let me go."

The gun was cocked and ready to fire.

I saw the rage in her eyes and confirmed that she was very able to carry out the threat. She was also alcoholically intoxicated enough to, and I wasn't going to take any risks.

I played along and lifted both my hands in the air. "What do you want, Freya?"

"I want out of here. I want a car."

In that moment, and especially at the look in her eyes I was more worried for her than for myself. If she made the wrong choice, everything from then on would truly be ruined. It would be the end and I would never be able to forgive myself. "You're going to drive in the condition you're in?"

For a moment, she seemed stumped.

I pressed my advantage. "You could kill someone."

"I won't be driving. You will."

"Okay."

She held out her phone. "Tell your guys to bring a car around and then I'm going to get in it with you. And if any one of them even try to follow me, I will blow your fucking head off."

I hesitated.

"Do it," she screamed.

I called them and gave my instructions. There was no way they were not going to react badly to a request like that from a number they did not recognize.

Seconds later, a gang of armed guards burst into the room. All five men gazed in shock at the incredible scene in front of them. Their next reaction was to point their guns at her.

I was almost deranged with anger. "What the fuck are you doing?" I roared.

They looked at each other in confusion.

I glared at them. "What the fuck are you going to do, shoot her?"

In a flash, they lowered their guns.

"Just do what she says," I instructed. "She won't harm me."

"Don't be so sure of that," she scoffed.

I turned to glare at her. "Are you sure you want to get out of here alive? Then you better shut up and wrap this up quickly."

She glanced at my men, but didn't say anything.

"Did you bring the car around?"

"No," Otari said, even as he produced his walkie-talkie and gave instructions for the Range Rover to be brought to the elevator doors.

"Move aside!" I said to my men and they parted ways. With the gun pointed to my head, I walked ahead of them towards the elevator.

As the elevator doors shut on us, I turned to look at her. "Where are you planning on going?"

I could hear her pausing for a moment to think of how she was going to make this happen. "That's my business."

"Right."

The door swished open.

The Range Rover was parked a few feet away. Both driver and passenger doors were open and the keys were in the ignition. Vasily was standing by. I jerked my head in his direction to indicate that he left.

"Get in!" she said.

I got into the driver's seat, the gun still on me. She rounded the vehicle, one eye on me, and the other on Vasily. As she climbed into the high vehicle her footing slipped and I lunged forward to grab her hand to stop her from falling backwards and cracking her head on the unforgiving concrete sidewalk.

In that moment, when my hand was circled around her soft flesh, time stood still. Everything became crystal clear. The shocked expression on her face, her mouth slightly open, the noise of the gunshot echoing through the car park, my unwillingness to let go of her flesh even though the pain that blast through me was staggering.

She had fired the gun.

I heard Vasily begin to rush towards us, but everything that had been so crystal clear began to seem farther away. As I tightened my hold on her hand I saw the gun fall. I could feel my strength ebbing away. Before it did, I pulled her into the car. She came barreling in and nearly landed on top of me.

"Maxim," she cried.

I looked down to see where I had been hit. It was right in the chest. She was going to be in so much trouble.

"Oh fuck," I cursed and felt myself begin to fall back onto the seat.

The lift doors opened and my men burst through, the car park began to fill with them.

"Don't fucking touch her," I roared, but I could feel my voice getting fainter and fainter as pain spread through me.

"If any of you lay a- hurt a hair on h-her head... I will kill you myself," I warned.

"I'm sorry. I didn't mean it," she sobbed hoarsely.

"Get out of here!" I said harshly. "Right now. And don't come back until I'm alright. Do you hear me? Do you fucking hear me? If I'm not okay—"

She laid her hand on my chest. The pain that hit me stole my breath.

"Maxim," she sobbed.

"Don't fucking come back," I croaked out. "If I'm not okay, don't ... you d-dar ... come ba—"

Then everything went black.

Chapter Forty-Two

FREYA

O h God. What have I done? I couldn't believe what was happening.

I was pushed out of the way by his men, and within moments the vehicle zoomed off.

"Leave!" One of them who had remained suddenly yelled at me, his eyes so mean with fury I instantly remembered Maxim's warning. I hurried back up to the apartment I saw my phone on the ground outside the elevator. I was shaking so badly it took three tries before I could pick it up. I pushed it into my pocket and ran towards the exit. Outside, I stood on the street for a moment. In disbelief and shock. Cold sweat poured down my back.

I had just shot Maxim.

My God.

What if I had killed him?

My eyes welled over with tears. Tears of fear and horror at

what I had done. I turned back to go to him, but a ringing sound stopped me. For a few seconds I froze. The sound was so loud and jarring I couldn't think. I shook my head to clear it, and realized it was my phone. I pulled it out of my pocket and stared at it stupidly. It was my father. My fingers were so sweaty, they slipped on the screen and refused to let me take the call. Roughly I wiped them on my jeans and tried again.

"Papa," I gasped.

"Get out of there right now," he said to me. I tried my best to stop shaking.

"Papa?" I said again.

"It's all going to be okay, *moya Printsessa*. All you have to do is turn left at the end of the street and keep walking as fast as you can until you get to a small park. There will be a green Toyota waiting for you there. The driver will be wearing a blue cap. Get into the back of that car. Say nothing to the driver. He will take you to my plane. It will fly you to Moscow immediately."

"Moscow?" I breathed.

"Yes, Moscow. Don't waste another moment, Freya. If Ivanov catches you in New York he will kill you! Do you understand me? You just shot his son. Whether he lives or not you cannot remain in the same state with them. He will kill you on sight. Move, right now!"

He ended the call. I didn't want to leave. The last thing I wanted in this world was to leave. It seemed cowardly. I wanted to stay and see Maxim. I wanted to make sure he was okay. I had to be sure he was okay.

My heart was pounding so hard it was like one of those African drums. I called Bianca.

"Freya?" she asked sleepily.

"Can I stay with your friend, Aldie? Something bad has happened. I ... I ... accidentally shot Maxim. I didn't mean to. I was drunk and it all happened so suddenly. My father wants to take me out of the country, but I can't leave Maxim. I need to be *here*... to know what happens... how he fares... I have to make sure that Maxim is okay. Can I stay with her? Just for a little bit until Maxim gets better. Please. It's okay if you can't help me but please don't tell Levan I called you."

"Where are you?"

I swallowed the sob. "Outside the car park of Maxim's home."

"Got it. It's not safe for you to stand there. Move to the next street. I'll tell Aldie to pick you up in about twenty minutes. I won't tell Levan a word."

"No," I choked out. "My father's people are everywhere. I'll find a way to give them the slip and sneak away. Send me her address and I'll go to her."

∾

Thirty minutes later, I arrived at the upscale apartment in Bushwick. Both Aldie and Bianca received me at the door. Bianca immediately pulled me into her arms. I didn't want to unravel all over again, but I held on to her as tightly as I could, and tried my best not to fall apart.

"He's okay," she whispered to me. "He's going to be alright."

My heart slammed painfully in my chest at her words, and I instantly pulled away to search her gaze.

"He is?"

I saw her gaze shift, and knew instantly that she wasn't telling the truth. "Bianca, please don't lie to me."

She held my hand and led me over to the couch.

"Do you want something to drink to calm your nerves?" Aldie asked, but even the thought of alcohol at that moment made me feel sick to my stomach.

"Bianca?" I called as I stared into her eyes.

"He's not completely in the clear," she said. "But Levan said that the bullet missed his heart. He is undergoing surgery right now so we can only know for sure in a few more hours."

I buried my head in my hands and pressed them against my mouth to muffle my sobs. I had never hated myself, but I did then. Why did I get drunk? Why did I provoke him like that? Why did I go back with the gun? When I was around him, I was a different person. An unrecognizable person. He truly brought out the worst in me.

"I didn't mean it," I sobbed. "I was just so scared... of every goddamn fucking thing."

She put her arms around me and I felt even worse at the pity party I was evoking. He was the one lying on an operating table not me.

"I'm fine," I said and raised my head. "He's the one I hurt so... I have no right to cry like this. He'll be fine. He has to be."

"It's alright to be upset," she said to me. "It only means you care."

I nodded my head in agreement, and at the shocking realization of just how much I did care. I had always deemed him indestructible, and not deserving or even needful of any caution whatsoever. What a freaking heartbreak it was to find out that he was just human, like the rest of us.

While I, on the other hand, was a total and complete idiot.

Chapter Forty-Three

FREYA

https://www.youtube.com/watch?v=eGoIYV6GoIo

I was sitting on the bed in Aldie's spare bedroom when Bianca called me.

"What?" I breathed.

"The surgery went well. He's still in Intensive Care, but he's awake now, and the doctors are pleased with everything. He was lucky. The bullet just missed his heart. Since he is young and healthy they expect a normal recovery, but he has to remain in the hospital for a few days in case any complications develop."

"I understand!" I nodded profusely, my hand on my mouth as tears filled my eyes.

Maxim was out of surgery. He was going to be all right. I tried to sleep but I couldn't get him out of my mind, and neither could I do much about my business, especially since Britney was not around. After Aldie left for work I called up one of the sports bars that I had rejected as an unsuitable place of employment and told them I was accepting the job.

I didn't want to be a burden to Aldie so I lied to everyone and told them I had found a small room to rent close to the bar. I sent my father a text to tell him I was safe, but since I didn't want him or Maxim's father for that matter, to find me I decided not to go back to my apartment. Over the next two days I worked as many shifts as I could, mostly so I wouldn't have to think, and afterwards went to sleep on some blankets on the floor in our staff room. The manager knew I was doing that, but I told him it was just a temporary measure. He really needed the staff so he told me I could do that for a couple of weeks.

It was exactly two excruciating days later that I dared to ask Bianca if I could go visit Maxim.

"Freya ... I didn't tell you earlier because I didn't want to make things worse. With Maxim's position, they've done their utmost to keep this news quiet, but in their world that is almost impossible. His father is furious and has been on the hunt for you." She paused. "Also, his father has called your father. The big wedding to unite the two families is off, and there could be a war brewing right now."

"What?"

"I'm sorry. Levan is trying to calm his father's wrath before anything more severe happens. So things are truly sticky right now."

I shut my eyes. "I want to see him," I whispered to her. "Even if it's for a minute, and from afar. I don't want to cause trouble, but I just need to see that he's okay. I feel so guilty. So torn apart."

"You can go now," she said, "but please be careful. Levan is still with him so if anything goes awry please call him and he will help you out. I'll text you the address of the hospital."

My gratitude to her was boundless. "Thank you so, so, so much, Bianca. I don't know how I can ever repay you, but there is a thing called karma and you will get your good turn somewhere down the line."

Then I immediately grabbed my bag and less than an hour later, my taxi pulled into the hospital grounds. I found my way up to his floor easily, but when I arrived in the corridor however, I saw a couple of his guards in the hallway. His father was standing a little further away outside the door of one of the rooms. He had the most bitter look on his face. At the sight of him, my heart nearly gave out.

I waited, hoping that he would leave soon, but instead the door was slid open, and Levan appeared. The guards moved away and then they began to speak in very low tones. To my luck, they also began to take their leave. My heart jumped for joy and I waited, hoping that they would soon turn away from the corridor and soon they did.

I immediately began to walk as casually as I could towards his door. I placed my hand on the door handle and was about to open it, when another hand slammed down on mine. I turned around to see Levan staring down furiously at me.

"You're here to finish what you started?" he rasped his eyes strained with anger and exhaustion.

"No. I never meant to hurt him. I'm so sorry... I just want to see how he is doing. Please."

"Did you really think you could get in here without us spotting you? I had to move my father away to keep him from blowing your head off on sight. Please leave. There's a limit to the leniency that I can afford you."

I could see just how angry he was with me, but I couldn't leave without seeing Maxim. "Please, Levan," I pleaded. "Please I beg of you. Just give me a second and I'll be out of there. I need to see that he's alright.

"No!" he refused, and grabbed my hand to pull me away.

"Levan," I cried, but my pleas fell on deaf ears.

"This is something between me and him. Please, Levan. You know he will never thank you for keeping me away."

He hesitated.

"I didn't mean to hurt him. It was an accident," I whispered, my eyes filling with tears of desperation.

"Go on. You have five minutes, then I'm coming in."

Without another word, he let go of me and began to walk down the corridor. I turned around and hurried into Maxim's room.

Chapter Forty-Four

MAXIM

She crept into the room like a thief... quietly and warily. But when she appeared by my bed I almost couldn't recognize her.

She jumped the moment our gazes met. She was startled to see that I was awake. She immediately turned away to wipe the tears off her face but it was too late. I'd seen the distress in her eyes and the sorrow that she carried. She was grief stricken and full of remorse.

When she faced me again her face was different. "You're awake," she breathed. "I just thought I'd see how you're doing."

I wondered if she was upset because I had been hurt, or simply because she had almost killed someone. The first kill was always the one that haunted you forever.

"I told you not to show yourself unless I was okay."

I saw the fear instantly cross her eyes. "But you're awake."

"I'm still lying here," I replied, my voice hoarse and void of energy. "If you're attacked there's very little I can do."

She lowered her head again and took a step forward, her hands linked together in front of her. "I'm really sorry I hurt you. You know, I didn't mean to. I would never have shot you even if you had stopped me from leaving. It was all bravado."

I watched her and felt disturbed. This was not my wild mustang! Where had all her confidence disappeared to? Her docile shift was strangely painful. I could only hope she wouldn't remain in that state for long. Despite the fact she'd held a gun to my head, and threatened to kill me, I would rather have her tearing down the world than for her to be beaten by it. "It was strictly not your fault. I should have let you fall on your ass."

She lifted her head then to meet my gaze. She bit her lip. "I agree. I deserved it."

I smiled. "Yes, you did."

She licked her lips and took a step forward. "How are you doing?"

I glanced towards the bandaged wound on my chest. "Okay, so far. Apparently, I was very lucky."

A strangled sound escaped her.

I didn't want her pity. That's the last thing I wanted. "I'll be alright and very soon. They'll be releasing me from here in a few days and everything will be back to normal.

"I'm so sorry, Maxim," she apologized again.

I sighed. I hated seeing her like this. "I'm fine. Let it go."

She nodded then and I saw the longing in her eyes. She wanted to come closer... she didn't want to leave.

I hoped that she would take the leap, but there was a light tap on the door and Levan put his head through. "Time's up. My father's on his way."

She gave me one last look then turned around and walked away quickly.

Chapter Forty-Five

FREYA

https://www.youtube.com/watch?v=ZSM3wIv-A_Y

Three days passed and it felt like I was losing my mind.

Given Maxim's recovery, I was no longer a target of the Ivanovs, but it still didn't give me the pass to show up in front of any of them without expecting some form of hostility or revenge even.

Bianca kept tabs on his recovery for me when he had returned to his home, and countless times I almost had to tie my hands behind my back to stop myself from calling him.

But then I *broke.*

I'd been so lost with thoughts of Maxim I was staring emptily at a bottle of beer in my hand. It was only the honk of a car in the street outside that startled me back to life. The world around me came back into focus again. I shook my head in wonder. Unable to hold back anymore I found my phone and hit his number.

To my surprise, he immediately picked up. My stomach flipped a bit.

"Uh ... it's ... it's me, Freya," I stuttered.

"I know."

Silence.

"I wanted to check up on you. Er ... how are you doing?"

"Okay," he replied.

"Oh, that's good."

I wanted to see him more than anything, but it seemed like that was an impossibility. All marriage talks were gone. Not that I was leaning towards it, but it would have been a good enough excuse.

"Alright," I said. "Take care."

"You too," he said and ended the call.

I threw the phone in the trash can by my desk.

Twenty minutes of fuming later, and I picked it back up and called Britney. It was time for me to move on with my life. The way it had been before he came into it. But Britney didn't pick up.

Chapter Forty-Six
MAXIM

https://www.youtube.com/watch?v=RQUuqbzQVsY

Bianca and Levan's wedding was in three weeks and their rehearsal dinner was being held at Rice and Gold, a restaurant with stunning views of the Brooklyn bridge.

The candles, the flowers, and the music created a very romantic ambience. It was expected to be a fairly quiet evening with about seventy of our closest friends and associates in attendance. However, they were also some of the most powerful men in the world so the restaurant was also crawling with guards.

I was happy for Levan as I stood nearby and took in his regal appearance. He was wearing a white tuxedo suit and on his arm was the woman he was ready to give his life up for. The bliss in their eyes was unmistakable. It made the troubles we'd all endured to make their union possible seem more and more like a small price to have been paid.

Bianca seemed extremely nervous. She kept touching the heart shaped necklace around her neck while her eyes darted around the room as though she was expecting someone. Finally, they settled on me.

I took a sip of scotch. "Gift from Levan?"

"No, it's from Freya," she replied. "I'm going to be wearing some pieces from her collection to give her some publicity."

I asked no further questions, as I knew that Bianca would take the reins all by herself for whatever she was trying to do.

"She's actually meant to have arrived here already." Her voice lowered. "I sent her an invitation. I hope you don't mind."

My whole body felt like it was on fire, but I kept my face stoic. "What if my father walks in?" I took another sip of my drink. "Will you be able to protect her?"

"She'll probably not come, but if she does, I'll look out for her," she said bravely.

"Good luck with that," I said, and moved away from them to take a seat on the stool by the open bar. I felt a fucking mess. The more I tried to talk myself out of wanting Freya, thoughts of that night when I almost made her mine wrapped themselves around my mind. Sometimes I woke up with the smell of her pussy in my nostrils and wrecked with an insatiable longing for her. She hated my guts, she held a gun to my head, she was too hot tempered, too wild, too everything that was wrong, I reminded myself. And then I would remember the taste of her mouth and all those objections would disappear like mist in the morning sun.

But no matter how I felt it was beyond clear she wanted *absolutely* nothing to do with me. I had the message engraved into my chest forever. The fact that she had agreed to come here and put herself in my vicinity infuriated me.

I finished my drink and ordered another.

Normally, I would have been immediately approached by the myriads of politicians and business associates my father had invited solely for political liaisons, but I had beckoned to Viktor and Nicolai to stand next to me. Their presence usually discouraged most people from approaching. Those who found the courage felt the sting of my chill almost instantly, and quickly found an excuse to move away.

My gaze never left the entrance.

I realized at some point that I'd been so severely affected by the news of her arrival I'd consumed far more alcohol than what was appropriate at a function like this. My brain felt woozy. I hadn't eaten since lunch. I signaled to a passing waiter carrying a tray of tiny little bits of food. I waggled my forefinger to indicate he should leave the whole tray on the counter. As he left I picked up something that looked like a little biscuit topped with lobster meat and some white stuff, probably mayonnaise piped over it. I put it into my mouth and reached for another. It must have been delicious, but my mouth was numb with whisky. I looked again at the entrance and ... there she was.

I stopped chewing. My heart stopped beating. They say redheads should never wear red, they had never seen Freya in red. She was like a goddess! Proud, tall, defiant and indescribably beautiful. She was the most beautiful woman in the world.

Her gaze met mine and the world stood still. Everything stopped for me. All the other people, the sounds, the movements, the smells, everything fell away. There was only her, in her red dress. Then she simply turned her head and looked away. As if I was *nothing*.

Aggravated, I rose from the stool and exited the room.

Yeah, message received, Freya. Loud and clear.

Chapter Forty-Seven

FREYA

https://www.youtube.com/watch?v=kOkQ4T5WO9E

I couldn't move. I felt as if I had turned to stone.

I wanted to see him again... it was the whole reason I was quite possibly risking my life to be there, but I hadn't expected it to be that soon. My heart was beating so fast it felt like there was a small bird fluttering inside my chest. I wanted to walk up to him and tell him how I felt. I wanted to kiss him and tell him I dreamed of him. I wanted to do so many things at that moment, but I heard Aldie call my name. I couldn't ignore her. Not her. She had given me a roof over my head when I was at my worst. I owed her a lifetime of gratitude.

I had to acknowledge her. My heart felt as if it would break, but I turned my head towards her.

She looked beautiful, with her blonde pixie cut hairstyle and a short baby pink ruffle dress. She enveloped me in a warm hug. Her eyes were more sparkly than usual, I imagined she was quickly approaching her alcohol threshold for the night. Familiar enough with her now, I took the drink from her hands.

"Hey!"

"I need this more than you do," I said, draining the flute.

"Thank you," I heard from the other side of me, and turned around towards Bianca.

Dressed in an olive-green, wrap-around dress she was stunning. Her hair was up in a bun with stray tendrils framing her face.

I was delighted to see her. "You look beautiful. Congratulations."

"Thank you, babes," she said, and placed a kiss on my cheek. She seemed so put together I had to remind myself sometimes that we were the same age.

"Aldie, I don't want to see you with another drink for the rest of the night," she said.

Aldie gave her a pout.

"Please take care of Freya. Show her where the food is. I need to be by Levan's side." She sighed. "It almost seems as though I'm getting introduced to the whole of New York. I've met the Governor and Warren Buffet. Can you even believe it?"

She shook her head and I suddenly noticed my heart shaped necklace on her neck. "Oh my," I gasped and lifted the delicate diamond heart. "It's beautiful on you."

"It's beyond beautiful on its own," she replied. "I can't wait for you to launch officially. You'll do amazing."

"I have one of yours on too," Aldie said, holding her hand up.

I turned to see my Notte, half-moon bracelet around her wrist.

My eyes misted with gratitude. They could have worn something from the top designer brands and yet they had both chosen to wear my stuff. "Thank you both so much."

"You're welcome, sweetheart," Bianca said. "I've been getting compliments all evening from everyone about my piece so it's not like I did you a favor."

I bit my lip. "The people here are pretty high profile. I hope the jewelry doesn't seem too cheap to them. I didn't exactly make it with this kind of crowd in mind. Everyone here seems to be able to have jewelry costly enough to buy a house."

"It's affordable, beautiful, and just my style," Bianca said firmly. "If they are too rich to appreciate it then that's their loss. I'm wearing your diamond earrings with my wedding dress tomorrow and its mention will be in the magazine interview I'll be doing after our honeymoon along with your name as the designer."

"Thank you so much, Bianca," I said and hugged her again.

Then it was time for her to mingle again. While she was saying something to Aldie, I took the opportunity to look around the room for Maxim, but he was nowhere to be seen.

I went with Aldie to the bar where we caught one of the waiters who continually passed by with endless trays of canapés. I popped the tiniest mushroom pizza in the world into my mouth. It was delicate and delicious.

"Bianca seated you beside me at the table," Aldie said, looking at her watch. "Good, it's almost 7:30. I can't wait to eat."

"What about Levan and Bianca?"

"They're opposite us."

My heart began to pound again. "Their whole family?"

She gave me a reassuring look. "You're worried because of Maxim, right?"

I smiled nervously and she looked amused. "You'll be fine. He doesn't seem to hold a grudge, although I still can't believe you shot him."

"I still can't believe it myself," I replied as I sipped champagne from the flute I snagged from a passing waiter. "And I'm sure he must be silently furious. My saving grace is he's really good at keeping himself in check. Hopefully, I won't be seeping out blood at the dinner table."

She shuddered at the statement. "You mafia peeps are too gruesome for me, and by the way, I'm officially impressed."

"Impressed?"

"What a hell of a way to refuse a marriage proposal," she teased. "Bianca says Levan told her that Maxim's never been shot before, and he's been in more than enough situations to attract bullets. So they've always seen him as almost indestructible. Well, you ruined that for them."

I buried my head in my hands in mortification and she laughed and patted my shoulder in consolation.

Suddenly, a reduction in the volume of the music and the sound of metal tinkled to get everyone's attention.

A graying man in a tuxedo stood up to speak. "Please take your designated seats at the tables. The dinner will be starting now."

People began to head towards the candlelit tables, and I felt myself begin to tremble.

Lifting my glass to my lips I drained my glass.

"Hey, you don't have to finish it all now. You can take it with you to the table."

I placed the emptied glass on the counter. "At the table," I said to her. "I'll need more."

Chapter Forty-Eight

FREYA

I was right.

Three glasses of champagne later and I was still wired and unable to relax.

All jittery and anxious and all because of the man seated a few seats across and down from me. I didn't even dare sneak a peek at him, too afraid of being caught, but at the same time, I couldn't get him off my mind.

I felt hot, as though just being in the same room with him was charring my skin, and it all made it too difficult to breathe. The dinner went on and on. Course after course that I pushed into my mouth and swallowed. Duck breast and Yellow Wax beans mixed with truffle pasta parcels, washed down with lime and blueberry sorbets. And I tasted nothing. There were well wishes and toasts given to the couple. I smiled when everyone else did, and clapped when others raised their hands. For more than an hour I ignored Maxim. Then, in a moment of weakness when I truly couldn't take it anymore I picked up my champagne flute, raised it to my lips as a cover, and let my gaze dart over to him.

And crashed right into his!

His were hard, unflinching... and angry

I was so startled, I nearly choked on my drink.

"You alright?" Aldie asked.

I turned red with embarrassment as I nodded and tried not to choke to death in front of everyone. I was in a bad way because that wrong turn of the drink down the wrong pipe was anything but comfortable. I needed to cough in the most unladylike, uncivilized manner possible to clear the blockage. Leaping up to my feet I hurried off to the bathroom.

In there, I coughed as hard as I needed to clear my throat. Finally, when I got myself back in control, I stared at my flushed cheeks and restless unhappy face in the mirror.

As I gazed at the sad woman in the mirror I stopped lying to myself. The realization of what was really going on was striking, and a thousand times as devastating. I wasn't just at that party because I wanted to confirm he was okay. I was there and scared to even meet his eyes because I wanted Maxim. Wanted him to the point of obsession.

His icy gaze came back to mind, and I felt a zap through my body.

It had always registered in my brain that he was handsome, but tonight especially, he seemed to outshine every other man I had ever come across. How had I ever hoped to be able to resist such an aggressively profound and effortless sexuality?

I was starting to realize just how terribly blind and dumb I'd been all along.

I pushed my hair out of my face, and decided I had had enough. The longer I stayed the more the profound the need for him became. It was not even like he returned the feeling. Hell, the way he looked at me, was as if he hated me. I squeezed my eyes shut. It could have all been so different. I had done everything wrong and now it was too late to go back or make amends. I had nearly killed him, for God's sake. I opened my eyes. In the mirror I looked like a woman defeated. The red dress that I had agonized over and paid too much for seemed like a joke. I was ridiculous. Coming here after what I had done.

It was time to go home, with my tail tucked between my legs.

Exiting the restrooms, I grabbed my coat from the hatcheck girl, and made it to the exit without being spotted. I stepped out onto the steps feeling a little guilty for leaving in the middle of dinner, but I couldn't go back. I sent a text to Aldie to tell her I'd left because I wasn't feeling too good and I would speak to her in the morning. Then I descended the stairs onto the main road and stood on the sidewalk, breathing in the slight chill in the October air.

Cars zoomed past on the busy street, and horns blared in the distance, the night alive with lights from the innumerable skyscrapers that soared into the sky.

I should have taken the subway home. The walk would help clear my head, and I'd save money, but the alcohol and a strange heaviness in my heart made the journey seem trouble-some. So I put out my hand to hail a taxi.

A black town car stopped next to me. Absent minded, I

moved ahead to continue my search for a taxi, and felt annoyed when the car moved forward again to halt in front of me.

I frowned at the window. Then the glass was rolled down.

"Get in," he said, and my heart dropped into my stomach.

For a second, I hesitated, but then I couldn't let this chance, whatever it was, and whatever would be the outcome of it, go. Time with him had been all that I'd wanted for the last several weeks. I pulled the door open, and stepped into Maxim's car.

Chapter Forty-Nine

MAXIM

---

https://www.youtube.com/watch?v=p47CgsSz4dE

Where had the feisty woman I had known for so long gone?

She was like a frightened kitten, although she remained still and tried to hide it, but I knew Freya. And right now she was frozen. She barely breathed. Had she become afraid of me?

"Where to?" I asked.

She nearly jumped out of her skin.

It would have been amusing if it didn't sadden me. This was never what I wanted from her.

"A-anywhere would be fine," she responded, still refusing to meet my gaze. "Sorry for making you leave the wedding. I mean you probably didn't do it for me, but uh... I mean because of me uh…" She shook her head in exasperation with herself, and turned towards the tinted windows. I could tell she wished the ground itself would open up and swallow her whole. I was perplexed. Was it guilt? Why was she so … lost?

"I'll take you home," I said.

She only nodded.

When we arrived at her apartment in the Bronx, she finally turned to face me.

"Thanks for the ride," she mumbled without meeting my gaze and turned to pull the latch open. It remained jammed.

She looked at me then. "I … it's locked."

I leaned forward and addressed the driver and bodyguard occupying the front passenger seat. "Leave," I said in Russian, and they immediately got out of the car and closed the door shut behind them.

Only the two of us remained, and I could have sworn I heard the thumping of her heart against her chest. Without a word, my hand went to the buttons that held my tux together and I unfastened the top one.

"What are you doing?" she asked, her eyes wide with shock.

Silently I continued to undo the buttons of my white dress shirt.

She looked at my hands, her mouth slightly parted. When my shirt was open, I turned towards her. The wound was still fresh and pink, but it was healing quite well, with no sign of inflammation. I wanted her to see it so that she could get back to the wonderful, wild, stubborn, independent creature she was.

"See. I'm fine," I said. "You can stop being so jittery now and get back to what you were."

Her gaze was on the scarred flesh. "Does it still hurt a lot?" Her voice was barely a whisper.

I shook my head as I watched her watching me. My breathing hitched when I saw her hand lift. The seconds seemed to drag on forever as it reached for my skin, and then at the last moment it stopped mid-air.

"Can I?" she asked breathlessly.

"Of course."

Her slender fingers brushed lightly across the wound.

"I'm so very sorry," she whispered, and I saw her eyes fill with tears and roll down her cheeks. A warm drop fell onto my hand and for the longest time I just stared at the moisture on my skin. Finally, I lifted my gaze to hers and she leaned forward, and with a soft, shaky hand on my neck, slanted her head and *kissed* me.

The air was knocked out of my lungs.

In that moment, I could process nothing as her heated, delicious taste tangled with mine and set my blood roaring. The kiss went on and on, until like a dream it ended.

She had broken it off.

I couldn't open my eyes. I didn't want to. I was so full of longing. For so long I had wanted her. So long. My whole body ached for her. I wanted to see her without the red dress. I wanted to see her naked and impaled on my cock. Then I felt her begin to move away and my hand closed around hers. I pulled her back to me.

She melted against my hardness.

I sucked passionately on her bottom lip, and then slipped my tongue into her mouth. Her scent was heady and it made me feel unstable. The deviously sweet pleasure of her taste sent all the blood rushing from my brain and straight to my cock. It tore a moan out of me.

Before I could get myself together, she had moved and was sitting astride me.

My gaze shot open to meet hers, and this time around, she held it boldly. I understood exactly what she intended. There were no words needed.

In that moment, it felt as though I had been gifted the entire world.

I covered her lips with mine again, and gave her a hard kiss. There was gratitude in that kiss, because I didn't think I could go on without this surrender from her. Then I began to trace sensual kisses of pure excitement and desire along her jaw.

Unsnapping a few buttons from her coat, I pushed it off her shoulders. Her nipples were straining against her dress. They were hard, just as I was, and alive to the deep attraction that crackled like static electricity between us. I felt my heart thunder in my chest. Her sex settled unashamedly against the bulge of my cock, and then she began to roll her hips against me.

I had dreamed about this intimacy for so long and so intensely that it almost felt unreal. As if I was hallucinating, but as her warm, sweet breath tickled my face, I knew I was not. This was real. Maybe I would only have this one time with her.

Swearing to make it one that we would both remember forever, I covered the silk covered hard bud with my mouth. Her moan sounded melodiously in the darkened car. The harsh light from the streetlamp was softened by the dark glass. It was the only thing illuminating us.

I needed to feel her skin against mine. I found the zip of her dress and pulled it down. She shrugged and the dress fell around her waist. I undid the clasp of her bra and tugged the material off her shoulders. Whoa! I felt my stomach flip at the sight of the breasts that I'd tried to picture through her clothes. Yeah, at least a million times.

They were as perky and beautiful as I had imagined.

She was perfect. Everything about her was perfect.

She intoxicated me like no other woman had ever done.

She was made for me. And only me.

I weighed the firm mounds in my hands and squeezed them softly. I was in complete awe of the woman's body. With my arms encircling her, I held her in place and took as much of one sweet breast as I could into my mouth. She writhed against me as I sucked hard on her succulent flesh. Then I moved to the other. God, I had been starved for way too long.

She cradled my head in her hands, her moans reverberating through the car, and sending dangerous chills down my spine.

"Maxim," she gasped in my ears.

The way she called my name made my cock jump.

I lifted my gaze to the breathtaking woman I had wanted for so long. "Do you know what you do to me?" I breathed, my throat choked with emotion.

It felt as though all the screws that kept my logic and senses intact had unraveled. I was wholly and fully at her mercy. It was not a state I would ever have chosen, but I was helpless to resist her. She was a green-eyed witch who had cast a spell on me. I pushed her hair away from her cheeks and kissed her. Her eyelashes fluttered as her green gaze locked with mine. I felt my chest expand dangerously.

I yanked her dress over her head. All she was left was her underwear. I exhaled. An insignificant black thong stood between me and my dream.

With one pull, it snapped away from her skin. She gasped in shock when I suddenly grabbed her knees and pulled them apart so that her body was leaning back and her pussy was wide open to my gaze. For a few seconds I could do nothing but stare at the glistening, pink petals. I could see it throbbing. An unfamiliar but strong sense of possessiveness filled my body. This pussy was mine. She was mine.

I slid my hand up her cleft, parting the slick wet folds to tease her swollen bud underneath. She was so wet and so tender. As I circled the hard bud, her thighs began to shake. I inserted a finger into her softly pulsating, pink slit and her juices ran down my fingers. As my finger slid deeper, her eyes fluttered closed, and she moaned.

God, I wanted to taste her.

"Open your eyes," I commanded.

Her eyes were no longer green, but almost gold with lust. She watched me, her eyes burning with fascination as I brought my fingers to my mouth. They were heady with her scent. Greedily, I lapped at her arousal. It was like tasting heaven. I was terrified I would never get enough.

I slipped my finger out slowly, then back into that warm, wet opening and finger fucked her as I reached for my cock. When it sprang free I grabbed her hips and lifted her up. She took the cue and moved into position. She crushed her lips to mine and ground her wet sex against me, rocking her hips back and forth in a crazed rhythm against my hardness. Enjoying the sensation of my hardness stroking her clit.

For the first time in my life, I doubted my ability to last. I slipped two of my fingers inside her and her channel immediately gripped them greedily. She was so fucking tight I was surprised.

Her head fell backwards in a gasp and I moved to position the wide crest of my cock at her opening. I began to guide her on to me, but she was too tight. I looked up to watch her face and saw the pain on it and suddenly I knew.

I was so shocked that for an instant, I froze.

"You're a virgin?" I whispered.

She nodded.

I leaned forward and buried my head between her breasts. Her perfume filled my nostrils. I felt a sense of loss. I should have done better for her. Not this quick fumble in the back of my car. I was such a fucking idiot.

"Maxim," she called, her voice shaky. "What's wrong?"

"You deserve better than this, Freya."

"Fuck you," she said and immediately got off me and began to haphazardly dress herself as quickly as she could. She grabbed her purse and pulled the latch so that she could get out of the vehicle. But it was still locked.

I wanted to tell her how I felt, but I couldn't explain myself without exposing myself.

"Fucking let me out," she muttered.

I tapped hard on the window and the two men returned back to the car. They pulled the door open for her and she got out. She headed back into her building and the moment I was sure that she had gotten in safely, I tapped on the window and the car pulled away.

Chapter Fifty

FREYA

I had never felt such shame in my entire life.

The minutes passed, and I remained behind my door, staring ahead and seeing absolutely nothing.

I had let him go where no other man had gone. I had been ready, and more than willing to give myself to him ...

And he had rejected me. There was no place lower than this to sink.

I turned around and knocked my forehead against the door. There was no coming back from this. I realized then that I'd left my torn underwear in his car. God, my thighs were still damp, and my pussy was swollen and throbbing with desire.

It was times like this that I missed Britney so much. I'd called her a few times and each time she said she just needed a bit more time. I walked to my bedroom and stood in front of the mirror. I looked at my crumpled red dress, my wild hair, my smudged lipstick. I looked like a slut, a two-bit hooker.

Between my legs was a throbbing that would not be denied. Slut or not the need was alive and calling greedily. I'd seen his cock and I wanted it. I turned away from my reflection. Then I walked to my phone and called his number. He answered on the first ring.

"Freya," he said.

"I just wanted to tell you," I began, "that you're a fucking, rude, bastard for what you did and I never want to see you again."

"Freya ... I'm sorry," he said to me with a deep sigh. "Very sorry. I wasn't expecting you to be a virgin."

My plan was to hang up, but somehow I couldn't pull the phone from my ear.

My mouth moved. "I thought you wanted me."

"You have no idea how much," he admitted, his voice a low tortured groan.

"Then how could you treat me that way?"

"We were in the back of a fucking car, Freya. I couldn't do that to you... to disrespect you in that way, especially with what you were about to give to me."

"Then finish what you started."

For a few seconds, there was a tense silence. Maybe he didn't think I was being serious.

"What's the problem?" I asked. "Do you or don't you want me?"

"I do," he said immediately.

"Then meet me at the Ritz Carlton in about an hour," I said.

"I'll be there. Let me know if you change your mind and decide not to come."

"I'll be there," I said.

I ended the call. He thought I might chicken out. No chance.

Chapter Fifty-One

MAXIM

https://www.youtube.com/watch?v=n-D1EB74Ckg

I gave my revised destination to my driver and sat back, a frown on my face as we glided on to meet her.

She was going to give herself to me... so she said.

I was... worried. Worried that for her I would be simply someone she gave her V card, but for me it would mean I would never let her belong to anyone else. To start with I wasn't one to obtain a treasure, then let it go. My nature was such. But my discovery of her purity had multiplied her value many times over. All the alarm bells in my body were sounding off willing me to step away from her to save myself before she completely took control.

I arrived at the hotel and, true to her word, saw her waiting in the lobby. She was wearing a loose black tee shirt tucked into baggy dark pants. Very, very unsexy and a great contrast to how she had been attired earlier. It didn't quell my passion one bit. I already knew what lay underneath.

"You're late," she pointed out.

She was too fiery and if I remained too much in a dance with her I was going to be burnt beyond recognition. "Why do you want to do this, Freya? I thought you loathed me."

"And I still do, especially right now, but for some crazy, inexplicable reason I can't get you out of my mind... sexually I mean. And you say it is the same for you. So let's do this so we can extinguish this fire and we can both move on with our lives. It's actually interfering with my business. I want to sleep better at night. You can also consider this an apology," she said, turning to look into my eyes. "For shooting you. Nothing more and nothing less."

I gazed into her eyes and saw the steely determination in them to be free of me. At that moment, I decided to take it as a challenge. I had experience, she was untouched. It wouldn't be a quick fuck in the back of a damn car. I would worship her body and give her the kind of pleasure that would make her as addicted to me as I was to her. I would teach her that pouring oil on a fire does not extinguish it, it only makes it burn brighter and hotter.

Unable to hold my stare she looked away to the influx of people going about their business, putting out their daily fires. None of theirs was as dangerous as the one that I was about to jump into.

"Alright, let's go," I said, knowing by now Gary would already have booked me their royal suite.

In a few minutes we were in our suite. I turned around to

look at her. Her face was closed off and her spine was ramrod straight. She was so close and yet so far. She was precious, not special, I cautioned myself. Precious like gemstones and diamonds. Special was what I kept for myself.

"A drink?" I asked, jerking my head towards the complimentary bottle of champagne sitting in an ice bucket.

"No," she said tightly.

She was determined to make this quick and nasty so she could walk away and say it was a fuss about nothing. She was going to learn different.

I took my jacket off, sat on the bed and began to take off my shoes. My tux was next to come off. I threw it carelessly over a chair nearby, then turned around to face her as I began to take off my cuff links.

"Having second thoughts?" I drawled, when I saw her standing very still and watching me. I didn't miss the sight of her hand tightening so desperately around the handle of her purse that her knuckles showed white. I wanted her just as ferociously.

She shook her head slowly and pulled the purse over her shoulder and let it drop to the floor. Then she pulled her T-shirt over her head, and my eyes devoured the lacy bra underneath designed to perfectly cup her generous alabaster breasts.

My throat tightened and I could barely move in anticipation. I was reminded once again of just how dangerously irresistible this woman was to me.

Like a man hypnotized I watched her unzip those deliberately ugly pants and let them fall. They slid like water *all* the way down those long, smooth legs and pooled around her feet.

She stepped out of them and held her hands loosely by her sides. She was trying her hardest not to appear intimidated or shy, but I knew she was a hot mess inside. I could have gone to her, made it easy, but I wanted her to come to me.

To make the final leap.

Chapter Fifty-Two
MAXIM

https://www.youtube.com/watch?v=jUe8uoKdHao

I shrugged out of my shirt and flung it towards the chair. Only a matching lacy bikini thong covered her sex, the slight bulge making my mouth water. Holding my gaze and began to walk towards me.

It seemed like forever before she stopped in front of me.

I looked onto her eyes. "One last chance to change your mind."

"I don't want to," she retorted.

"No regrets?"

"No regrets," she echoed softly and I knew then that there was no turning back... for either of us. There never was. From that day I saw her hanging upside down from a tree on my father's land.

I placed my hand on the side of her thigh, my skin looked dark and beastly against her fair skin. She had no idea how much pleasure the contrast gave me. I began to trace my way slowly up her white skin.

"Take off your bra."

While she obeyed me I cradled her hips in my hands, before I slid them behind her to grab her round ass. Cupping the voluptuous flesh hard, I pulled her to me and took a fierce sniff of her sex. Instantly her smell intoxicated me to the point I feared I would climax right there and then.

"Turn around, spread your legs wide, then bend from the hips. Touch the floor if you can," I ordered.

She looked at me with surprise.

"Well," I mocked softly.

She pulled away from me and obeyed. She was all woman, much more than I had imagined and I had imagined plenty. The way her ass and pussy hung in front of my face was more than I could bear. I leaned forward, covered her sweet flesh with my mouth, and blew hot air through the light fabric.

"Maxim," she breathed.

Gripping the thong in my hands, I ripped it apart with a sharp tug, and threw it on the carpet. I now had a full view of her shaved, smooth sex. All that lovely, swollen, wet, pink flesh were there for me to take, do what I wanted with. I leaned forward and licked the liquid pearl that was running down her slit. She staggered and nearly fell.

I caught her hips and speared her deep with my tongue. She did not expect that and she groaned. She was soaking wet and her taste was like once again coming home to fine wine. I licked the walls of her pussy while she squirmed and twisted. Her thighs were shaking and her breasts jiggled with the effort she was making to stay upright. I knew she was going to come. I moved my mouth away and laid back on the bed.

"Come up here and sit on my face," I invited.

She turned crimson, but she straightened. It took her a few seconds, but soon her knees were astride me and she was shifting over until she was directly positioned over my mouth.

I grabbed her hips and rammed my mouth into her cunt. I glided my tongue down the lips of her sex, and hollowed my cheeks to suck her clit into my mouth.

At first I ate her slowly, taking my time, but it was impossible to be sated and I began to eat her like a starving man, sucking hard on the drenched folds, lapping up all of her juices hungrily. I drove my tongue deep into her entrance, and felt her jump as though she'd been struck by a live wire.

"God," she screamed.

Her breathing was loud and hard above me as she fought to remain in place, but it was close to impossible. With her hands buried in her hair and her eyes clenched shut, her hips began to rock in a sensual rhythm against my mouth. Until the inevitable happened.

"Maxim," she moaned. "Ohhhh fuck ... *Maxim.*"

I felt her entire frame freeze for a moment. All she was capable of then was indecipherable choking sounds followed by the violent trembling of her whole body as her release poured straight into my eager mouth.

She grabbed the sheets of the bed and, completely uninhibited, rocked against me even harder, as her climax tore through her.

When it was over, she collapsed beside me on the bed, her eyes closed, her chest heaving, and her hands clutching at her swollen, throbbing sex.

"Oh my God. What the fuck ..." she gasped.

I vaulted to my feet, unbuckled my belt, and in one moment pulled my pants and boxers down.

Her eyes fluttered open, and slowly her gaze took in my body until she got to my cock. Then her mouth rounded into a circle, and she sat up.

She licked her lips, and I almost came right there.

Chapter Fifty-Three

FREYA

https://www.youtube.com/watch?v=725WlG1idPc

This, then, was the great Maxim, all stripped down and brought to my tent!

To say I was impressed would have been the understatement of the century. The man was built like a god.

True, I didn't have any experience viewing real life dicks in my life, but I knew enough to understand that the man before me was hung much, much, much more generously than most. Without doubt he had a beautiful body, but his cock ...

God, I could not take my eyes away from it. It was just ... amazing. Thick, long and carved with pumping veins, it stood proudly away from his body. Actually, he was so fucking hard his cock bounced in a very horizontal position against his stomach. As if it was alive.

I was almost afraid to take that hot angry boa inside me.

"Come over," he commanded.

Like a trained puppy I got on my knees and crawled over to the edge of the bed. My hand reached out ... eager to touch the beautiful pale hardness, but for a second I hesitated and looked up into his eyes.

"Go ahead," he said, approval in his eyes.

I took him in my hands, delicately, and then found the courage to circle my grip around the satiny thickness. There was no turning back. This monster was going into me. Anyway, I couldn't even resist him if I wanted to. I was dying to taste him. At that moment a drop of pre-cum appeared on the eye of his cock.

I leaned forward and licked it with the tip of my tongue.

And was instantly sold on his taste. I gave his entire length a long sensual lick before returning to the taste of his pre-cum at the head.

I tried to remember everything I had learned from watching porn stars give head as I opened my mouth wide, took as much as I could of him, and sucked hard.

"Fuck," I heard him breathe, but he pulled his dick away from my grasp.

"Today is not about me. This is your first time so I need you to be so wet I can fit in," he said.

I wanted to protest. A fire was roaring in my belly. I wanted to suck that big cock and have him at my mercy. But at the same time I couldn't wait to see how having him inside me would feel.

"Lie down," he said.

I moved towards the pillows, but for some bizarre reason I felt a sudden wave of self-consciousness so I grabbed at the comforter to half cover myself up, but he snatched it away and threw it aside.

Before I could say another word, he was on top of me, and my breast was in his mouth. As my back arched off the bed with the pleasure shooting from my nipple, I wrapped my hands around his broad back to keep me somewhat still on earth.

He moved his mouth from one nipple to the other, tracing wet burning kisses across my goose-pimple covered flesh. He dragged his mouth upwards and found the pulse in the crook of my neck. There he placed a kiss on the soft flesh before he did the thing I had only seen on other women. He marked me. And I loved it. I stretched my neck and offered it to him.

"More, Maxim, more."

He lifted his head to see what he had done. His eyes were full of possessive, victorious light. It was as if he had won me in a great battle. He swooped down on my lips and drove his tongue into my mouth, and I was completely lost. I could feel his fingers playing with my sex, gently travelling in and out. Circling. One finger, then two, then gently ... three. When he removed them, I moaned into his mouth.

I felt the moment he began to position himself at my entrance, but I was too preoccupied with the sensation of him sucking my tongue to care until he tried to push in.

I stilled suddenly.

He whispered to me, "It'll hurt a little, but It'll be okay."

I nodded, and felt him inhale and release a deep breath.

"Look into my eyes," he said, and I held his beautiful blue gaze.

"You're fucking beautiful," he said as I tried not to show how painfully stretched I felt.

He inched further and further into me.

When the pain became too much I shut my eyes and he immediately stilled.

"Freya?"

"I'm alright," I muttered. "Just keep going."

He did as I asked, until it seemed as if he was fully sheathed inside of me. "You're so fucking tight it must hurt like hell. How do you feel?"

"Like I have a freaking football pushed inside me." A small nervous laugh escaped me.

He smiled down at me and I lost myself in the tenderness of his gaze and smile. This was what was behind that cold, hard mask he showed to the world.

He remained inside me without moving and slowly, I felt my body begin to accept him. There was no discomfort, instead it felt good to be so full of him. It felt as if I was finally whole. That hole was meant to be filled and this was how it should always be.

"More?" he asked.

I nodded profusely, my heart rate picking up.

He retreated once again, and when he thrust back in, my hips rocked forward to meet his. A guttural moan slipped from my throat at the ethereal pleasure. He began to fuck me slowly gaining speed. I shut my eyes and let all my senses focus on our joining as one, and the rapturous waves of pure bliss he was sending through my body.

"More, Maxim, more," I gasped.

I was sure I heard his laughter somewhere in the distance. He picked up his pace, and my hands dug into his buttocks, guiding him, urging him on ... faster and harder.

I was now in the frantic race towards release, and it was a delicious one. Sweeter than any fantasy I could have ever imagined. He captured my mouth with his again, and I moaned into his kiss, my body buzzing with anticipation.

"Oh God!" I heard him gasp as his restraint snapped. I could tell he was trying his hardest to be gentle, but both of us were too feral, too needy to take such a precaution.

We fucked each other, feeding the ferocious fire that had been burning within us, for the other, for way too long. I felt myself begin to quicken, and my hips moved frantically to meet his.

When I could hold back no more, I came, hard. No, not hard, but viciously. The force of the orgasm coursing through me in a maddening torrent that jerked my body and turned it into a trembling, pulsating, mass of jelly.

My cry rang out in the room, and as though that was the push he needed, he exploded inside me, a burst of hot semen shooting straight into my core.

I heard his fist pound furiously against the headboard as he roared out my name. My fluttering eyelids caught glimpses of his reddened face and the strained network of veins that bulged down his neck as he threw his head backwards and let himself go over the edge.

"Freya!" he called over and over again, while still pumping into my limp body.

He hid his face in my neck to recover, our chests heaving with similar rapid exhaustion.

"I knew it," he muttered. "I knew you were going to blow my fucking mind."

I didn't know how much time passed, before I came back down to earth, but when I did, I could sense him beside me, breathing hard.

I didn't know what I was supposed to do, but I did know that if he turned around and pulled me into his arms I was going to go to him... whole heartedly and beyond ready to bask in the aftermath of what he had just done to me. So I waited, my body stiff with anticipation.

The moments passed by and then... he got up.

Immediately, I hid my face away from his as I pulled the covers around my naked body. I heard him start to put on his clothes, and rose to my feet to pick mine up from the floor.

He was ready before me, and when he rounded the bed on his way out I forced myself to meet his gaze.

"I had a great time," he said.

"Sure, me too," I replied.

It looked like he was about to say something else, but then he shook his head and went on his way. I watched him leave and disappear into the foyer and felt my eyes mist with tears.

Was that the last I would ever see him, I wondered. If it was, then my heart would be thoroughly and irrevocably shattered. If I thought sleeping with him was going to free me, I was dead wrong.

Oh God, I was falling in love with him.

Chapter Fifty-Four

MAXIM

https://www.youtube.com/watch?v=jUe8uoKdHao

I hadn't been able to get out of that room fast enough. I knew she had broken something inside me. I wasn't the same man I was before we had sex.

I arrived at home, dazed and disturbed and the last person I wanted to see was Levan. He was waiting for me in my living room and I couldn't help the frown that dug into my forehead at the sight of him lounging on my sofa and working on his laptop.

He put his laptop down. "Bianca and I are going to hold on with our move to South Africa," he said. "Until everything blows over with Freya's family."

My frown became deeper. "There is no need. My security team is working tirelessly on it."

"Good, then it should be resolved very soon. Until it is I'm not going anywhere."

I headed over to the alcohol cabinet by the corner and poured myself a generous measure of whisky. I downed a significant portion in one swallow, and his eyebrows shot up in surprise.

"Is everything okay?" he asked.

"Yeah," I replied. "Now if you have nothing else to discuss, I'll see you tomorrow or something."

"What happened?"

He started to walk towards me, but I was not ready to speak to him or to anyone for that matter. All I needed was to be alone, to try to pick up the pieces of myself that she had blasted to smithereens.

"What's going on, Maxim?" he repeated.

And I fucking lost it. "Fucking leave!" I roared, my arms flailing like a mad man.

Everything stilled, especially him. He noted the look in my eyes, but before he could see too much, I turned away from him.

A few seconds later, the door shut behind him. I sank into the sofa.

I wanted to call her, to tell her she had been the very best fuck of my life, and I didn't know how I could go on from here onwards because I was craving her like a drug, but I knew she didn't feel the way I did. After we had finished back in the hotel, how I had wanted to hold her in my arms even for a second. To bask in the pure magic of what we had just shared with each other. But she became as stiff as a corpse.

I knew then she regretted what she had done.

My intuition had been right. I had been correct to avoid her in the first place. She always scared me shitless and yet I waded in there. I basically hung myself out to dry.

I wondered how the fuck I was going to recover. Now that I knew how she tasted I would never be able to forget it.

I rose to my feet restlessly.

The answer was work. It was always work. I needed to work. That was the only thing that could save me.

Chapter Fifty-Five

FREYA

I slept badly and after making myself a mug of coffee went into the room Britney and I used as an office. I looked at the mess of papers and magazines across Britney's desk. Behind it was a gigantic cork board, filled with hundreds of jewelry cut outs for photography concept inspiration. My gaze wandered around the small space which seemed so empty without her, and wondered if she would ever come back.

Putting aside my feeling of sadness, I went to my desk and tried to focus on designing a layered necklace with the unique Burgundy Tourmaline stones I acquired from a dealer a very long time ago. Then I knew they were beautiful, but I did not have a design for them.

But these rare burgundy ones spoke to me now at this moment of darkness in my life. I had an idea for them. I inspected the stones and began to draw quickly on my notepad. For a while there was nothing in my mind but the design and the strokes I was making on the paper. Then I dropped the pencil and leaned back on the chair.

The design was complete. And it was beautiful.

Sounds and thoughts rushed in my consciousness again. I put the stones back into their plastic envelope and walked out of the office. I went to my bedroom and looked at the tie Maxim had left in the hotel bedroom. In his rush to get away from me he had even forgotten he came in with a tie.

It was a silk Christian Lacroix with an intricate gold pattern. I tried not to, but I couldn't help myself. I raised the fabric to my nose and sniffed his very familiar and just plain intoxicating scent of wealth and arrogance.

This tie was a reason to contact him. He didn't need it returned, probably had a hundred more abandoned in hotel rooms all over the world, but still ... I breathed his scent in.

What would be the harm?

I picked up my cell phone, and before I could change my mind, I hit Call.

It rang three times.

Just as I was about to chicken out and disconnect the call, he picked up. I had a lump to work through in my throat before I could speak.

"Hey," I croaked out.

"Hello," he replied formally.

I tried my best not to think of the way I had whimpered and shuddered underneath him. "I have ... uh ... You uh ... left your tie at the hotel." I clenched my eyes tightly shut at the clear note of anxiousness in my voice.

"I'll send someone to pick it up," he said softly.

I received the message. As clear as day. It felt as if I just swallowed shards of glass. It cut me all the way to my stomach.

He got what he wanted and now he wanted nothing more to do with me.

"Sure," I replied and quickly ended the call.

Chapter Fifty-Six

MAXIM

https://www.youtube.com/watch?v=BxuY9FET9Y4

It was nearing 9pm, and getting the report that she was still at work, I hadn't been able to hold myself back from stopping by. I sat in the car and watched as she moved around in her little office.

She was wearing a navy-blue dressing gown and her hair was up in a gigantic and messy bun on top of her head. Time after time, she walked past the window with a pencil in her mouth and papers in her hand. I took a deep breath and knocked on the glass partition.

One last time, Maxim. One last time.

Viktor pulled the door open for me and I stepped out onto the dirty Bronx street. The lift had stopped working and I had to take the stairs. The sound of my shoes echoed in the empty stairwell. A few minutes later, I knocked on her door and waited for a response.

"Who is it?" she called out.

"Maxim," I responded and everything seemed to go still. I waited. More than a few seconds passed, the door was pulled open. Her hair was now falling down in a cascade down her shoulders and she had put on lipstick. I was shocked to see she had made an effort. My words came out wooden and cold.

"I came for my tie."

"Sure," she replied airily, and turned away from me.

I followed her into her living room. It was dimly lit by a small lamp on the floor. The whole space seemed filled with papers and magazines and loose sheets of papers filled with drawings. A cup of half-eaten ramen noodles was on the coffee table. I presumed this then was Freya in work mode.

She turned around suddenly, the way someone nervous would do, and her long dressing gown caught the cup of noodles, spilling its contents on the floor.

"*Damn!*" she cursed. "Excuse me." She headed over to her desk and grabbed some paper towels. A few minutes later she had the spill under control. I didn't move from my position by the door. I found it fascinating to watch her in her own environment. I even liked her apartment. It seemed cozy and sweet.

"Sorry about that," she said, straightening. "I'll get you your tie now."

"No problem," I murmured.

She fished it out of a drawer, neatly rolled up, and came towards me holding it out.

"I don't have a clean bag here so perhaps just take it by hand. Hope you don't mind."

"It's fine," I said, and stuffed it into my jacket's pocket.

She pressed her lips together and swallowed.

"Your partner isn't back?"

She shook her head. "Sadly no, but perhaps soon."

"Why don't you hire someone for the meantime?" I asked, looking around at the whirlwind around her. "It seems like you have quite a lot going on."

Her smile was sad. "Hiring someone requires money, which I don't have now, so I'll have to make do."

I didn't understand her need to do everything all on her own, but I admired it. I had never met a woman who was so strong and independent. So determined to be free.

"Any news on the pizza delivery man who was harassing us?" she asked.

"Hmmm ... that."

Her eyes narrowed. "What do you mean, hmmm that?"

"Do you really want to know?"

"Of course, I want to know," she said crisply.

"Well, something didn't add up about that whole episode. So I got my men to do some digging around. It's unconfirmed, but I think he was working for your father. His job was not to hurt you or Britney, but just to scare you. I believe your father might have thought it would bring us closer together."

"What makes you think it was him? Maybe it was your father," she challenged.

"Did you know your father owns apartments on the second and fourth floor of this building? Through off-shore companies, of course."

Her eyes widened.

"It was the fact that the guy just disappeared into thin air that gave me the idea. He obviously had access to one of the apartments. Also, the way he gave your father's men the slip was very suspicious. Your father runs a very tight ship and even after such a security breech, none of your security detail were given the boot."

She sank down on the floor and sat cross-legged. "Wow! My father is something else. I can hardly believe it."

"Your father likes to win. The end always justifies the means."

"But what about when I was stabbed? My dad would never allow me to get hurt like that."

"No, that was not your father. I don't know who that was or why they tried to hurt you. It was most probably something to do with our wedding, but since that is off ..."

"Right."

I was left helplessly staring at her red, parted lips. Memories of them stretched around my cock flooded into my brain. It had driven me wild to see her like that.

"What?" she asked suddenly.

Shit. I must have been staring at her like a demented fool. "Nothing. I should be going."

"Wait," she said, jumping to her feet.

"Yes?" I replied.

The dimness of the room cast her in a glow that was just so soft and perfect she looked almost ethereal. I knew not to go any further with her, but the look in her eyes. It made me *burn*. She started to walk towards me, her gaze unblinking, and I couldn't move.

"I have been thinking," she said softly. "What if we meet up once in a while?"

"To fuck?" I asked, almost in disbelief.

Her gaze faltered from mine, but her voice was sure and strong. "Yeah."

Chapter Fifty-Seven

MAXIM

https://www.youtube.com/watch?v=ja-n6my6rKQ

"I don't think that'd be a good idea ... for either of us."

"Why?" she asked, a frown on her lovely forehead.

"I already have someone for that. You met her the last time at lunch on Madison Avenue."

I felt a pain in my chest. What was wrong with me? Shouldn't I take the crumbs I was being offered? Why hold out for more when more was not forthcoming? But I refused to take the words back. I did have someone and she was perfect because she threatened nothing within me, unlike the woman before me right now. With Freya, my sanity was at stake.

I thought she would stop then, any other woman would have, but she kept going. "You can't have more than one?" she asked, a defiant light in her eyes. "I'm not that bad, am I?"

I realized then she had convinced herself we could have something that was purely sexual. If only she knew the fire she would be playing with if I agreed to what she thought she wanted.

"Come here," I murmured.

I knew the moment the words left my mouth I'd made a mistake, but there was only so much self-control that I could wield in her presence. Hell, I probably deserved a medal for how much I had held back.

She came forward. When she was about two feet away, I reached out and pulled her to me and kissed her. Fire *seared* through my veins. Her response was fervent. I matched her passion and we expressed in that joining what words could not convey.

I would never again be able to kiss someone and not think of her. Her taste seemed like it was made exclusively to fit my palette, to quench a thirst I'd never even realized I had.

Eventually, we broke apart, our chests heaving and I stared into her eyes. She grabbed the belt of my pants and I let her take control. The power went to her head.

Her hands were shaking by the time she pulled my cock free. She stroked the hard length while I could do nothing but stare greedily at her. What was it about her that knocked the air out of my lungs?

She slipped her pants and underwear down her hips and reached up on the tips of her toes to slip her tongue into my mouth. I grabbed her ass and held her in place while she took my dick between her folds.

She was so hot and wet.

I picked her up and moved to the desk closest to us. With one hand, I swept away all the junk on it and set her down.

Jerking her legs apart, I cupped her cleft hard before driving a finger into her. I followed that with another. Head thrown back, she emitted a gasp of pleasure as I began my thrusts.

My thumb circled the engorged bud of her arousal, in precise rhythmic circles and it drove her wild.

"Maxim," she breathed, her hands gripping the edge of the table.

I shuddered at the sound of my name in her mouth. Her voice wasn't intentionally sultry. It was soft but with an unmistakable note of steely determination. I loved it.

"Hold onto me," I instructed hoarsely.

She threw her arms around my neck and I lowered my knees to position myself at her opening. Then I hooked my hands underneath her thighs and rammed my cock into her so hard, her ass left the table.

At the brutal thrust, her unrestrained moan rang out into the quiet room and blended with the distant buzz of the city's noise.

I fucked Freya hard, and felt things that I didn't want to. My eyes remained on hers as I committed her features to memory. The wild movement of her hair as I slammed my cock over and over into her, the sweet grimace of pleasure and pain on her face, the noises coming from her parted lips, the light perspiration across her forehead.

When she climaxed, I followed right after. It was long and

earth-shattering. I shuddered through it all, my stomach in knots.

It should have been just a quick and easy fuck, but there was nothing quick or easy about the fuck or the hold Freya was beginning to have over me.

I said something stupid to her, zipped myself back into my pants, and stumbled out of there like a drunken man.

Chapter Fifty-Eight

FREYA

I was buttering my toast when the timid knock at the door came. I wasn't expecting anyone so I headed quietly over and peeped through the hole. Just in case it was another 'delivery' that no one asked for. But when I saw who was at the door I swung it open with a cry of joy.

Britney smiled at me, her eyes misty with tears. "I'm sorry," she said.

I ran into her arms. For the longest time I couldn't speak, the weight of the world seemingly lifted off my chest.

Eventually I pulled her into the apartment and hit her hard on the shoulder. "Why the fuck did you ring the bell like some stranger? And why didn't you tell me that you were coming?"

She shrugged. "I made the decision late last night and just booked a flight."

"Your mom pissed you off?"

"Honestly?"

I began to laugh.

She sucked in her breath through her teeth. "I can't believe I forgot why I left home in the first place."

"Hope you didn't also forget why you left here either? I can't exactly delete my criminal background."

Her face fell with remorse. "I deserve that. I was too scared, still am but …"

I playfully knocked her on the head. "Hey! I'm not dead yet, so perhaps you'll be fine too?"

"Don't do that," she scolded. "You might damage the last two brain cells I have left."

I laughed. It was so good to have her back. "Come on. I'll make you some toast."

Together we headed back towards the kitchen. At that moment a message arrived on my phone.

"What's been going on?" she asked. "How is Maxim doing?"

My mind went to the previous night on her desk. I planned on telling her everything, but not yet. I hid my face from her and quickly looked at my phone.

"Just a second. I just received a text from my bank."

I opened the text, and for one wild incredible second, I thought I was seeing things. I shut my eyes, and reopened them, as if I would see something different. I knew exactly what it was, but I didn't want to believe it. I couldn't believe it. I looked up at Britney, my whole body in an uproar of disbelief and hurt and words, normal words came out of my mouth.

"Did you uh ... did you hear from Barney's yet?"

She nodded vigorously, her curls bouncing "Yes, I have. They've agreed to stock us when we officially launch, special thanks to the mention from Bianca's wedding. I'll have the website done by next week."

"Hmmm ... How much will we need for the first order?"

"For the first collection?"

I nodded.

I grimaced. "At least seven thousand dollars. That will meet the minimum order for all the pieces in the collection."

I dragged my gaze back to my phone and reread the notification. A million dollars had just been sent into my account. "Give me a minute. I'll be right back," I told Britney and went to my room.

To my horror my eyes filled with tears, and before I could stop them they dropped to the phone screen. Pain like this I didn't think I'd ever feel again. Only my mom's death had ever hacked my soul apart like this. I took a deep shuddering breath and tried to get my thoughts together. The longer I thought about it the more livid I became. I got into such a rage I started shaking.

How dare he?

How dare he?

I made some excuse to Britney and quickly got ready. A few minutes later I hailed a taxi in front of our apartment building and headed straight to Citigroup bank. On my way there I called Hailey Carpenter. She handled all my father's financial dealings in the country before I had completely broken away from being his beneficiary.

It would only be through her that I would be able to go in to do exactly what I wanted to, without being delayed. She knew exactly who and what the name Fedorov meant.

"No need to involve the IRS," I said to her. "The money will be gone soon. There was an error in transfer from Ivanov holdings."

"Oh! Ah ... alright then," she said uncertainly. "So what do you want me to do?"

"Arrange so I can withdraw the whole million in cash."

"Uh ... that will not be possible, Freya."

"Then I want as much as you can get me right now."

"Maybe ... a quarter of a million?"

"That'll do," I replied. "I'll be there soon."

Chapter Fifty-Nine

FREYA

hree hours later, I arrived at Ivanov Holdings with half a million dollars in cash in a shopping bag. I headed straight to the receptionist's desk and knew in an instant that they recognized me.

The last time I had arrived in a wheelchair, wild haired, and under dressed. This time I was out of a wheelchair, but looked no better. The real difference was my eyes were reddened with rage.

"I want to see Maxim," I announced.

She tapped away at her computer and then raised her gaze to mine. "Mr. Ivanov is not taking any meetings without an appointment today."

"Tell him its Freya Fedorov."

"I can't do it while the do not disturb sign is on." She took great delight in telling me that.

I was shaking. "Can you please connect me to his secretary?"

"I need to know for what purpose ma'am. We have to screen callers to the executive secretaries too."

"Just tell him my name please, he'll know who is calling."

"Just a second ma'am." She tapped away at her computer. "I'm sorry, but its lunch time and he's currently not at his desk."

I walked away from the desk and pulled out my phone. I called Maxim, several times and the phone simply rang out. I was running out of patience, tears of red hot anger close to blinding me. I felt so utterly broken, beyond hurt.

I had given my body, and a precious part of me to a piece of shit. He had labeled it worthless and thrown it back into my face. The level of disrespect he had shown me, I was sure, would haunt me for the rest of my days.

All I wanted to do was return the money back to that unfeeling beast.

But that was proving impossible.

I felt a sob grow inside my chest. *No, no tears, Freya. He's not worth it.*

I put the shopping bag on the floor and pulled it open to reveal the bundles of cash. I snapped the band of the first bundle of cash and threw it up into the air. Hundred dollar bills flew into the air and rained back down onto the ground. I worked quickly through the bundles. The entire room... I stopped at the sight, but I didn't give a damn. Security guards started running towards me.

"Excuse me ma'am," they shouted. "You're not allowed to do that here."

"Tell Mr. Ivanov," I shouted back to them, "that I will keep doing this every day until the money is all gone, and if I am blocked tomorrow from entering the building, that I will do it out on the street."

I cut another bundle of ten thousand dollars, and flung the notes into the air.

I wiped the tears from my eyes and kept going.

Gary burst into the conference room.

I raised my head from the acquisition documents we were reviewing and turned my gaze to him with irritation. The room was filled with twenty executives from seven countries.

"Uh ... sorry to interrupt," he apologized, before adjusting his glasses, and walking over to me. "You should see this." He held his phone in front of my face, and there she was, and for a while I couldn't understand what I was seeing.

Then it hit me. Jesus! I rose to my feet.

"Gentlemen, please excuse me. I won't be too long," I said to the curious faces around, and walked out, Gary's phone in hand.

Levan caught up with me as I reached the elevator. "What's going on?"

I tossed the phone to him and he caught it.

It took him a while too for what he was seeing to register. "Isn't that Freya? What the fuck is going on?"

I tried my best to but I couldn't stop the smile that spread across my face. Never had I felt more exhilarated in my life.

"What's today's date?" I asked Gary.

"Uh the uhh- 29th sir, of October."

I noted it.

It was the day that I claimed Freya Fedorov as mine.

I pulled my phone out of my pocket and called Viktor. "Where are you?" I asked.

"I'm on the second-floor sir," he answered. "I'm almost at the lobby."

Chapter Sixty-One

FREYA

https://www.youtube.com/watch?v=02luJPh6h_A

The guards had obviously had enough.

They came for me, and before I could defend myself, it was after all four against one, they grabbed me.

"Let me go," I said trying my best not to cause more of a scene than I already had. Truthfully, I wasn't here to exhibit my fury. I was simply just here to dispose of the money. To return it to the jerk who sent it to me.

It would have been the entire million if the bank had agreed to give it to me, but they had not.

The guard's grip was rough and nearly tore my arm away from its shoulder sockets. I didn't blame him... I was putting him at risk of losing his job for even allowing my debacle to go on as long as it did. This was meant to solely happen in the privacy of Maxim's office, but since his people had refused to let me see him, I had no other choice.

"Get your hands off her!" an imperious bark sounded.

Instantly, the callous hands holding me prisoner were gone. I turned around and saw two of his guards. Viktor and the one with a vicious scar down the side of his face. I couldn't remember his name. Britney and I just called him the one with the scar from the time we saw him at the house.

They glared at me, but I was unfazed. It appeared as if I had created quite some scene at the Ivankov head office. People from the lobby and several floors up had stopped to watch me. Others had heard the news and were running out of their offices to see what was going on. It felt as though a thousand fascinated eyes were on me.

I looked down at all the money and saw the three approaching pairs of tailored pants. One of them was him. I could just tell by the way his feet moved. He prowled like a panther.

I looked up and Maxim was standing in front of me, his expressionless gaze boring directly into mine. It seemed like a lifetime passed before he eventually spoke.

"What are you doing?" he asked casually.

"Returning what you sent to me. I would have brought it straight to you, but," I jerked my head towards the reception desk, "they wouldn't let me go up."

"Let's go up then," he said to me, stepping aside so that I could go ahead of him, but I scoffed at the offer.

"No need," I replied. "I've delivered what I wanted. I'll return tomorrow with the rest." I gave him a smile, turned around and started walking away. I wanted to run, but I wouldn't stoop to it. The revolving doors were right ahead of me, and I prayed to God I would be able to get to them and away from that place before I crumbled with tension and heartbreak.

I almost reached it.

Almost.

Suddenly, my hand was grabbed firmly and I was spun around. Before I could even begin to protest or fight back, I was unceremoniously lifted into the air and swung over someone's broad shoulder.

Of course, it was him... no one else would dare.

"Fucking put me down," I ordered through gritted teeth.

Of course, I was totally ignored. He walked with me further into the building seemingly completely unembarrassed to behave like a damn caveman in front of all his staff.

"Maxim," I screamed into his back. "Put me down. Right now!"

I rained blows on his back, but I might as well have been punching a brick wall. I only hurt my own fists.

He took me out of the arena like a spoilt child. I could hear people begin to giggle and laugh. Some even started clapping and as he carried me to his private elevator. It was already open, one of his men was waiting inside of it. Maxim took me in with him, and the guard immediately exited the elevator and the door dinged shut on us.

He put me down then and I headed straight to the keypad to try and open the door. I did but just before I could press it, he grabbed my hand and my contact was interrupted.

Furious, I turned around, and my hand went on a rampage of its own. It struck him, hard across the face.

Everything stopped.

My blood felt like it was steaming in my veins, my heart was pounding hard enough for me to hear it, the breath, going in and out of my nostrils came fast and furious.

The blow had turned his face aside and he held it still in that position as though he could not believe what had just happened. Neither could I.

There were innumerable lines in this world that would have been forgivable to cross. Hitting Maxim was not one of them. I turned around then and pounded my fist against the emergency stop button. It was only after I did that I realized what the button did. It didn't stop the elevator to let you out, but stopped it to keep you trapped. I was losing my mind. I punched the stop button again.

"You are a very problematic woman," he said from behind. "All this because I gave you the million dollars that I promised I would?"

"Ever since I've known you Maxim, I've truly hated you, but this time around you've really behaved despicably."

He straightened and adjusted the sleeve of his suit jacket. "You almost killed me? What do you call that?"

"What you deserve," I retorted. "How I wish that I hadn't missed your heart. Oh, hang on. I didn't miss. You just don't have a heart."

It was impossible not to see the rage that was burning in his eyes.

"You're a hypocrite, Freya. You say one thing with your mouth and then do another. Why exactly are you offended about this money? Wasn't this what we discussed? What you requested? In fact, what you *need* to get your business off the ground? If you weren't so fucking proud you'd take it and do something great with your life. For both you and Britney. You're holding her back, Freya."

I couldn't respond. My entire body was trembling. I wasn't offended. I was hurt.

He took a step closer to me. "You've just hit me," he said in a tone that sent shivers down my spine. "A lot of people have been killed for much less."

"Are you threatening me?" I choked out.

He locked his gaze with mine. "We're both vulnerable now. We've now both been backed into corners that we never want to be in. So let me ask you... why does this offend you so much? Why does it hurt?"

My head fell. He might as well have been asking me if I had feelings for him. He took another step closer to me, and I staggered backwards until my back hit the steel wall.

"Maxim," I breathed, hating how weak I sounded... how spineless. But in that moment, the earnestness in his eyes... it felt as if something invaluable was being dangled in front of me. I told myself that it could be a trick. If I reached out to try to grab it, it would be snatched away and I would be mocked.

So why wasn't I breathing... and why did I want it so bad?

"Answer me," he demanded. "You have feelings for me, otherwise the money wouldn't have hurt so much. You gave me a piece of your heart when you slept with me, didn't you? You became mine... solely mine."

It felt like I had been hit on the head with a block. All I could do was pretend to be unaffected. To scoff. "And you? Do I have a piece of your heart?"

"Yes, you do," he said softly. "The question is would that be enough for you?"

"What's that supposed to mean?"

"I'm not an ordinary man and I won't give you an ordinary life. There will be bodyguards at the zoo."

The elevator stopped then, and I nearly jumped out of my skin. I glanced to see that we had arrived at his floor. I swallowed the lump in my throat. The doors swished open. He walked out of the elevator and stood looking at me.

I didn't do anything and the doors closed on him. I told myself I had done the right thing.

Chapter Sixty-Two

FREYA

"Britney, what was your first big dream?" I asked.

I was standing by the window in our office, a steaming cup of coffee in my hands. Below, an elderly Asian woman was squatting by a corner of the street, with a cigarette in her hand. She was watching a dread-locked man playing a guitar.

"What?" Britney asked.

I turned around to see she was completely focused on her computer screen. She had not even heard me. "What was your first dream?" I asked again.

"Uh... other than being one of those kids Barney used to play with, I wanted to be a top chef. My mom was big on child labor so she had me in a helper tower from the minute I could well, stand. She had me mixing flour and cracking eggs and munching on dough. That's why I grew up so chubby."

I smiled at the image she painted. "Why did you change your mind?"

She laughed. "I realized I didn't give a fuck about cooking. What about you? What was your first big dream?"

I smiled. "I just realized it a few days ago."

"What?" She laughed.

"Yeah. My first dream was to be in love," I answered.

She looked at me as if I was speaking Chinese. "What?"

"Yeah, I was fourteen and I wanted to fall totally, and deeply, and absolutely in love with someone. At that time, I had just finished reading my first harlequin about this broken actor who finally found love in the arms of his high school sweetheart. Somewhat cringey now that I think about it, but back then, it made me want to find that one person that would love me beyond anything else."

She began to cackle. "You're joking, right? You? Love? You don't even fucking date."

"It's not that I don't date. I didn't have the time. I was busy with the idea of setting up a business."

"You were too busy to date? Yeah, pull the other one."

"Okay, maybe I wasn't too busy to date, but I had my dream at the back of my mind. It was either I got the right guy and everything or nothing. I'd never settle for anything less."

"I think with you though, it's worse than you not wanting to *settle for something less*. I seriously doubt if someone you wanted came along right now that you'd even give him a glance much less agree to him."

I returned my gaze to hers. "What do you mean?"

"You're too closed off, Freya. I used to think that you were just being stubborn but now I'm beginning to understand all that Mafia/Bratva stuff must have made you wary. Which is not a bad thing in itself, but sometimes I wish you'd allow yourself to just jump at the opportunities life throws at you, even if it will be a mistake."

Actually, I did jump and ended up falling down a great big hole.

Chapter Sixty-Three

MAXIM

"We got a lead on Freya's attacker," Levan said, placing two photos in front of me.

I stared at the two heavily tattooed men.

"Well, first of all brother, you have a pretty extensive hate list."

"Get to the fucking point," I prompted.

He chuckled and pointed to the man in the first picture. "Well, this one is part of the MLBOA gang. We had nothing on him at first … until, they got this picture of him last night." He slapped another photo on my desk.

The man he referred to had his face slightly turned away from sight, and a baseball cap sitting low on his head so it was almost impossible to make out his feature.

"That's Boris Arakas. Now he's the Death Angels' Sergeant at Arms. Ring any bells?"

I thought about it. "Isn't that the club house we had Detective Clay raid for Sarah Dale's grandson?"

"Exactly. His brother was killed in the raid and I have it on good authority that he holds you responsible."

"Hmm." It was all starting to come together, but something else occurred to me.

"We reasoned, especially with the attacks on Freya instead of you, that this was personal. He wanted you to suffer the same loss and pain he did."

"Seems like the closest lead we have until something new pops up," I said thoughtfully.

"The thing is I want to clear this mess up before I leave. The fastest way to do it is to dangle some sort of bait in front of them."

"Why don't you leave? You've done good work until now, but I can easily handle this on my own."

"No. I leave when it's all over," he insisted stubbornly.

"You keep finding reasons not to. I hope you don't plan on disappointing Bianca."

He rose to his feet. "Not on my life or yours. And how the fuck am I supposed to leave with a target on your back?"

I sighed. "After you resolve this one, another will pop up. It's the curse of our trade."

"Well you can handle those on your own then, but this, I need wrapped up for my own peace of mind." His lips twitched with amusement. "Besides, I need to see how you sort things out with Freya."

I ignored his mention of her and went on. "So what's the plan?"

He produced a key and tossed it on the desk. "You, are going to move. The new jersey compound is too protected. We need to give them clear access to you."

I grinned. "When you said bait, I didn't think you meant me."

"This is the only way to lure them out."

I picked up the gold key chain and key and gave it a once over. "Where?"

"Midtown, 172 Madison Avenue. 63rd floor."

"Okay."

"Am I ever going to find out why Freya lost her shit on you last week?"

"Get out of here. I have work to do."

His laughter rang out until the door shut on him.

Chapter Sixty-Four

FREYA

I placed the empty tray down and picked up my vibrating phone. It was a quiet night at the bar so I had brought my phone behind the bar with me.

"Aldie?"

"Hey," she greeted excitedly. "I'm at Bianca's place, how are you?"

"Um, I'm great," I replied. "You?"

"I'm doing okay."

She laughed. "I heard about what happened at the Ivankov's building," she drawled, and I felt my heart sink to my stomach. That episode was going to haunt me for life.

"Bianca's too polite to ask but I'm dying of curiosity. Why did you get so mad? Why did Maxim have to carry you away like some scene in a romantic comedy? And what was all the money about? Also, I am butt hurt that you didn't come over to my place to rain some down on me, but I'll try my best not to hold that against you."

I couldn't help the grin that slipped onto my face. Aldie was a busybody, but a loveable one. One I couldn't resist.

I looked around. It was still pretty dead. "Why don't you come over to my bar and I'll make you a drink... on the house. To make up for not raining cash at your place."

"I'm hailing a taxi as I speak!"

Forty minutes later she waved vigorously to me from the door. I set her Dirty Martini on the counter and she took her seat opposite me. She had an air of excitement around her as if she couldn't wait to hear my story. I leaned on the counter while she took a sip of her drink.

"Thank you, babe," she said. "I needed that. Now, quickly tell me what happened before I burst from curiosity."

I wasn't really ready to talk about any of it yet, but I figured talking to someone objective could only help. I spelled it out simply. "It was kind of a joke that if I slept with Maxim he would pay me a million dollars. I slept with him, and he transferred a million dollars into my bank account."

She went still, the hand holding her toothpick with an olive stabbed on it, suspended in the air.

"Which part are you appalled by?"

"Uh... oh... uh..." She shook her head to get her brain working again. "You... did you... a million dollars? As in... seven figures? As in real money?"

"Yup," I agreed crisply.

Her hand covered her mouth as she stared at me. "They always say you have to watch out for the quiet ones."

"Just a second," I said, and walked away to take a customer's order for a beer. After serving him I returned to her and by then she had processed the information.

"Okay. Um ... why did he send it to you if it was a joke?"

"Because he's a piece of shit."

She opened her mouth, and shut it again.

'How much did you disperse that day?"

"About a quarter of it," I replied.

She began to fan herself with her hand. "Where's the rest of it?"

"Still in my account, but not for much longer."

"I can't believe this," she gasped.

"Neither could I," I agreed sourly.

"Well, mine is for a different reason. What I can't believe is... you threw all that money into the air when you still have to pull shifts in a bar to make ends meet."

I shrugged. "I guess the only money that excites me is that I make myself, no matter how little."

"Right. Makes complete sense. Now, if you really have no interest in Maxim can you put in a good word for me?"

"Aldie!" I scolded.

She couldn't hide her blush. "I'm sorry but have you taken a good look at Maxim? The first time I saw him I almost went into a coma."

"Yes, he is hot," I admitted.

"And tough, and loyal. Sure you have absolutely no interest in him?"

I bit my lip. I hadn't even confessed how I felt about Maxim to Britney. It was too confusing. Too intense. Too crazy.

"Bianca once said that she wondered what kind of woman would ever be enough to attract and keep Maxim. I wondered the same too, but now ... especially with that scene you pulled at his workplace, you both actually seem perfect for each other."

I had to serve another customer and when I got back I tactfully steered the conversation to a different topic. When she left an hour later, I mulled over her words.

During my break I went outside and called Maxim. My heart was pounding so hard in my chest, that I was sure if he picked up, I wouldn't be able to speak. He picked up on the second ring.

"Apologize,' I said. "Apologize for sending me that money."

A small silence followed. Then he shocked me.

"I'm sorry," he said.

My heart stopped.

"I'm very sorry about that. I wasn't trying to degrade you. In my world you keep your word." He stopped and I knew that he wouldn't be going any further. Even that little glimpse of him being vulnerable was something hardly anyone ever saw.

"Can I see you? Sometime soon?" I asked. "To ... er ... talk."

"Talk? Okay, how about tomorrow? In the office? I'll shift things around to make time for you."

"I'm never coming to your office again, in my lifetime."

He laughed softly. The sound was low and deep, and it rumbled through me like good liquor.

I held my breath. "How about tonight?"

"You're at work now, aren't you?"

Of course, he was aware of my every movement. "I mean afterwards. Will it be too late?"

"I'll wait up," he said. "But I'm no longer in Jersey. I have a place in Midtown."

I noted that whiff of danger in his voice. I was coming to like it way too much. "Oh, ah okay then."

I wanted to ask why, but I didn't have to because he offered up the information.

"We're trying to smoke out who's behind the attacks. Better chance of doing that if I'm perceived to have less security around me."

My stomach roiled at the danger involved in their tactic, but I kept my concern to myself.

"When you come over can you be as inconspicuous as possible?"

"Oh, okay. You mean, I should come dressed as someone else?"

He laughed again and my heart soared. It was rare communicating with him in such a light-hearted manner.

"You couldn't come as someone else if you tried for a year, Freya."

"What is *that* supposed to mean?" I demanded immediately.

"Maybe one day I'll tell you. Look, I gotta go. I'll send you the address. See you later."

I ended the call and gave a little skip of joy.

Chapter Sixty-Five

FREYA

https://www.youtube.com/watch?v=yCC_b5WHLX0

t twenty minutes to two in the morning, my co-workers and I ordered pizza. The moment it arrived at the bar, it was pounced on by them.

I turned to pay the pizza guy and noticed his cap. It was scuffed and painted in red and white with Johnny's pizza stamped in front of it. Apart from that he had a plain black bomber jacket on. Mine would do, but the helmet, I needed to have.

"How much will you take for the cap?" I asked.

"Uh," he was stumped by the question.

At the end of our strange discussion I walked away with his old busted cap, and he with an extra $20.00 tip.

I arrived at the high-rise residential building in midtown

Manhattan and with my cap pulled low, I quickly went into the building. I was greeted by the night porter and upon the confirmation of my visit, I rode the elevator to the 63rd floor.

The building was finished with marble floors and gigantic centerpieces. It stank of extreme wealth. I saw my reflection in the mirror and couldn't believe how shabby I looked in those surroundings. Neither could I believe I was once again going to the man that I'd sworn I hated to the depths of my soul.

Life was sometimes such a sick, twisted bitch.

I arrived at his door and knocked. The busted old hat was still on my head and for a moment, I thought to take it off, but I couldn't decide fast enough because the door suddenly clicked open... and there he was!

He was wearing only his pajama trousers, and it instantly scrambled my brain. In the soft yellow lights of his apartment his skin glowed. I swallowed hard at the sight of the pure slabs of muscle and the strength radiating from them. When I saw the fairly healed bullet wound I had given him on his chest it made me sad all over again. I wanted to reach out to touch it, but he quickly brought me back down to earth.

"Creative," he said, his gaze on my hat.

I rolled my eyes at his sarcasm. "Are you going to let me in?"

He stepped aside and I walked into the gorgeously decorated apartment. "How much do I have to tip you?"

I turned back around to face him and summoned up the boldness to say exactly what I wanted to. My gaze lowered to and settled on the bulge in his pants. I could see that he was already excited and growing.

"About nine inches." I pretended to shake my head as if to clear it. "I mean, nine dollars."

He smiled. A dark and sexy smile.

I felt my throat tighten at his amusement. Fuck... but he was beautiful, in a dangerous way that made me begin to drip with arousal.

He came forward and took the box from me, found it a bit light, and shook it. "You ate all the pizza before you got here?"

"My coworkers did. Did you want some?"

"I could eat a pizza."

"Well, uh ... I'm sorry," I said. "I'll bring you some next time."

He threw the box aside and placed his hands on my hat. I shut my eyes as I suddenly felt too heated, and remained still as he pulled it off my head and flung it behind him. I felt him lightly brush his fingers down my hair to arrange it, and then tuck some flyaway strands behind my ear. I had held it all together and secured it to the nape of my neck so that the helmet could sit properly on my head. I shifted uncomfortably at the strong throb of the bud between my legs.

"You look beautiful," he whispered.

With my gaze on the floor I began to shrug off my jacket. He took it from me and draped it across the couch. The huge ceiling to floor windows with their breathtaking view of the city's skyline in the middle of the night was impressive.

"Beautiful," I said.

"I'm actually hungry," he said, holding the door to his refrigerator open. "Do you want something to eat?"

"Uh ..."

"Maxim, uh, we both know why I'm here, so I say we just... uh get to it. I have to go home and be up early to go to the office." Establishing control and power right from the get go. I was doing great.

"Well I'm starving," he said. "I'll get to you soon."

Ouch. I chose not to feel sore about his response, but I did deserve it. Choosing not to care, I went over and sat in front of the counter. I watched as he brought out a plastic bowl of salad and dug a fork into it.

It was quite strange seeing him in this way, so homey and almost human when the rest of the world was used to seeing him more as a walking weapon.

"Do you always eat this late?" I asked.

"I got carried away and forgot to eat. Sure you don't want some?"

I shook my head and he took his seat opposite me and continued to eat quietly. He ate the way he did everything else. Carefully, purposefully. I couldn't stop looking at the way he chewed.

We remained that way with him intently watching me as he ate. I was sure that this was some kind of tactic to keep me drooling over him. I was unable to wait for the moment where he would most probably lay me flat across the counter and fuck the living daylights out of me. I wanted that. I craved that. And I couldn't wait any longer.

"Why are you staring at me?" I asked.

"It's strange," he said. "You being here."

"That's putting it lightly," I responded. "And you. You seem so human."

He snickered in response. "What do you mean?"

"I don't know. You're quite perceived as ..." I didn't know what words to use that wouldn't show any affection or awe whatsoever. "I guess you're aloof, and it commands a sort of reverence. Not many people come off that way."

"It doesn't seem like I ever commanded any measure of respect from you though."

"I've always hated you," I said. "I still do."

"Then why are you here?"

"Well there's a part of you I just recently discovered that I can tolerate. Why deprive myself?"

He laughed.

My stomach did several flips of excitement. I wanted his mouth on me... his tongue inside of me. And I really, really couldn't wait any longer.

Chapter Sixty-Six

FREYA

https://www.youtube.com/watch?v=9kp3N3wQPOo

I summoned up my courage and pulled my shirt over my head. My breasts beautifully displayed in my favorite lace bra, so when his hand froze in mid-air with his fork on the way to his mouth, I couldn't help my smile.

I went further. I reached behind me and unhooked my bra and the perky mounds spilled out. I pulled the material away and placed it on top of my shirt on the counter.

He wasn't smiling anymore, his gaze hot and intense, zeroed in on me like a hawk on its prey.

I rose to my feet. I headed over to the refrigerator and pulled it open to retrieve a bottle of water. I couldn't face him fully. I wasn't that confident, but he was quite close to me and I was well aware of his gaze charring the skin off my back.

I took my time drinking the water. Until I heard the stool

scrape against the tiled floor as he got off his chair. I waited, my breath bated, as I put the cap back on the bottle. "You have quite a lot of fruit," I said. "Did you shop for these yourself?"

I felt him behind me, and my skin began to overheat, despite the cool air coming from the open refrigerator in front of me.

His hands slid around my waist, and the bottle fell from my hands.

I couldn't breathe. He leaned forward, his warm breath against my neck. I leaned into his body, the hardness of his cock pressed solidly against my ass. His hands moved, splayed out against my stomach, and then they went to the button of my jeans. He made short work of unbuttoning and unzipping my jeans. He must have a lot of practice. The thought jarred and annoyed me.

His hand moved, slipping down my panties to grab my mound. All the blood left my brain. I moaned aloud as I writhed, breathless with anticipation of all that was coming.

His fingers slipped between the slickness of my folds, teasing and stroking my swollen clit, and my feet nearly left the ground.

"Maxim," I gasped, my eyes clenched shut at the shock of arousal that flashed through me like a bolt of lightning.

I held onto his hand as he slipped a finger into me, and then another. Then he slammed my body against his. His left hand curved around my body to hold me in place while the other took me to places that I couldn't believe I had waited so long to explore.

His fingers fucked me, his thumb joining in the dance as he worked my swollen sensitive bud in rapid torturous circles.

I saw my hand reach out to hold onto the fridge and it never did quite make it. It froze in mid-air and clenched at the agonizing pleasure that was coursing through me.

"Maxim," I breathed as he nibbled on my ear, but then suddenly, he stopped and pulled out and I almost cried.

"What the—"

He lifted me off the ground, and threw me over his shoulder.

"Maxim," I squealed and in no time he had me on the counter.

"I want you to be mine, Freya. I want you to be my woman." He wrapped his hands around me and held me tight. "God, I've missed this," he whispered.

I threw my hands around his neck. He nibbled my neck and my jawline, then moved to my nipples. One after the other, he sucked feverishly and ran his teeth over my pebble-hard nipples. I closed my eyes as jolts of pleasure shot through me. I caressed his shoulders loving the masculine hardness under his shirt.

Then, he knelt between my splayed legs and caressed my inner thighs. He bent his head and kissed my thighs going higher and higher. My pussy was hot with arousal. I screamed when his tongue connected with my clit.

"Yessssss."

The pressure of his tongue on my clit eased. His licks became feathery light movements that barely scratched the itch. I pushed my pussy into his face. He moved back and continued with the light licks. I was going crazy with frustration.

"Maxim, please," I begged my body aching for release.

"What do you want?" he said.

"I want you to eat my pussy," I said between clenched teeth.

"Like this?" Another feathery lick.

"No, like you can't get enough," I said, almost shouting.

A finger circled my clit, and I made jerky humping movements. I needed some friction desperately. "What do I get in return?"

"What do you want?" I groaned.

"I want you to stay the night," Maxim said.

"Yes, yes, I'll stay. Now give me satisfaction."

"With pleasure," he said and proceeded to eat my pussy with great fervor, as if he had been starving for years.

I was still calling his name when my body exploded with an orgasm. He continued licking my pussy, long after the vibrations had ended.

"I want your cock now," I gasped.

"I thought you'd never ask," he said.

I watched him drop the pajama bottoms. He was magnificent to look at, with his muscular chest and ripped abdomen. I stared at his huge cock. I still couldn't believe how damn big it was.

My pussy tingled at the thought of his cock filling me.

"You want this, my little stubborn minx?" Maxim asked, his hand stroking his rock-hard cock. In that moment he was like a beautiful Roman centurion standing proudly while holding his spear, only in this case, it was his impressive cock.

"Yes, please," I said, my mouth watering. Maxim had made me shameless in my need for him.

"I'm going to make you scream," he promised.

He pushed my legs up to my chest. I looked down and I could see how completely exposed I was. My pussy wet and glistening.

"Fuck," Maxim growled and in the next second, his cock was poised above the entrance to my pussy.

He dragged the smooth tip of his cock up and down the dripping slit of my pussy. I cried out when the thick head slowly pushed in. I could feel juices gush out of my pussy. I thought I was going to die from pleasure.

"You like that, baby?" he growled.

"Yes, yes, it feels so good. I want all of you inside me," I gasped.

"Balls deep?"

"Balls deep," I muttered.

And he slammed into me, so brutally, my ass slid on the counter.

"Again," I groaned.

"I'm going to fuck you until you can't walk." Gripping my ass tightly he began to pound me relentlessly, like a madman.

He went so deep it felt as if his cock was in my belly and I knew I couldn't last much longer.

"Oh God. Oh God," I shouted as my pussy began to clench. I screamed his name as the orgasm rolled into my pussy, then spread to the rest of my body.

Maxim pumped harder and faster until hot seed shot into my pussy. With us both spent, he stroked my back softly. "That was hot. You're hot, Freya Federov."

Chapter Sixty-Seven
FREYA

I had the sensation I was drifting on a soft cloud. But I wasn't on a cloud. I was in... Maxim's bed.

Memories of the previous night rushed back to me. Maxim completely possessing me on the counter, then carrying my limp body over to the shower. In there, he fucked me once, my palms pressed against the cool tiles, hot water rushing down my body. Then while cleaning me between my legs, he got aroused all over again, and proceeded to pump into me all over again. In the end I was so exhausted he had to carry me to his humongous bed.

There I had fallen into blissful sleep in his arms after he ate me out.

I carefully turned my head to see that the other pillow was empty. Instantly I sat up, holding the sheets around my naked body. From the open door I could see the sun had long risen.

It made me feel strangely sad he hadn't stayed around, but I told myself not to be so pathetic and clingy. This was clearly just a sexual thing. I should get out of bed and find out where the hell my clothes had ended up.

But just as I started to get out of the bed I heard him approaching and instantly fluffed my hair and got back into a sophisticated, nonchalant lounging pose. Anyone would have thought I'd been staying overnight at my lovers' homes thousands of times.

He appeared already shaved and dressed in a navy-blue striped suit. God, he was heartbreakingly handsome. He also had my clothes in his hands. He placed them at the foot of the bed. I debated whether I should rise confidently and get dressed in front of him, but I wasn't sure I could carry it off.

"I'm sorry for... uh... sleeping in. I guess I was tired."

"That's alright," he said and pulled two cufflinks out of his pocket. "I have a flight in about an hour. Can I call you when I get back?"

My heart leapt for joy. "Yeah, sure," I responded casually. I was dying to ask when he would be returning, but that would probably look as if I was desperate to see him again, and I wasn't desperate, was I? Well, I wasn't the only one. I let the sheet drop to my waist, and he made a strangled sound.

"Jesus, Freya," he muttered.

"What?" I asked innocently.

"Nothing," he said, and turning on his heel walked out of the room.

I was grateful for the space. Being naked in the harsh light of day is harder than at 2.00am in the night. I quickly got dressed, used the bathroom, then went to the kitchen to see him sipping at a cup of coffee as he scrolled through his phone.

The stoic look was back on his face, and his aura of the intimidating billionaire that the rest of the world knew was now fully in place. The playful, hungry, passionate Maxim of last night was gone, but it was a part that I felt privileged to have seen. This part of him however, although incredibly attractive, was very familiar.

I didn't know what the protocol was for these kinds of situations. Should I announce I was leaving? As it happened I didn't need to.

"Do you want some coffee?" he asked the moment he sensed me standing awkwardly at the threshold.

As a sexual hook-up I had probably already overstayed my welcome, and he was just being polite and so I shook my head and refused the offer. "No thanks."

"Juice then, or tea?" he insisted, getting up and walking towards the refrigerator.

Maybe it was customary to drink something before leaving. I didn't want to seem gauche and inexperienced so I said, "I'll have some juice, thank you."

He closed the refrigerator door and held up a jug. "Freshly squeezed orange juice okay for you?"

Just by that same door the previous night, he had grabbed my breasts and licked my sex, and I had writhed against him like some animal. I couldn't understand how we were looking at each other in the eye and behaving in such a civilized way this morning. I cleared my throat. "Yes, that would be lovely."

He poured the juice into a tall glass for me and put it on the counter opposite his coffee. Oh well, maybe I should sit and have my drink then. I walked over and sat on the stool. I took a sip of the cold drink.

"Um ... do you travel a lot?"

"At least every week," he replied. "What about you? Do you—"

"Oh, I don't go anywhere," I interrupted, then laughed nervously.

He looked amused. "I was about to ask if you liked traveling."

"Oh," my cheeks flushed. "No, I don't."

Why on earth did I say that? I loved travelling. I drained my glass then. I should be on my way before I spontaneously combusted and became a pile of ashes in his kitchen.

"I should go," I said, sliding off the stool.

"Okay. Let me call you a car."

"No, don't do that. It's a fine morning and I'll enjoy the walk to the subway."

He frowned. "Are you sure?"

"Yeah, I'm sure," I said walking backwards, only to catch my hip painfully on the hard corner of a piece of furniture and nearly catapulting to the floor.

He stood up in alarm. "Are you okay?"

"Yeah, everything is fine," I sang out as I quickly straight-ened. "Bye," I shouted as I almost ran out of there, hiding my flaming cheeks.

"Bye," he said, just before I slammed his front door.

Outside, I took deep breaths. Idiot, I scolded myself. I'd completely ruined my exit.

Chapter Sixty-Eight

FREYA

"Whenwill you have the funds for the tourmaline piece?" Britney asked. "My sample request has been finalized so they're just waiting on us now. Next week?"

"Uh," I thought to the $750,000 still parked in my account and experienced a barrage of emotions ranging from nausea to guilt.

"I have it already. I'll send it to you right now. How much is it?"

"About $950."

"Done," I said a few minutes later.

"Wow, do you earn more at this new job? I thought this expense would be a bit difficult since you've already covered so many expenses this month."

"Some nights I get lucky with tips."

"Nice," she said.

And my spirits sank even lower. I didn't want to lie to my best friend and business partner. But ever since she left there was now a sort of unspoken strain in our relationship. Even though I understood her decision and where it came from, it had reduced my faith in her just a tiny bit. I stared down at my phone and wanted so badly to tell her the truth. I raised my head.

"Britney, I need to tell you something."

"What?" she whispered immediately.

"While you were away I slept with Maxim."

"What?" she screamed and covered her mouth with her palm. "Oh my God, tell me everything. Right now!"

I laughed and just like that we were best friends again. We sat on the couch together and I told her everything. About the money too.

She sat back. "Wow! So you guys are just going to hook up for sex."

I nodded. "That's the plan."

"Quite frankly, I think that's a bad idea."

"Why?"

"Because, trust me, you'll just end up falling in love with him."

I opened my mouth to deny her statement, but she held up her hand. "Wait, hear me out. I have more experience than you in this department. The thing is. Men seem to be able to compartmentalize their sex life really easily, but it's really hard for women to do. Forget about Hollywood fantasy movies where the woman is all macho and wanting only sex and the man is the one who falls in love with her and desperate for commitment. From what I've observed, eventually, someone ends up falling in love and getting hurt, and it's almost always the woman. I mean, you almost stand no chance with a guy who looks like Maxim."

I chewed my bottom lip. She did have a point. If I was truly honest I was already kind of in love with Maxim. He was just so perfect ...

At that moment my phone dinged with a message. I quickly snatched up my phone and looked at it. For the first few seconds I just stared at it, then a smile slowly spread across my face. I felt my toes curl with pleasure.

"I'll be back from Belarus in three days," he'd written. *"Will you have the time to meet?"*

Fuck yes my mind screamed, but I took the more respectable route in real life.

"Sure." I texted back.

I looked up and Britney was looking at me with an incredulous expression. "It's already happened, hasn't it? You've already fallen for him."

"No, of course not," I denied automatically.

"Don't kid yourself, Freya. I know that look. It's unmistakable."

"Okay, maybe a little, but I have it under control."

She burst out in laughter. "Famous last words, if you ask me."

"Anyway, I need to return the rest of his money."

She put her chin on her fists. "I know you have to return the money, but how about we keep some back. It can be a loan. About $10,000 would solve all our problems and we can pay it back in about six months with interest. It'll be like he invested in us. He'd make money and you wouldn't have to kill yourself to fund our first order."

I grinned at her. "You know what, Brit. That is a damn good idea."

She grinned right back. "Right. I've got to get back to work." She walked to the door and turned back to look at me. "You know what, Freya. I'm really happy for you. You deserve someone special and I'll be praying it works out with Maxim." She grinned. "Men with dicks anything over seven inches are rare so you make sure you have fun."

"Get lost you," I said throwing a pillow at her.

She ducked and was gone.

I began to type a message to him.

I'm going to return all the money you sent except for $10,000. I will consider that as a loan from you. For six months. You'll get interest, of course. Thanks.

I read it through. Perhaps that was too cold.

I'm going to return all the money you sent, but I was wondering if I could hold back $10,000 as a loan from you. For six months. You'll get interest, of course. Thanks.

I studied it. It still sounded too emotionless. I crafted another message.

Hey Maxim,

I'm going to take your advice. You were right. I shouldn't let my pride hold Britney and me back from achieving our dream. So I'm going to return all the money you sent except for $10,000, which I will consider as a six-month loan from you. You'll get interest, of course. Thanks.

There. It was polite, not condescending or aggressive and gave him credit.

Two minutes later, his response came, and my heart jumped in my chest.

"Brilliant idea."

I thought to send a thumbs-up emoji, but then decided I should stop while I was ahead.

Then I made an appointment with my doctor. So far I had been very careless with birth control. I could already even be pregnant. Strangely, the thought didn't make me feel any dread at all. In fact, I kinda wished I was. How great it would be to see a little cutie of a Maxim running around.

I smacked my cheeks to pull myself together.

What the hell was the matter with me? Why was I even thinking these strange thoughts? The last thing I needed was getting pregnant, especially to a man who was unemotionally unavailable to the world.

Chapter Sixty-Nine

FREYA

https://www.youtube.com/watch?v=GOJkoHW_hJw

Three days later, my feet were off the floor and my back slamming into the wall of Maxim's foyer. He had been unable to wait, and the moment I arrived at his door he pounced on me. One moment I'd been holding a pizza box and the next, I was pulled into the apartment, the pizza was on the floor, and his cock, thick and hard, was ramming into me.

With my legs wrapped around his body and my hands clinging to him like a monkey he took me to his bed. There, I changed the power structure and got on top of him.

I ground my hips sensually against him, riding him fast and then slow, and near driving me out of my own mind. I put my hands over his face to hide what I was doing to him.

"*Fuck,*" he roared into my hands and I couldn't help my laugh.

I was light-headed with the high that I was on from being with him again. From feeling his cock inside me. Life felt more beautiful, vibrant, full of purpose that I could barely contain the marvelous sensations inside me.

"*Freya,*" he called.

I fucked him even harder. Rising on his shaft and slamming down hard. His hand glided down my body to grab my ass, shoving me even deeper inside of him.

"I fucking love the way you feel," he grunted. "Oh *fuck*, just like that."

I was already quaking and I could tell he was also close. I waited for it eagerly. This part I treasured so much. Racing towards a release that always completely shattered the both of us. The sensation of his seed hot and thick bursting deep inside me, filling me up. Sometimes I squeezed my thighs together to keep it a little longer.

I cried as I shuddered against him, my system overtaken by such strong spasms of raw primal pleasure, I froze.

He flipped me over onto the bed, and shoved his hips at me, milking out every bit of pleasure before he followed me over the edge into the abyss of pure bliss. He collapsed on top of me, and I held on desperately to him, a new fear filling me. After what Britney said I had started to think more deeply about our arrangement.

How was I ever to let him go when he made me feel like this? When he made me fucking come like this?

He kissed me then, sweetly, but I kissed him desperately and with a silent plea. What I was asking for however, I didn't have a clue.

He must have felt the difference in me, because he lifted his head and looked into my eyes with a questioning look. I felt as if I couldn't breathe, let alone speak, but my phone ringing did register. It gave me the perfect excuse not to face his curious eyes, so I lurched over to my bag where it had been flung across the floor, and fished my phone out.

It stopped ringing as I got it. It was Bianca.

As I was about to call her back I felt Maxim come up to me. He slid an arm around me and pressed me against his gloriously naked body. He had an apple in his other hand and he brought it to my lips. I took a bite out of it and sank into his hold. He took another bite then both his hands covered my breasts.

"I need to call Bianca back," I managed to say.

"Later," he grunted.

I shook my head and clicked the green call button. "Maybe it's important."

"Yeah?" Suddenly, he picked me up, and I squealed as he threw me over his shoulder. Next, I was deposited on the couch and my legs pulled wide apart. Then my greedy lover got on his knees, and covered my whole sex with his mouth.

I tried to stop the call from going through, but Bianca had already picked up.

"Hey you."

"Hey," I croaked back.

"Are you alright?"

I tried to stabilize myself. "I'm fine. How are you?"

With an evil grin Maxim shoved two fingers inside me and I couldn't sit still anymore. This call needed to end quick.

"I'm great," she said happily. "Its Levan's birthday today so I want to organize a little soiree with some intimate friends at the Lexington Avenue club. It's one of the bars that their company owns.

"Oh... uhh ... ah."

Maxim sucked my clit into his mouth.

"*Fuck*," I breathed and I was sure she heard me.

"What?"

"I'm so sorry, Bianca. I stubbed my toe."

"Oh dear. So can you make it?"

"Yes, oh God, yes, I mean ... I'll be, oh ... be there. Please ... mmmm ... send me the addr—"

My words were cut off because Maxim had grabbed the phone from me and flung it away. I heard it smash hard against something.

I didn't care.

He captured my mouth in a hot kiss, and slammed that massive cock of his straight into me.

A t 10 pm later that night, I walked into the Lexington Avenue club with a broken, but still working phone in my purse. The music was loud and the ground floor bar and dance floor was filled with hoards of people gyrating to the music.

Britney was with me. However, I was nervous about how Maxim and I would conduct ourselves in front of our friends who knew nothing beyond the fact that we were sworn enemies. Would we be able to maintain the facade or would our friends instantly be able to see right through us?

After placing a quick call to Bianca, we were invited up to one of the big glass cubes hanging above the dance floor. Of course, theirs would be a very private and exclusive gathering amongst the mayhem. Britney and I walked in to see Bianca, Levan, Aldie and a man I did not recognize, already seated and laughing uproariously at something.

Bianca gave me a hug and a kiss on the cheek, while Levan

gave me a pleasant smile. Aldie squealed with excitement and instantly poured me a glass of rosé champagne, while I introduced her to Britney. I could see immediately that Aldie and Britney were going to become fast friends.

Levan introduced me to the man I didn't know. Timothy Barnett, one of their company's main attorneys. "Call me Tom," he instructed.

He was dressed in a beige suit, his face was clean shaven, and his hair was slicked back from his face. He was handsome and imposing, almost flawlessly so.

"Maxim's on his way," Bianca said to me, her face filled with a mixture of guilt and devilish match-making. "I hope you don't mind. He will be civil and decent, I swear."

There was a twinkle in Levan's eyes, I wondered if he knew what was going on.

"It's alright," I replied with a sage smile. I turned my attention to something else. "Happy birthday, Levan," I said, handing over a pair of customized cufflinks that Britney and I had bought from a supplier we knew.

"Thank you, but you didn't have to," he said, and squeezed my shoulder in appreciation.

"I hear you make jewelry," Tom said smoothly to me.

I turned to focus my attention on him. "Yes, Britney and I do."

"Do you have a store, or a way I could buy from you?" he asked.

Britney instantly switched to business mode and preoccupied

herself with selling our business. She was impressive. Without being pushy she gave him the details of our site.

"How fascinating," he murmured. As they were sucked into a deep conversation I began to relax. Perhaps this night was going to be good after all.

"Oh good, here comes Maxim," Bianca called gaily.

I felt my body become tense again.

Tom and Britney continued to speak, but I couldn't hear a word they said any more. I leaned forward and grabbed my flute. Two men began to approach and I didn't know where to look.

"Here he is," the lawyer announced.

Pretending to be completely normal I turned and looked into the eyes of the man who had fucked me senseless just a few hours earlier. I felt the wind knocked out of me. He was dressed simply in a black shirt, grey slacks and highly polished black shoes, but the man himself always made simple look unattainable.

I instantly wanted him ... right there and then.

Almost everyone in the room stood up to receive him.

"Aldie," he said with a nod, and she nodded back, then threw a naughty, knowing glance at me.

Bianca went in for a hug.

And Levan and Tom just grinned at him.

Then Maxim turned to me.

"Freya," he murmured.

I gave him a quick nod before lifting my glass to my lips. No one made a big deal out of anything and I was grateful for that. I did feel quite disappointed though when he took his seat beside Britney at the opposite end of the couch.

Chapter Seventy-One

MAXIM

https://www.youtube.com/watch?v=aJOTIE1K9ok

She acted like she didn't know me, and I got off on knowing that was our little secret. At least, for now, keeping it as a secret ignited my blood and gave me great pleasure to know I had sucked on her sweet pussy only a couple of hours ago.

As the night went on I tried to keep my eyes off her but it was almost as though she was dressed to torture me. Her blouse was sparkly, and low cut and the glimpse of her full breasts was more than enough to remind me of how they felt in my hands and tasted in my mouth.

Her dress ended somewhere on the middle of her thighs, the fair skin of her legs glowing softly in the dim ambience of the club.

She smiled at something Tom said to her, and the way he

leaned in close to her churned my stomach. Her eyes sparkled as she gave all her attention to him and suddenly my temperature began to rise.

"Now that Maxim's here does anyone want something to eat?" Bianca asked. "We can place any special orders to the kitchen and they'll have it made for us."

"Perks of owning the place," Levan said.

"Perhaps some sashimi?" Aldie said. "I'm craving some."

"Alright," Bianca said and started to move away, but Levan caught her by the waist and pulled her back down on top of him. "Everyone here should take care of their own damn selves, instead of having my wife run around."

"Stop being such a bear," she protested, but to the amusement of the room, he began to instead nuzzle her neck.

"I'll handle it." Freya rose and Aldie did the same.

"Relax everybody. The manager will be here in a minute," I announced, tapping at the screen of my phone.

Soon enough the manager arrived accompanied by two waitresses.

"Sir," he greeted, while the waitresses placed bottles of champagne and liquor on the table. Bianca ordered platters of sushi rolls and sashimi.

"Freya detests fish," I said.

The whole room turned to me and then to her. She turned bright red.

"Why didn't you say anything, Freya?" Bianca asked.

"Ah, it's alright. I'm quite happy with the rice and seaweed rolls—"

"No, that won't do," Bianca said firmly. "How does some tacos sound? Or grilled chicken sandwich?"

"Tacos would be great," Freya replied.

"How do you know that Freya doesn't like fish" Aldie asked mischievously.

I turned my gaze to hers. "I think she mentioned it to Gary once."

"Ah," Aldie said knowingly.

The issue was clarified, I poured myself a glass of scotch and settled in to enjoy the show.

"You knew Levan when he was a boy, didn't you, Freya? What was he like then?" Bianca asked Freya.

Freya turned to him. "How much is this worth to you?"

Levan laughed. "Play your cards right and we can come to a suitable agreement."

She smiled at Bianca. "Levan was a charming child. Even then a lot of girls were besotted by him, but he ignored them all, of course."

"See, I was always waiting for you," Levan said, kissing Bianca on the tip of her nose.

"What about Maxim?" Aldie asked.

Freya didn't even bother looking at me. "Um ... I didn't know him very well then."

"You were closer to Maxim than you were to me, Freya," Levan pointed out, a golden smile on his face.

"Actually, I was not!" she said heatedly.

Levan was just trying to bait her given what he suspected of our relationship recently, and I couldn't fault him. I was thoroughly entertained.

"Does uh anyone want to dance?" Britney asked.

"I'll dance," Freya said, and Aldie drained her glass. "What the hell? I'll come too."

"I'll accompany the ladies," Tom said, and got up to go with them. Just before he left however, Levan warned him, "You better not hit on the wrong woman if you don't want your head on a platter by the end of the night."

Tom looked confused and then turned to me. "Who is the wrong woman?"

I sipped quietly on my scotch.

"You'll find out..." Levan said, "when your head is off your neck."

He left the room and Bianca looked between the both of us. "Am I missing something?"

"Maxim here is in a passionate relationship with Freya," he said.

Her eyes almost popped out of their sockets in shock as she ran her gaze between me and her husband. "Levan, I'm going to smash your head into this table," I said.

She hit him on the shoulder. "Why didn't you tell me? So it

means that when I called earlier this morning and Freya was... because I swear she sounded like..."

"Yup," he said. "He was probably in the sack with her."

"I need some air," I said rising to my feet.

"She's loosening you up, man," Levan called out after me. "And I like it."

I didn't disagree. I liked it too.

Chapter Seventy-Two

FREYA

I danced with Britney and Aldie, but couldn't help sneaking peeks at the cube above the dance floor. Suddenly, I realized he wasn't even sitting there anymore and felt silly for being so obsessed with him. I let out my pent-up anxiety and tried my best to have fun with the girls. Britney came close to me as she danced.

"Do you think I have a shot?" she asked over the loud music, and gyrating bodies around us.

"What?"

"A shot!" she yelled into my ear. "With Tom."

I stared at her with surprise. "Uh... I don't see why not. He looked pretty interested."

"He smells fucking amazing. I swear I couldn't breathe properly when he was next to me."

"You know he is the lawyer for a criminal family, though," I reminded her.

She laughed. "I think I can handle it. There's nothing a smoking hot guy with great dick moves can't resolve, right?"

"Oh, there's Maxim," she suddenly called out.

My heart jumped in my chest. I turned at her nudge and saw him with the manager who had taken our order earlier. They were standing on the top floor and over the railing. The manager was gesticulating with his hands to emphasize whatever he was saying, and Maxim looked around while he listened, until his gaze collided with mine.

I instantly turned away.

"He just looked at you," Britney squealed.

My phone began to vibrate then. I pulled it out of my pocket. It was Bianca.

"Food is here," she said.

"Be right there," I told her and informed the girls. Aldie managed to pull away from the man she was dancing with, and we were on our way. Tom had received a call on our way down, and stepped away to receive it before we'd gotten to the dance floor so I didn't know where he was.

We returned to the room to find Levan's hand quite high up Bianca's skirt. He didn't want to pull away when we arrived, so she smacked him away.

I knew whose hand I wanted that high up my thigh, but he was nowhere to be found. This I told myself was how it would be. Outside the bedroom we were nothing more, but as I watched Levan unable to take his eyes from Bianca, I became more and more sad and even envious of their love and passion. We dove into the food, and soon Tom returned and joined us. He made a point of sitting next to Britney, which made me wink at her.

I was happy for her, but I needed a breather from it all, so I excused myself.

"There's a private bathroom just down the hall. Go past the mural and take a right," Levan said to me. The code is 3768."

"3768," I repeated, and went out.

I stepped out of the box and began to head down the hallway in search of the mural. I found it easily enough, but just as I turned to the right... I saw Maxim. The manager was speaking to him along with two other men in suits.

At first, he didn't notice me, but then he lifted his head and saw me. His gaze lingered on me, but I quickly escaped and headed over to the bathroom.

My cheeks felt overheated. I wanted to pat some water on them, but I was worried that would ruin my makeup. So I just washed my hands, fixed my hair and exited the room.

And almost passed him, if not for the fact that all the hairs on my body tingled with a familiar awareness. I stopped in my tracks and turned to my left. He was leaning against the wall, his arms folded across his chest and just looking at me. I felt my knees go weak.

His eyes ran down my body, a knowing smile on his face, and it reminded me of what he had done to me that afternoon. I couldn't help the heat that ran up my cheeks.

"I didn't know you were going to be here," I said.

"If you did, you wouldn't have come?" he shot back.

I straightened my shoulders and flipped my hair back airily. "Don't be so big-headed. Bianca invited me and I had no reason to refuse." I paused and raised an eyebrow. "Would you rather I wasn't here?"

"I'd rather you were on top of me," he said.

The pang of arousal in my belly was real. I turned away, but he stepped forward and caught my hand, and drew me towards him.

I accepted the fact I had no will anymore when it came to him. Then he slipped his hands around my waist, and held me tightly to him, his face in my neck, and his nose breathing in my scent.

I didn't move. I couldn't and I never wanted to. It stunned me how such a simple, intimate touch, could mean so much. To the rest of the world he was so strong and impenetrable, but right now it felt as though he were in the palm of my hands.

I drew back to look up at him. I felt as if I was drowning in his eyes. The way he looked at me terrified me. There was so much intensity in his gaze. My hand moved to the side of his face.

If, or more like when, our relationship ended there was no doubt it would haunt me for a very long time, maybe even forever.

I stood on the tips of my toes to kiss him, and my heart felt as if it was close to bursting with emotion. The kiss was soft and sweet until he deepened it.

My legs left the ground as his hands went around my ass to lift me up against him. I giggled when he turned around to place my back against the wall. I was thankful for the billowing dress I was wearing because it made it easy for me to wrap my legs around his waist.

"Do you know I've always loved your hair?" he asked. "It was the first thing I noticed about you."

I began to grind my sex against his hardness.

"The first thing I noticed about you was how beautiful but cold your eyes were," I told him. "They don't seem cold anymore, though."

"That's because I'm looking at you," he said.

I felt my heart stop. For the longest time, we just looked at each other and it seemed as if we were in a world of our own. A beautiful world where there was only him and me. Then I realized we had company. I whirled my head around and found Britney was staring at us, completely astounded.

"Uh... I-I'm sorry," she stuttered. "I was told the bathroom is this way."

Maxim put me down gently.

"It is," I smiled at her. "Come on, I was just about to go too."

Maxim to my surprise, placed a kiss to my cheek, and left me staring dazed after him as he took his leave.

Britney approached me carefully, as though she didn't recognize me and then we went into the bathroom together.

We used the stalls then washed our hands under the faucets. I looked at Britney in the mirror and she looked at me curiously. "I thought you said it was purely sexual."

"It is," I said.

She looked at me incredulously. "You didn't see the way he was looking at you? I know you don't have much experience, but let me tell you that man is completely and utterly enamored with you, Freya."

Chapter Seventy-Three

MAXIM

"I'm going to Spain in the morning. Meeting with my father. I'll be back Sunday evening. Will you have time for me?"

Her reply was almost instant.

I will indeed.

I couldn't help the smile that spread across my face. Having Freya in my life had done something to me I never thought would happen. I felt lighter in her arms, more excited about things around me, more hopeful. It only served to affirm my earlier prediction that if we had married things would have been good between us.

I put the phone away, and that was when I noticed the old Holden Calias Sedan. It had been parked at a corner close to the bar. What had drawn my attention to it was a girl using their window as a mirror, but she jumped and moved away after a few seconds when she must have suddenly noticed the passengers sitting quietly inside it.

A man got out and started walking quickly up to me. Immediately Viktor placed himself in front of me, but I knew from the man's expression he was not there to hurt me. He was a messenger.

"It's all right," I said to Viktor.

As he moved the man thrust an envelope into my hand and walked away without saying anything. I tore it open and there were pictures of Freya. Working at the bar, walking on the street, at her window with a towel around her head, arriving at my home wearing a pizza delivery man cap. There were hundreds of pictures and there was no part of her life that had not been captured.

I could feel my hands start to shake with fury. My phone rang and I picked it up and said nothing.

"Right this minute your girl is wearing a rather fetching navy-blue dressing gown, drinking tea, and working furiously at her desk. She has big, ambitious plans for her design company, poor thing doesn't know there is a sniper in an apartment across from her. One word from me and her brains will be splattered all over her designs. All her young dreams will be gone. It would be a pity because as you know, it's not her I want."

"What do you want?"

"I thought you'd never ask. I want you to tell your team to stand down. Then I want you to drive to the carpark of your building. My men will meet you there. If you would be good enough to go with them it will make things much easier."

Roman had just pulled up to the curb. He got out of the driver's seat and hurried over to pull the passenger door open, but I stopped him and held out my hand for the keys.

"Dismantle the surveillance on me and don't follow me," I said harshly.

"What?" he muttered.

"You heard me. You and Viktor get to Freya's apartment immediately and take her to a safe house." Then I got into the driver's seat, and drove away. The Holden Calias Sedan followed me from a safe distance.

I headed straight to my apartment complex and pulled into my parking spot. There was a gun in the car. I got it ready and looked at the ring I had been given on my eighteenth birthday. There was not a day it hadn't been on my little finger since then. Then I got out of the car and waited for them to make their move. Soon enough, I would know exactly whom had been pursuing me for the last few months.

There were three of them. They had their guns pointed at me. They had masks covering their faces, but that was probably because of the cameras.

"Lose your gun!" One of them roared, and I instantly stilled, but I knew that their goal was not to just kill me. They wanted to take me with them.

I moved my hand to the back of my pants.

"There are three guns pointed at your head and heart right now," one of the men warned. "If you even blink the wrong way, you will be dead. Throw the gun away, over there!"

I took a deep breath and did as I was asked.

"Tie him," one of them ordered, and another moved forward with a plastic tie in his hand.

"Don't even think of trying anything funny. Your men are

racing to your girl, aren't they? But they will be too late if we get any trouble from you."

The man bent forward, secured the tie around my wrists. I saw his yellow teeth through the face cover just before he raised his fist. He was a gigantic man, just about a head shorter than me but disturbingly thicker, so I wasn't surprised at the power that the punch packed.

The impact of his fist driving into my jaw made me stagger away. As I tried to recover from the agonizing blow, I heard his roar. I looked up, and saw the knife slicing through the air.

Chapter Seventy-Four

MAXIM

xcruciating pain woke me up. It felt like my shoulder was on fire. I tried to touch the wound, but I couldn't move my hands. I realized I was still tied up.

Through the haze of pain, I blinked and looked around. I had been tied to a chair in a room that stank of rust, oil, and a foul stench of death. I turned to the throbbing wound and found darkened blood. My body felt weak, incredibly so, and sweat beaded my skin all over. I had to get out of here.

Through the small, barred window in front of me I could see that the sun was now high in the sky, which meant I had been held for about six or seven hours. In that time, I had been stabbed, beaten close to death, and still not been told why. I wondered why Levan had not found me yet. Then I looked at my ring and saw why.

My ring was gone. I also noted my watch was gone, which hopefully meant they didn't realize the significance of the ring. I looked desperately around the room for it. It didn't have to be on me but it had to be at this location otherwise they would never be able to use the tracker inside of it to find me. For the first time since I had been taken, I panicked.

"Where's my ring and watch?" I demanded to the camera watching. My voice was gruff from the torture.

I heard voices and footsteps approaching. The door was banged open and in walked the three men, who had long discarded their masks. They didn't care if I could see their faces any more because I wouldn't be walking out of here alive.

Otherwise I would come for them.

Nevertheless, I committed them all to memory. Life had a funny way of throwing you a line when you least expected it.

None of them however, I was certain, was the boss.

The bald one with the beaky face laughed aloud. "He's awake!" He raised his hand in the air for a salute and stomped his feet on the dirt blackened floor in a parody of respect. *"The almighty Ivanov."*

"Almighty my ass," the skinny one, who was almost certainly Albanian, piped up.

"If by some sick luck he gets out of here alive, I hope you understand that you'll be running from him for the rest of your lives," the only Russian among the trio said. I could feel the fear in his voice even though he tried to hide it.

"Well he's not getting out—"

The door was pulled open suddenly, and all three men quickly arranged themselves. Whoever had come into the room was obviously the boss. I turned to finally see who it was.

It was indeed Boris Arakas, just as Levan had suspected.

He was a short, bulky man with the face of a bulldog. In his eyes was a bitterness I could almost taste. The other men quickly and quietly moved to the edges of the room, while he dragged a chair and sat across from me.

He watched me for the longest time before his ugly face split into a smile. From a simple smile, it grew to a full out grin, until he could no longer contain himself and he broke into uproarious laughter. When he was done, he rose to his feet, his hand on the chair, and with a deafening roar of rage swung it at me.

I shut my eyes as I awaited the impact. The metal chair smashed against my head and threw me to the ground. The pain was soul splitting.

Everything around me began to darken, but before I could catch my breath he rained me with kicks. His heavy boots slamming into my body while he cursed me.

"You. Fucking. Bastard. You've. Ruined. My. Life. Every. Fucking. Thing. Around me."

He stopped to catch his breath, and I shut my eyes to contain the strength I still had in me. With a cry of rage he rolled me over on the floor so I was flat on my back and then slammed his feet into my wound.

I roared out at the pain, and prayed to God that Levan was on the way.

Then he calmly picked the chair back up and then sat on it in front of me. "Do you know me?" he asked.

I was so close to passing out even the sound of his words

were becoming faint to me, but I could still grasp some of what he was saying. I knew if I blacked out, I would truly be finished, so I held on as long as I could.

It was just as Levan had discovered. It was revenge for the death of his brother and the way his life had fallen apart after that. I had destroyed him and now he wanted to return the favor.

However, he had his demands.

He grabbed my shirt and pulled at me until I was almost sitting up. My head was drooping low from the torture and exhaustion. With one hand around my neck, he held me up till I was at face level with him.

"Open your eyes," he ordered.

I managed to do so because I wanted to remember him. To commit every feature of his to memory.

"Marlow! Marlow!"

The Albanian stepped forward.

"Bring the gas!"

My breathing quickened.

A red can was brought in, and through the blood dripping down my eyes, I watched him uncap it. He brought the red can to my nose, and forced me to inhale.

"Do you smell this?" He cackled like a demented man. "I am going to fucking burn you alive."

He began to squirt the gasoline all over me, even into my mouth. He raised it over my head, and I was doused with it until I was drenched from head to toe. I heard laughter both in the distance and in my ears.

Afterwards he threw the empty can aside and asked for a cigarette.

I spat out the gas that had gotten into my mouth, and tried to open my eyes, but the mixture of blood and gasoline as it dripped down my face and into my open wound, stung with unimaginable pain. I wasn't certain how long I'd be able to hold much longer. I felt myself hanging on by a thread.

I watched as with a wicked laugh he lit the cigarette in his mouth. He took a long puff and then came forward to blow it into my face.

"How does it feel?" he asked. "Being so close to your end? You don't deserve to live Maxim... the things you've done... so ruthlessly, so selfishly."

"To save your brother you kill another's, to fill your pockets, you empty another's?"

He inhaled deeply again.

"You have behaved like a monster, but I just might spare you," he said, "after all every man deserves another chance. Do you think you deserve another chance, Maxim?"

I found I didn't want to nod. I didn't want to give him the satisfaction.

He frowned with irritation. He had expected me to beg him for another chance. He pulled out his phone from his pocket.

"This is what you're going to do," he said. "You're going to dial your brother, and you're going to tell him to admit to every crime your family has ever committed. The murders, the thefts, the bribery, the fraud. Everything. Within three days. I want it all in writing. That is the only way, that I'll let you go."

He held out the phone to me "Are you ready to speak to him?"

I looked him in the eye, and managed a crooked smile. If he asked, no doubt Levan would do whatever was required to save my life. Even to the extent of harming himself and the conglomerate we had given our whole lives to. But after all that I would still not be spared. Because they all knew I would not coexist in the same world with someone who debased me to this extent. I had no interest in life if that was the cost.

At that moment I knew my time in this world was nearly over. I refused to go out cowering like a dog. I evoked the spit from the base of my throat and shot it at his face. It splattered against his eyes and he shut his lids and jerked away.

"You must be out of your mind," I muttered. "Since the day I was born, I've been at the top of Death's list. You must... indeed be a great... fool to think that threatening... to kill me would have any effect on me. Go ahead. Set me on fire. Right *now*."

I shut my eyes, and dropped my head, resigned to my fate ... and all I could see was her. She was the only regret I had. The only thing that made me want to save myself by any means necessary, even if I had to grovel.

For the chance of one last glimpse of her... to look into her eyes, to taste her lips, and to sheathe myself in her bliss. She was the heaven I'd been granted in the midst of the hell on earth.

I smiled.

I had truly been blessed... to know her for a period, to own her heart and body, for the period I did. I wondered if after I was gone, if she would realize her feelings for me? I sighed and allowed the tears to pool in my eyes, but never to fall.

Never.

Boris rose from his chair, and once again picked it up. With a jarring shout, he swung it into the air and I was once again flung to the ground, broken and battered beyond belief.

"Alright," he said. "It seems that you need greater incentive. Since you don't value your life, then let's go for the next best thing. Fedorov's daughter. Did you really think you could save her?"

My heart slammed into my chest.

He laughed. "Do you really think your men got to her in time?"

I stared at him in horror.

"Yes, that's right. I have her." He was gloating. Finally, he had me. "What if I bring her here and set her on fire, right in front of you? No, I'll fuck the bitch first. In the ass. While you watch. She has a good ass on her." He grabbed his crotch and moaned aloud.

It made me sick to my stomach.

"And if that's not enough motivation for you to speak, then

we can put her on a grill, start burning off parts of her while you watch."

He turned to his men. "Keep him here until I get the girl."

With those chilling words he stormed out of the room. My mind was blank with shock. I could not even begin to...There was absolutely no way... Not that animal... Not Freya... Nooooo... Oh God... Please...

Chapter Seventy-Five

FREYA

I was concentrating on a design and totally lost to the world when the doorbell rang. I knew Britney was expecting some samples so I quickly went to the door. Sure enough a man in a UPS uniform was standing outside holding a package. I quickly opened the door, but something made the hair on my body stand to attention.

I recognized the alarm from years of ingrained caution from being around my father's circles. He handed me the package. On the top was a photo of Maxim, he was lying on a concrete floor with a knife sticking out of his prone body. My mouth dropped open in shock. I couldn't move. I couldn't think. I just stared stupidly at the photo in my hand.

"No, he's not dead. At least not yet," the man said.

I nearly fainted with relief. My knees went and I landed in a heap at my doorstep.

"But he will be if... you do not come with me willingly."

As soon as I heard the words strength poured back into my body. I rose up and said. "Let's go."

"Do you often go out in your dressing gown?" he mocked.

I looked down. For a second I felt a confused, then I threw it off me. Underneath I had a little T-shirt and leggings. I pulled a coat from the coat rack and turned to him. "I'm ready."

"You're going to walk out of this building as if nothing is wrong. Anybody watching you will think you are going out to the shops to get a pint of milk. You will see a woman wearing a blue coat when you get out. Follow her. When you see a dirty white van on the curb around the block on the way to the convenience store you will get in quietly. If you even look to your left or right, or try to call for help at anytime, your man will die. Look normal. If you trigger suspicion in your security detail and they start to follow you he will die. If you try something clever, he will die. If you try to pass a message on to someone he will die. Basically, his life depends on your good behavior. Do you understand me?"

I nodded quickly.

"Good. Start walking."

Blankly, I began to walk. Down the stairs I went like a zombie. He followed behind. As if he had nothing to do with me. When I got on the street outside, he turned and went in the opposite direction of the woman in the blue coat. The woman never looked at me. I began to follow her. All I could see in my head was the image of Maxim on the ground. A knife in him. The knife quite close to where I had shot him.

Around the block I saw the white van parked by the curb half hidden behind a news kiosk. The side door was half-open and once I disappeared into it, it would drive off and my security detail would not know until they realized I did not appear from behind the kiosk. That would give the driver of the van precious time to get away.

In the side mirror I could see the reflection of a man on the passenger seat, I imagined there must be at least one man at the back, and of course, there must be a driver. Just seeing the van snapped me out of my zombie-like state.

My heart began to pound furiously in my chest.

I realized that if I got into that van and went with them, Maxim was a dead man. If they wanted to kill him they already would have done so. They *needed* me to go with them. I knew Maxim was as tough as they come, but the only reason he was still alive was because whatever they wanted him to do for them, he had not yet done. The thought came to me crystal clear. *They were going to use me as leverage to get him to do something.*

I slowed my pace as I tried to formulate a plan in my head. My hands were shaking, but I forced myself to calm down. This was not the time to be paralyzed with fear.

The side door of the van opened all the way and a man with black hair looked out of it. Our eyes met. "Hurry up," he urged harshly.

I was only a few feet away from him. A thought circled in my mind and it was dangerous, extremely so. It could cost me my life and Maxim's if I calculated wrong. The other option was letting myself get captured and become their leverage over Maxim. Right now, I had some advantage. I was still free on a busy street and in sight of my security detail. The man must have seen the hesitation in my face, because he said urgently. "Come on."

I dropped to my knees and simply, but very loudly, began to bawl.

My voice was loud and piercing, my words indecipherable. It was enough to confuse and get the attention of anyone within a mile from where I was. The man panicked and rushed over to try to pull me up forcibly. Whoever he worked for hadn't told him to be careful of me. That I was Igor Fedorov's daughter and was taught to fight since I could stand.

The moment his hand closed around my arm, I had him.

Immediately, I struck his neck, right on the Adam's apple, and it instantly had him howling. With one hand he held the source of his agony, but with the other he reached for his gun. A vicious kick to his gut and he was on the ground. He lost his grip on the gun and I dove for it.

I spun around on the floor and had it on him before he could even think about rising.

I glanced quickly at the door to see that his friends had gotten down from the van and were advancing. From the other direction my father's or Maxim's security detail were running towards me.

As if on cue, the sound of sirens blared in the distance. I saw the terror and panic in his eyes. "Fuck," he cursed. "You fucking bitch!" He scrambled upright and stumbled towards his friends and in seconds they had zoomed away.

Even before my security team reached me I had pulled the phone out of my pocket and dialed Levan's number.

It was picked up even before the first ring was over.

"Freya, I was just about to call you. Are you alright?"

"Levan? What's going on. Where's Maxim? Is he alright?"

The silence that followed almost knocked out my knees.

"Levan, what's going on?"

"Get into the SUV. I'll be waiting for you."

Chapter Seventy-Six

FREYA

I remained in terrified silence until we arrived at an old warehouse. I jumped out and was escorted through the cavernous space to an office. It had about ten members of their security team in it. Levan stood when I came in.

"What's going on?" I asked Levan, my heart in my throat. I tried my very hardest to keep my composure, but I was a nervous wreck. All I wanted to know was that he was alive.

"Maxim's missing," he said.

Obviously he did not know more than me. "I know. I saw a picture of him. He was lying on a concrete floor with a knife in him, but he was still alive... then."

"What?" Levan gasped, shocked.

"They wanted me to go with them. They said he would be killed if I didn't go, but I knew they were only keeping him alive to get me to go with them. They needed me."

Levan fell heavily into his chair and shook his head. "I don't understand it. We had a clear plan. We had everything in place. Why did he tell his men to stand down and deliberately leave himself vulnerable to his captors?"

"For the same reason I was almost going to go with them," I whispered. My knees began to wobble, but I couldn't even think of sitting down. "So what do we do now?"

He stared at me, with a frown on his face.

"Levan, what do we do?"

"I don't know. Maxim has a ring with a GPS tracker on it."

I knew the exact ring he was talking about. "The one with an anchor a cross and a heart that he wears on his little finger?"

"Yes, that one."

"Well?" I tried to control my tone before impatience got the better of me.

"There's a problem. It shows its location as a hostel down in Harlem. We've sent our people, but he's not being held there. The ring and his watch were inside a mattress on the fourth floor."

"They were stolen?"

"More likely taken off him after he was captured. So we put it back and left. What we need now is to find the owner of that bed. No doubt he won't leave things as precious as that there for too long. The moment he comes back for it, we will be able to capture him and make him lead us to Maxim. He is probably one of the hands that was hired to capture him."

"What? So we just wait like sitting ducks?" I asked desperately.

"That's all we can do," Levan replied heavily.

I could feel my heart begin to sink.

Levan stood and began to pace the floor. "They probably wanted to use you to blackmail him."

"To do what?"

"He's probably been tortured, severely, but he has refused to do whatever they wanted so they came for you."

I got up then, unable to contain my frustration. "Levan, what are you talking about? What do they want from him?"

"We already suspect who is behind this," he said quietly, his face strangely hard. "If it is him then he would be looking for revenge or exoneration. With our influence we would be able to give him all the exoneration in the world he desires, but what good would that be to him if we will still have the power to hunt him down as soon as Maxim is free again?"

"That means..."

Levan's face was black with fury. "He wants us to destroy ourselves. With our own hands. And after that he will kill Maxim."

Someone burst into the office. He went to Levan's side and whispered in such low, but rapid Russian that I could pick out only three words.

Found him. Shop.

"The man has returned to the mattress to pick up his items," Levan explained to the room. "They have him captured now. I'll head over immediately and get him to talk."

I started to go with him but he turned and stopped me. "No, Freya. It'll get gruesome."

"That's not a pro—"

"No, Maxim wouldn't want that. It is better you remain here. The moment we find out where he is, I'll let you know."

Chapter Seventy-Seven

MAXIM

I was on the floor leaning against the wall to keep myself upright, keeping my hands hidden when he returned. Their mistake was letting the chair I was tied to break. Once I freed myself from the chair I was playing a completely different game. What these fools didn't know was plastic ties can easily be broken with a simple technique that a child can execute. A quick Google search would have told them.

Boris was so furious he almost took the door down. Two men followed him in. My mind automatically clocked the absence of the Albanian and wondered where he was.

"Ivanov," he roared, but when he spotted me he burst out into hysterical laughter. "Your woman is quite the soldier. Better than you. The idiots I hired couldn't get her."

For the first time since I got that phone call, I breathed easy, even though it now meant that his focus would solely be on me. I would probably be killed any moment now. It didn't matter much to me. As long as she was safe, and Levan kept her that way.

Boris grabbed the chair he had flung aside earlier and swung it at me. The impact seemed to knock the last bit of life out of me, but I knew enough to pretend my hands were still tied behind my back.

"Look at you," he jeered. "You're no better than a disease infested, dirty little rat living in a sewer. I should just fucking *end* you right now!"

As I fought to recover, he stood watching me, his chest heaving in frustration that Freya had thwarted his best laid plans.

"Well, looks like I'll have to work with just you then," he said. "There's pain and there's pain. At a certain point every man breaks and if he doesn't those that love him will. I'm going to start burning up parts of you. We'll start with your legs, and then when that is crisp, we'll put the fire out, and send the video to your brother. I'll use that to start the negotiation."

"Marlow," he roared again. "Get an extinguisher and a fucking lighter. The rest of you get in here and secure him back to the chair. And someone bring a fucking phone."

There was a flurry of activity, two of the men ran out to do his bidding. I was left with just him and I understood that it was either now or never. My only hope was I would have enough strength to completely decimate him. He looked thick and healthy, but I had desperation on my side. I had one chance and only one. I raised my head and looked him in the eye.

He lit a cigarette and took a long draw. "One of the things I hate the most about you is the way you look at people, like right now. As though they are all beneath you. Your life is literally in the palm of my hands and yet you would rather die than to plead with me. I am so going to enjoy killing you."

It was now or never. I had already loosened my gasoline soaked pants, I kicked them off me as far away as possible. Then I threw away my shirt and began to rise in my under-pants, slowly. I saw the expression in his eyes change.

With my face twisted, and my mouth open and screaming like a mad man, I ran towards him, but before I could ram into his bulk, the sound of a gun exploding shook the walls of the room.

I couldn't stop my momentum and I slammed into him. The pain was indescribable. We tumbled to the floor.

His laugh was bitter and full of disbelief. "You managed to set yourself free," he said, "and found a way to guide your brother here, but it won't be enough."

I heard the shouts from beyond. Levan. My heart came alive with hope. But before I could start to breathe easy again, Boris's hands circled around my neck. I looked into his eyes.

"This is how you die," he growled.

With all my strength, I tried to tear his hands from my throat, but he was like a man possessed. He was smiling. This was what he had dreamed of for such a long time. I could barely see, my eyes hazy with a raging fever, and a deathly exhaustion was starting to take over. The edges were begin-ning to go black. Then his hands were gone. My head dropped to the ground as I choked and coughed and took great gasping breaths of air.

"You're not going to make it out of here, and I am not going to strangle you. That's too much mercy for you."

He scrambled up and retrieved the can of gasoline from the corner and began to pour it across the ground from where I stood.

"You will be burned like an animal!" he swore to me. "That's the fate you deserve."

When he had emptied the can, he brought out the lighter from his pocket. He lit it and my heart lurched into my throat. He threw the flaming lighter forward and the room went up in flames.

With a howl of delight he ran out and I watched the flames begin to engulf the room. This would be the end unless I found a way to get out. The fire was growing and coming towards me, trapping me

Then I heard Levan call out my name.

"Maxim!" he roared, and I answered back at the top of my lungs.

"Levan! Levan!"

I needed to leave... right this moment even if it meant being set on fire otherwise no one would be able to get to me. I took a deep breath and aimed for the corner that was the only place that was not burning. I counted to three and was about to move, but fear stopped me. My body was too weak. I could barely even stand up straight. I would be too slow, and the flames would engulf me in seconds.

"Levan!" I howled.

And just like an answered prayer, he appeared.

He ran into the room but the flames were too high, and he immediately jumped right back.

"Extinguisher!" he shouted and disappeared once again.

The smoke began to get into my system and the heat began to char at my skin. I crouched down into a protective position but I knew I was only mere seconds away from being burnt to a crisp. I tried to contain the coughing, but the smoke itself felt as though it was seeping into my very bones.

I could feel the fire start to lick at my skin when Levan blasted the extinguisher and it killed the fire in the section where I stood.

"Come out!" he yelled, but the ground was too hot.

"Maxim, come out!" he yelled and continued to blast the extinguisher to make a path for me, but I couldn't move. He threw the fire extinguisher aside and came to me. Hauling me up, he dragged me out of the door.

"Come on," Levan ordered with a shout at his men. "The whole place is going to go up in flames soon."

"Freya..." I managed to croak out.

"She's fine," he reassured me.

With one of my arms around his shoulder and the other around Viktor's we moved along. Everything passed by excruciatingly slowly and then.... so rapidly I experienced it in flashes. One moment I was struggling to walk and near collapse from the pain, and in the next I was being carried on a gurney into the hospital. I was in a corridor. Moving fast. I saw the light overhead, bright and so beautiful. I kept drifting in and out of consciousness, the damage to my body no longer bearable.

Levan remained by my side, but after a while there was only very little that I could register.

"Boris..." I muttered. "Don't kill him. I'll handle him myself." I was going to finish him off just the way he had planned to do to me. Burn every single part of him to a crisp over an extended period of time. He was going to look for death and not see it.

"He's dead," Levan said harshly.

And I finally shut my eyes and let the blackness descend.

Chapter Seventy-Eight

FREYA

https://www.youtube.com/watch?v=ljoXD1NFa1I

L evan, Bianca, and I were seated in the hallway of
Maxim's hospital room, awaiting the moment when
he would finally awake. It had been two days now,
and his eyes remained shut.

They were speaking in low tones to each other and I felt
alone and afraid. My nails were bitten to the quick, and my
legs tapped nervously on the ground. Just thinking of all he
had endured made me feel lost and sad. Stab wound, broken
ribs, countless bruises, third degree burns on his hands and
feet, the more serious problem of a concussion.

What saddened me even further was that I had, so far, only
been able to see him a handful of times and only with Levan's
presence in the room. As if he didn't trust me with his
brother. As if he blamed me for what had happened to
Maxim.

I felt as if I couldn't take it anymore. I needed to be by his side, to watch even the rise and fall of his chest as he breathed, and to listen to the beating of his heart. To soothe his hand with my touch until he came awake. I knew I could will him awake.

I rose to my feet. "Levan, I'm going to sit with Maxim for a little while," I announced, but before I could get to his door, two of his guards stepped in front of me and blocked my path. I turned around to look at Levan's stern gaze, and Bianca's face, guilty and apologetic. She knew if it was Levan in there she would be in there with him.

"You don't have to," he said. "He's healing, let him be."

I was not going to back down. "I'm not going to disturb him. I just want to be by his side."

He sighed and came over to me. "Freya, the last thing I want is to be rude to you, but I think its best you keep your distance from him for now."

"Says who? You? I'm his woman and I deserve the right to be with him just as Bianca would have the right to be with you if you were lying in there hurt."

I'd never said the words out loud before, but I couldn't deny the warmth that they filled me with. I was *his woman*. And no one could take that away from me.

Even Levan was a bit taken aback, that I had finally spelt it out. Still, he pressed on.

"I don't think that you're good for him."

"That's not your call to make."

"My father could come by at any moment."

I looked him in the eye. "I'll step away when he does."

He sighed at the determination in my eyes. I was going to go in no matter what he said unless they carried me out themselves. He nodded to the two men blocking my entrance, and they stepped away. I walked into the room, shut the door behind me and walked quietly towards Maxim. I could feel the sob forming in my throat.

Only a few days ago he had looked so virile and indestructible, now he looked so pale and unwell.

His feet were wrapped in bandages as well as various parts of his arms and chest. Thankfully, he only had a few cuts on his face which had been stitched up, but everywhere I looked some part of his flesh was purple with bruises.

He had been hurt way too badly and it made my very soul ache. I sat on the chair by his side, and the tears began to roll silently down my cheeks.

I wanted to touch him, but there was hardly any place that did not look sore and hurting. I was worried that it might cause him some sort of discomfort. Eventually, I rested my head on the edge of his bed and softy laid my hand on top of his.

I thought of all the times we had spent with each other thus far, the arguments, the misunderstandings, the fights, all the bad blood, the twisted history, and in the end here we were. None of that mattered any longer. He was my heart. The reason I woke in the morning. The reason I breathed. I never wanted to let him go. I wanted Maxim ferociously. I wanted to care for him... bear his children. Grow old with him.

I wiped the tears from my face and wondered at the force of

my emotion for him. How and when had he snuck his way this deeply into my heart? I could have sworn that I had been on guard.

Suddenly, I felt a slight movement on my palm and almost jumped out of my skin. I realized that it could have been Maxim just stirring, but with hope bursting out of my chest, I lifted my head to study him. My heart nearly fell out of my chest as I breathlessly watched his eyelids flutter and open.

He looked at me and I remained stuck and frozen in position.

And then he opened his mouth to speak. His tone was low and weak, but I watched his lips and heard every word.

"Why are you crying?" he asked.

I quickly shook my head. "I'm not crying," I sobbed. "I'm really not."

"I don't want to see you cry," he murmured, and stretched his hand towards me.

Instantly, I leaned into his touch and his bandaged hand wiped the moisture from my cheek.

I shut my eyes and basked in the pure bliss of his touch and presence, and then I lifted my gaze to stare into his eyes.

"Thanks for being here," he said, and all I could do was smile.

"I will be fine," he said and I nodded heartily in response.

"You don't have a choice," I said. "You have to recover and quickly, so I can beat you up for being so reckless."

He smiled. "I love you, Freya Federov. My one regret while they were torturing my body was I didn't tell you that."

I began to howl with happiness. At the sound Levan and his guards rushed in.

"Get out," Maxim said, his voice stronger than it had been.

Levan had tears of joy in his eyes as he ushered his men out.

"Maybe you don't love me yet, but you will. I'll make you fall in love with me if it's the last thing I do."

I leaned down and kissed his mouth. Our kiss tasted strange, of the chemicals they had given him, but I didn't care. When I raised my head, I looked deeply into his eyes. "I'm so in love with you, I thought I would die when I saw that photo of you on the ground with a knife in your body."

He grinned. "Was that all it took? If you had told me earlier I would have stuck a knife in myself."

"That's not funny, Maxim," I complained. "You don't know what it's like to love someone the way I love you."

"Are you trying to pretend you love me more than I love you?"

"Are you trying to start a fight?"

He started to laugh and then had to stop for the pain. He looked into my eyes. "Can you just be a bit clingy for once?"

"You want me to be clingy?" I asked incredulously

"I like clingy from you."

I smiled. "You have no idea what you just signed up for."

"I know exactly what I've signed up for and I can't wait to start my life with you, my darling heart."

"Neither can I, Maxim Ivankov. Neither can I."

EPILOGUE

Six Weeks Later
Freya

I was looking for Maxim.

The store was a flurry of activity and excitement, but more than half an hour had passed since he said he would be here. I knew he had a meeting afterwards, but he had promised to make the time to stop by for my store's launch. Maybe he got held up. Never mind, I told myself. It was not important. There will be many other launches we will celebrate together.

A waiter passed by with a tray of champagne and without thinking I reached for a flute, needing the refreshment, but then I remembered, and drew my hand away. As I turned away I saw him.

He was seated at the welding station. His hand was

outstretched and Jeremy, one of our interns, was attempting to weld a chain bracelet around his wrist. It was a design I made and excitedly showed to him a week earlier.

Maxim had his hawk-like gaze on my newbie and I saw the terror on his face, and that was already more than enough to unsettle him. There were two guards in suits looming in the background, which did nothing to alleviate his fear. I saw his hand shake, and immediately hurried over to rescue him.

"I'll do it, Jeremy," I said, and he jumped to his feet gratefully and handed the machine over to me. I sat on the stool before my heart.

"I thought you couldn't make it," I said.

A gentle smile curved his lips. How I loved that my presence could do that to him, instantly brighten him up and put him in a better mood.

"I canceled my meetings for the rest of the evening," he said. "It's your big day. I want to be here through it all in case you need me."

His words struck my heart, and I watched him, tears filling my eyes, especially in the light of what I knew.

"Hey," he called and reached forward to catch the tear with his thumb before it ran down my face. "Hey, are you alright?"

I leaned my face into his palm, and reveled in the warmth of his touch. "I'm fine," I said and sniffed my emotions away. "I'm just happy and overwhelmed. I'm finally opening my own store. It's not been easy at all."

"I know," he said. "You've worked so hard. I adore you for that."

I laughed at his generous compliment. "You're one to talk Mr. Workaholic."

"I've slowed down greatly since you've come into my life. You have to acknowledge that."

"I do,' I said, and leaned forward and captured his lips for a quick kiss.

But he wrapped his hand around my neck and lengthened the kiss. Holding me in place he claimed me, our tongues dancing as I savored his oh so familiar and especially intoxicating taste. The whole world faded away and I almost fell from the chair.

Laughing softly he caught me and set me upright. My eyes opened wide in a daze. Sometimes I still couldn't believe that this man was mine. Suddenly I was aware of the people milling around me so I broke his gaze and focused my attention on welding the solid gold bracelet to his wrist. Just like mine, it was to remain on him until he intentionally broke it off. I gazed at it and wondered if it would last until the day he died.

"I want to go home," I said and rose to my feet.

He did the same, and looked down worriedly at me. "Already? Your event is still on."

"It's winding down. The main itinerary for the evening has been handled. Britney can handle the rest. I don't feel very well," I said.

"Of course. I'll get Roman to bring the car around."

Maxim

*F*reya went upstairs as soon as we got back because she needed the bathroom. I pulled the tie off my neck and went ahead to pour myself a drink, but a better idea occurred to me. Perhaps if I opened a bottle of wine instead, she would join me. I hardly ever had wine but this was a worthy exception.

I walked into our bedroom, placed the bottle and glasses on the dresser, and I heard her coughing. I hurried to the bathroom to find her on her knees spilling her guts into the toilet bowl. She lifted her gaze to mine and she looked miserable.

All the color had drained from her face, and her eyes where reddened and strained. She had tied her hair back and out of the way, but a couple of stray strands were plastered to the perspiration on her forehead.

My heart lurched at the sight and I dropped down next to her.

"Freya," I called and pulled her towards me.

She quickly wiped the vomit that stained the corners of her lips.

"What's wrong?"

"I'm alright," she managed a weak smile. "I think I ate something bad earlier."

She began to head towards the sink so I supported her and held her hair as she rinsed her mouth. When she was done, she turned to me with a smile and gave me a quick hug.

"I'll go lie down for a little bit."

"Should I call the doctor?"

"No, I'm alright, it'll pass. I just want to lie down."

I helped tuck her into bed. She turned her face away from me and suddenly I knew exactly what was wrong with her.

"Do you want some wine?" I asked.

She waved her hand in response.

"Er ... no."

"Perhaps later?" I asked, one eyebrow cocked.

"Uh ..."

"I'll get you some food then. Craving anything in particular?"

"Uh ... maybe some steamed rice rolls." She turned to glance at me. "I think I can stomach that."

"Alright," I said and placed a kiss on her forehead. The moment I exited the room, I placed the order for the food, and then called Bianca.

It was a six-hour time difference to South Africa, but thankfully she picked up.

"Hey, Maxim," she responded. It was 3am there.

"Bianca," I said. "I'm sorry for the late call but I have to ask you something. What symptoms did you have when you got pregnant?"

Freya

"*H*ow far along are you?" he asked.

My heart stopped beating. For the longest time, I didn't move. I waited for him to say something else but when he didn't, I knew that my period of grace was up. I sat up, too afraid to meet his eyes.

"Uh ..." I breathed. "About six weeks."

The room went silent. And then he moved to sit next to me on the bed.

"Why is your head hanging?" he asked. "Why are you acting like you've committed a crime?"

I choked back tears. "I wasn't careful. I'm so sorry." I searched his gaze. "I was going to tell you. I was just waiting for the right time. I know it will change things, but I promise I will take care of everything."

"Do you have so little faith in me?" he asked.

I raised my head.

He shook his head. "So your conclusion is that I am not going be happy with the inconvenience of having a child, the baby I created with you?"

My brain felt scrambled. "You've never ..."

"Never what?" he asked, one eyebrow arching.

"You've never said anything about wanting..." I couldn't complete my statement. I didn't want to cry again, but the tears rolled down my face before I could stop them. "I'm sorry for crying, but it's the hormones I swear. I'm so freaking out of balance."

Maxim placed a leather box on the table.

I stilled and stared at it.

"Open it," he urged softly.

I reached for the box with shaky hands. Taking a deep breath I pulled it open. Inside was the most beautiful diamond ring I'd ever seen. It sparkled like mad. Slowly, I looked up to Maxim's waiting face.

"Marry me, Freya Federov."

I opened my mouth but no words would come out.

"Yes," I replied. "Yes, yes, yes, I will. With all of my heart."

"Now we will make both our fathers happy." He reached me then and pulled me into his arms. I held on tightly to him and never wanted to let go.

"I love you, Freya. I love you so much it fucking hurts when I think anything is wrong with you."

"I feel exactly the same way," I said, and pulled away to look into his eyes. "I can't believe you're finally mine."

"And I am over the moon that you are pregnant with my child. I can't wait to have a little red-headed Freya running around."

I laughed. "Funny, I was thinking I couldn't wait to have a little black-haired Maxim running around."

"Well, how about we have both. As far as I am concerned we can have as many as you want to have, but I draw the line at sixteen."

I laughed. "I want three."

"I can live with that."

Then he slipped the ring onto my finger and bending his head pressed his lips to mine. The kiss he gave to me was the sweetest and most soul stirring kiss I'd ever received from him.

EPILOGUE 2

Maxim
Three Months later
https://www.youtube.com/watch?v=rtOvBOTyXoo
-I have loved you for a thousand years-

It was a grand church, the walls were grey with centuries of holy smoke. These ancient walls had witnessed hundreds of thousands of ceremonies and rituals. And here was another for it.

I stood facing the altar. The designer had decorated it with swags of greenery, baby's breath and roses that had been flown in from France for their sweet scent.

Behind me the pews were full of pastel colored hats, dresses and suits. There was a buzz of excitement in the air. I turned slightly and looked at my father. His shoulders and his spine were straight. There was no smile on his face, but I knew he was proud of me.

This was his dream.

He nodded formally at me. I felt a pang of sadness that my mother was not there, but I told myself she would be watching from wherever she was. She was a good woman and chances were, she was in a good place.

My brother stood next to me. The day he and Bianca would leave for Africa for good was looming closer and closer. I was going to miss him like hell, but he had his dream to follow. The music changed. I was told not to turn around, to wait for my bride to arrive beside me, but I had never been one to follow custom.

I was not missing this for the world.

I took a deep breath and turned around and saw the little flower girls in their sweet pink dresses and wide white sash bows, strewing petals on the carpeted aisle. Then she appeared at the entrance of the Church.

Ahh ... something inside me melted. My woman was here.

In the white gown and long veil she looked other-worldly, like a nymph or a spirit of the forest. She must have been nervous because she was clutching the flowers entwined between her fingers so hard they trembled. Then she began to walk down the aisle, the light caught her tumbling curls and turned them into glowing fire.

I remembered again the girl hanging upside-down from the tree.

Yes, I wanted to marry her that day. It was my big goal. The goal I never told anyone. The reason no woman would ever do. I was always waiting for the green-eyed witch. No more. She would be mine soon. Forever. Inside her was everything I ever wanted. When I laid my head on her belly, I could already hear the sound of my children's feet, their laughter, the happy life that we would have.

Flanked by her father, she walked slowly, in time with the music. It was so beautiful. My mind made a record of the moment. It would live forever inside me. No matter how hard or difficult the times get I would remember this moment and know I was the luckiest bastard alive.

Tears of joy gathered in my eyes. I wasn't ashamed of them.

As she got closer I could see her white face. I felt as if my heart would burst with the love I felt for that woman.

The butcher was grinning from ear to ear. When he caught my eye he made the thumbs up sign. I was too choked up to respond. He gave his daughter to me and went to sit next to his eighteen-year-old Italian model girlfriend.

I lifted her veil. "I love you," I whispered.

She raised her hand and wiped away my tears. "This is not a competition, but I love you more."

I laughed through my tears. The priest cleared his throat. I guided her to our place in front of him. He droned on and I didn't hear a word. I was so happy. When I was prompted I turned to face my bride and said, the right words. All of them were mere inventions of man. None of those shallow words that could only describe the feelings of the unimaginative could adequately reflect how I felt about her. The passion I had for her. A promise I made all those years ago.

Then my brother was turning to me, handing me the ring I'd picked out for her. I took it from him and it felt cool against my fingers. That felt wrong. It should feel like fire. That is how our love was. From the very beginning. Pure fire.

I looked into her beautiful eyes and slipped my ring and mark of possession onto her slender white finger. "With this ring ... I thee wed."

The End

Curious about how Levan and Bianca got together?
Pre-order their hot and passionate story here.
With This Secret

COMING NEXT: SAMPLE PROLOGUE

Unedited

Bianca
(College Days)

Help, I am about to do something insane, I wrote to my best friend, Aldie.

While I waited for her response to come into our chat room, my eyes fluttering above to reread what I'd just typed. I tapped my fingers impatiently on the desktop and wondered why I was waiting for her response when I didn't really want her to talk me out of my intention.

Ten seconds later I'd had enough.

Exiting the chat room, I pulled up his contact on my phone. The crazy message I'd just painstakingly crafted was there, still waiting for me to do something with it. Send or delete.

I glanced at the computer screen. Still no reply from her.

I took a deep breath and let my finger hover over the Send button, but to my surprise I couldn't let my message fly off into the ether. It was the sound of a message from Aldie pinging its way into my computer that jolted me into action. She was going to ask me to delete the message. I knew then what I wanted to do. I said a silent desperate prayer, let my finger drop on the Send button, then went after Aldie's message.

She had a one word answer for me. *What?*

My fingers got busy. *You're too late. I've just told Levan that I really, really, really like him.*

Her reply was as instantaneous. *You really used THREE reallys?*

I could feel my heart start sinking. *Is that really bad?*

The seconds ticked by without response, even though I could see my message had been read.

I hate you, I wrote.

She came back with a hysterically laughing emoji and a message. *What did he say back?*

I swallowed hard. *He hasn't responded yet.*

I could picture her sighing. *Paste what you wrote here.*

I did as she asked and a couple of minutes passed with a reply from her. I wanted to strangle her.

ALDIE! I punched in.

She responded with a giggling emoji. *Well, I guess, you were direct, if a tad bit dramatic, but... at least you're breaking out of your damn shell.*

When Aldie used words like a tad bit it was never a good thing. My nerves began to buzz with the very devastating possibility that I might have just blown up everything with Levan.

Do you think I made a mistake? I asked anxiously. *I know he is, you know, out of my league. His obviously from a very wealthy family. All those bodyguards hanging around outside the college gates. Not to mention we're still not certain of who he is exactly.*

Her reply was immediate. *He's not out of your league, babe. Yeah sure, he's gorgeous as fuck and obviously wealthy, but you're good enough for anyone, even him. Let's just wait and see what he replies back, okay?*

I closed my eyes for a second. *Okay, let's wait and see, but I really, really, really like him Aldie.*

It took a bit longer for Aldie's answer. *It's never a good idea to wear your heart on your sleeve or anywhere it can be easily trampled on. Men are class A bastards when they know you're crazy about them. So just cool it, okay.*

I didn't tell her I thought I was already more than half way in love with Levan. Sadly, I wrote my reply to her. *Okay. I will cool the ardor.*

That's my girl, she came back. *I just got out of class, I'm hurrying to an open house in East Village, but I'll stop by your bakery when I'm done.*

Nah, my mom is working there today. I'm in the library, then I'm going home, I responded. I paused a moment then added hopefully. *I'll text you when he replies.*

Cool. Can't wait to hear what he says.

I waited and I waited, but Levan never called or wrote back. He literally disappeared into thin air. It hurt like mad, but I took full responsibility for the disaster. I had pathetically worn my heart on my sleeve, and he, being the bastard he was, had stomped all over it.

SAMPLE CHAPTER

One

Present Day

Levan

I was sitting at the bar of a French seafood restaurant in Midtown Manhattan, and had just taken a sip of wine, when she emerged from the restroom area.

Doubling over in shock, I nearly choked on my wine.

My unguarded reaction immediately raised the alarm of the two men with me. They shot their gazes around instantly, searching for any signs of danger.

"Is there a problem?" Sergei asked in low urgent tones, his hand going to his concealed weapon.

"No, no," I said quickly, raising a reassuring hand. "There's no problem."

Both men settled down, but for me, my turbulence had just

begun. My restless, shocked eyes searched for her again, but she was nowhere to be seen. She must have gone into the main room where the diners were.

The barman, a smooth bastard, appeared to ask if I wanted a refill. I nodded and watched blankly as dark vibrant liquid flowed into the glass.

She was here.

She looked even more beautiful than she had been. I'd dreamed of this moment a thousand times and yet it didn't' seem real. I lifted the glass and drained it down.

Sergei gave me a funny look. Fuck him. What did he know of the sacrifice I'd made? My chest hurt with the memories.

"Will Maxim be present when Luka and Dimitri arrive?" Mikhail asked.

My attention snapped back to my men at the mention of my brother. "Maxim left for Spain this morning."

Both men nodded in understanding. Anytime Maxim was called out of the continent by our father, everyone knew it had to be for something extremely 'delicate'. He would only resurface when it was done to his satisfaction.

I leaned back as far as I could and tried to look into the French seafood restaurant. I had a good view, but I could see no sign of her. I knew she hadn't have left yet, so I figured she had be in one of the private dining rooms.

I started to rise to my feet to casually pass by them, but fell back heavily onto my stool when I saw her come out of the dining area in the company of a man. His arm was possessively snaked around her waist.

As if he owned her.

As she was fucking his!

I couldn't believe my eyes. I stared at them in disbelief. The irony was too much to bear. I'd walked away from her to save her from the life of a Mafia wife, and here she was with the biggest, meanest psychopath in our world. Calling him an animal or a beast was being unfair to animals and beasts. They didn't kill for fun.

This man was a heartless sadist who did his own wet work. Not because he was tight, but because he enjoyed inflicting torture. There were terrible rumors about him, the kind of stuff snuff movies were made of. I didn't usually pay attention to gossip, but there were too many stories from too many credible sources to dismiss. No smoke without fire and there was plenty of poisonous smoke hanging around him.

At first the shock of seeing *her* with *him* had completely floored me and I couldn't think straight, but as I gathered my wits together I knew something was not right. They were not opposites who are attracted to each other, they were night and day. They should never be together. I forced myself to focus on her face, and instantly, I felt it.

She *hated* the man who held her as if he owned her.

Her body was stiff with revulsion, and her face was tight with a mixture of fear and despair. She was staring straight ahead of her as if she wished she was somewhere else, someone else.

"Tell me that's not Semion Litvinenko," I asked, without taking my eyes away from her.

"That's him," Sergei spat out disgustedly, but in his voice I detected the touch of fear.

I ran my hands through my hair and felt as if the blood in my veins had turned to liquid fire. Damn. What hell on earth have you got yourself into, Bianca Russet?

ABOUT THE AUTHOR

Remember
I **LOVE** hearing from readers so by all means come and say
hello on my facebook page.

facebook.com/georgia.lecarre

ALSO BY GEORGIA LE CARRE

Owned

42 Days

Besotted

Seduce Me

Love's Sacrifice

Masquerade

Pretty Wicked (novella)

Disfigured Love

Hypnotized

Crystal Jake 1,2&3

Sexy Beast

Wounded Beast

Beautiful Beast

Dirty Aristocrat

You Don't Own Me 1 & 2

You Don't Know Me

Blind Reader Wanted

Redemption

The Heir

Blackmailed By The Beast

Submitting To The Billionaire

The Bad Boy Wants Me

Nanny & The Beast

His Frozen Heart

Printed in Great Britain
by Amazon

26057274R00229